THANKFUL FOR YOU

Visit us at www.boldstrokesbooks.com

By the Author

Visiting Hours

Bird on a Wire

Across the Dark Horizon

And Then There Was Her

Queen of Humboldt

Swipe Right

Two Knights Tango

Almost Perfect

When It Feels Right

Pumpkin Spice

Cabin Fever

Thankful for You

THANKFUL FOR YOU

by

Tagan Shepard

2025

THANKFUL FOR YOU

ISBN 13: 978-1-63679-884-4

THIS TRADE PAPERBACK ORIGINAL IS PUBLISHED BY
BOLD STROKES BOOKS, INC.
P.O. BOX 249
VALLEY FALLS, NY 12185

FIRST EDITION: OCTOBER 2025

CREDITS
EDITORS: ASHLEY TILLMAN AND CINDY CRESAP
PRODUCTION DESIGN: SUSAN RAMUNDO
COVER DESIGN BY INKSPIRAL DESIGN

Acknowledgments

There are so many people who make it possible for me to make my dreams come true, one manuscript at a time.

The BSB family is so amazing and I'm so proud to be a part of it. Thanks to Rad, Sandy, Ruth, Cindy, and, of course, Ashley, the most kick-ass editor in the world.

I couldn't do any of this without my Sapphic Lit Pop-Up family. They inspire me and make me laugh and give me a community I need the way I need oxygen. Cade, Louise, Serena, Bird, Rita, Anne, Nan, and Brooke are rockstars like no other.

I had an epic beta reading team this time around and I am awed by how friggin' good they are at this writing thing. Y'all make it look like I almost know what I'm doing. Cade, Cris, Sandy, Rita, Nan, Action Jackson, and Bird—I can't thank you enough for your guidance.

Thank you to Elizabeth for filling me in on what elementary schools are like these days. It was so much easier to be in the little desk!

What can I possibly say about Cris? She's my rock, my favorite person, my everything. The one I can't wait to talk to at the end of the day and the only one I ever want to wake up next to. She's the light at the end of the tunnel. My whole world. Thanks, baby. There's no one else I'd rather be an indoor cat with than you. I love you.

Dedication

For Cris—every single day I am thankful for you

CHAPTER ONE

The summer sun bore down like an oppressive blanket, making heat shimmer in waves off everything its light touched. The shingles soaked up the heat and returned it twofold through the worn leather of Karen's gloves and the even more worn denim covering her knees. Sweat pooled and dripped across every inch of her skin so her clothes stuck to her already uncomfortable body.

She drove a final nail into a new shingle and rocked back onto her heels, turning her face to the sun to spare her neck any more of its rays. The skin on the back of her neck was raw; there would be a deep burn there. She'd twisted her long hair up into a messy top knot as usual. She'd finally discovered a hairstyle that went with her personality and her work, but the severe undercut that stretched from temple to temple left her neck far too exposed on a cloudless July afternoon.

The screeching of hinges shattered the peace of the afternoon. Karen didn't have to turn around to know someone had come through the kitchen door of the main house. She'd tried more times than she could count to correct the hang on that door, but none of her efforts had been successful and she'd finally admitted defeat.

"Hey there, Cinderella. Aren't you going to relax at all during your summer break?"

Karen chuckled at the teasing tone in her brother's voice. "What did you have in mind, Derek?"

"Swimming. Boating. Fishing. Or just read a book."

Karen carefully scooted to her left and placed a new shingle, making sure to appropriately overlap the ones already in place. "Sounds like fun."

"We're heading out on Dad's new boat to show the boys Oyster Cove. Why don't you come with us?"

Karen took a deep breath as she positioned a nail. What did Derek expect her to do? Drop the shingles and hurry down the ladder to jump on the boat? Half the roof was exposed plywood. What if it rained?

"Not sure if you noticed, big guy, but I'm a little busy right now," Karen said.

"I hadn't noticed actually. Why'd you start replacing the roof when we had a boat trip planned for today?"

Maybe if she'd been invited on the boat trip, she wouldn't have, but she wasn't sure how to say that without sounding like a jerk. Fortunately, the squealing of hinges saved her from inventing a polite explanation. Instead, she blocked out the crunch of footsteps by hammering in the nail and grabbing another from her tool belt.

Her mother's voice cut through the muggy air. "Derek, honey, you need to come get some sunscreen on your boys before we head out."

"I don't know if we have any sunscreen," Derek said.

"You brought young children to the beach and didn't pack sunscreen?"

Karen could almost hear her brother shrug and her mother roll her eyes. She covered her laughter by hammering in another pair of nails.

"I guess that means you don't have any on either? Come on, your father and I have plenty."

"Have fun, Cinderella," Derek said, his voice fading as he hurried off to the house.

Karen positioned another shingle and laughed, an edge of bitterness coloring the sound. As she nailed the new shingle in, she grumbled to herself. "Yes, Mom, I did put on sunscreen. Thanks for asking. Oh no, I'm fine up here. I don't need any water. You all go have fun."

She hit the last nail a little too hard and the head bent. She smiled at herself as she worked it out and snatched another from her belt. That's what she got for throwing herself a pity party. It's not like she wanted to go on the boat. Her nephews were a lot, especially early in the day when they hadn't been tuckered out, and she loved working with her hands. Even more, she loved being useful and making sure her parents' property was well maintained. Still, her knees were aching and her neck was stinging and Derek was right, she needed a break.

Karen set down her hammer and looked out across the water. There was nothing quite so beautiful as the view from up here. If only there was a little cloud cover or maybe even a squall. As it was, there wasn't a breath of wind off Fleets Bay to cool her or any other resident of Kilmarnock. Although, admittedly, the locals probably weren't foolish enough to choose early July in Virginia as the time to patch a weak spot in their roof.

Karen didn't have a choice. Her parents' property consisted of the main house and two guest cottages. Her dad only told her about the leaking roof of her cottage a week ago. There hadn't been rain yet this summer and there wasn't any forecasted, so she'd put it off until today while she finished projects in the other guest house. She'd wanted to finish working in there before her brother and nephews arrived to occupy the place, so she'd added the leaking roof to the bottom of an ever-growing list. Derek and the boys had arrived a few days ago, so today was finally fix the roof day.

If she didn't get to the roof on this trip, it would get worse and her parents wouldn't be able to rent out the cottage to supplement their retirement income. They had investments, and honestly, their income was more than hers, but they were too old to get up there and fix it themselves and they would never spend the money to hire a handyman. That left it to their kids and Derek wouldn't know which end of the hammer to use. Like their parents, the only tools Derek was handy with were a corkscrew and a checkbook, so Karen had to keep the property in good working order. She didn't mind too much. She didn't get to be handy like this in her day job as a third-grade teacher. Sure, her back ached and her skin was unlikely to recover from the sun's torment any time soon, but her parents needed her and she loved them.

Karen stretched and ground her knuckles into the knot just above her right hip. As she tipped her head from side to side to loosen her neck, she was surprised to see the pier was empty. She hadn't heard the boat leave, but she had been focused on her task. The boys loved the new Cobalt A29 her parents had acquired in the spring and her parents loved nothing more than doting on their grandkids. They'd all gone out on the boat yesterday, too, while Karen was draining the hot water heater and the day before when she'd been replacing the leaking p-trap in the main house's primary bathroom. They hadn't invited her on those two occasions, just like they hadn't invited her today or the week she was here before her brother and nephews arrived. Was that because she was busy doing their maintenance projects or because they weren't interested in boating with her?

Annoyance bubbled up in her and she closed her eyes, starting a slow count to twenty-five. If she didn't stem this feeling now it would turn into full-fledged anger, and she didn't want that. She'd had an ulcer last year thanks to her habit of carrying all her stress in her core and she didn't relish another round. The annoyance dissipated, leaving emptiness in its place. This was exactly how it always worked. Every year she wanted it to be different. Every year she pulled into the driveway of crushed oyster shells and thought maybe this year her family would magically be interested in her company. Every year she filled her days with projects instead of having to focus on the fact that her parents just didn't really like her that much. Or at least didn't like spending time with her. Or asking about her life. She should just accept it, but she'd never been the type to give up hope.

Karen bent her head to the task and offered her neck back to the unforgiving sun. By the time she finished she was exhausted from the heat and the work, but the roof had never looked better. She slid down to the edge of the roof and checked that no one was lurking below before she dropped her toolbelt to the ground. She took a long moment to rest before descending the ladder. She'd emptied her water bottle an hour ago and skipped lunch rather than climb down before the job was complete. The last thing she needed was to pass out and fall off the ladder. Her family's boat still wasn't back at their pier. God knew how long it would take them to find her if she hurt herself now.

❖

The windows of the main house were glowing with the last rays of the setting sun and Karen was just taking dinner out of the oven when her parents came bustling through the door, her nephews and brother in tow. By the time she had the casserole dish on a trivet and the oven mitts off her hands, her dad had removed his boat shoes and was marching into the kitchen. She shouldn't expect praise for her day of hard work since it was too dark for him to have seen the roof. She shouldn't expect her dad to wrap her in a big hug that smelled like brackish air and Old Spice cologne. She shouldn't expect them, but her heart ached when he marched past her without a word and dropped heavily onto a barstool.

"What's for dinner, pumpkin?" he asked.

"Tortellini and zucchini bake," Karen said.

If she'd been expecting him to acknowledge that she'd made his favorite meal, she would have been disappointed. Instead, he turned to slap Derek on the back as he claimed the nearest barstool and started in on the state of fishing in the Chesapeake Bay.

Her mother arrived in the open kitchen next, bustling up beside her. "Oh good, you've started dinner. I'm starving. What can I do to help?"

"Don't worry about it, Mom. Everything's ready. It just has to rest a couple minutes before I serve."

Her mother made a little disingenuous sound of disappointment that she couldn't help, but she didn't seem too broken up about it. She went straight to the fridge for a bottle of wine, then the cabinet for three wineglasses.

"The boys baited their own hooks today." Her mother removed the cork in a few swift, practiced movements. "Little Charlie didn't even cry when we handed him the worm."

Charlie, Karen's five-year-old nephew, spread a wide grin evenly across the adults assembled in the kitchen, then turned back to playing with his older brother.

"He managed it at least three years before I did." Derek accepted his glass of wine and raised it toward Karen. "But you still have us all beat. You've got nerves of steel."

Karen accepted the compliment—and the first eye contact she'd received from any member of her family since their return—before getting a wineglass for herself from the cabinet.

While Karen filled her glass, her mother said, "Oh, I'm sorry, sweetheart. Didn't I get four glasses? I'm sure I did. The other one must be around here somewhere."

Her mom spun in a circle, desperate to find the wineglass she hadn't grabbed from the cabinet. Sometimes her mom's forgetfulness was hurtful, but this time she had to keep herself from giggling.

"It's okay."

"I do remember you drink wine. I meant to get four glasses."

"Seriously, Mom. It's okay."

And it *was* okay. Anything to make the hot prickling of embarrassment on her cheeks go away. The only thing worse than them not including her was when they belatedly realized their omission. Conversation stopped and everyone looked at her, but she had no idea what to do or say. She wanted the discomfort to end, so she changed the subject.

"How's the new boat handling, Dad?"

Her mom seemed just as eager to cover over the awkward moment. "It's a dream, isn't it, Arthur?"

"She's even-keeled and that's about all I can say for her now, but give me a few more months to break her in and she'll be a fine boat."

"Oh, come on, Dad. That boat's amazing and you know it," Derek said.

That was all it took to change the mood. Karen relaxed. In fact, the subject of how much better the boat would cut through the water once it had been put through its paces carried them all the way through their salads.

While her mother scuttled back into the kitchen for a second bottle of Chardonnay, Derek turned to Karen. "Did you get the roof finished?"

"Sure did," she said. "The leak shouldn't come back any time soon, but if you see anything, Dad, just let me know."

Derek squirmed in his seat. "I would've helped, but I had to entertain the boys."

Everyone kept eating, not bothering to call him on the obvious lie, but the boys shared a look over their forks.

"Thank you for doing that, honey." Her mother made a show of filling her glass first. "I'm sure you did a lovely job."

"You didn't have to do anything to that roof. It was fine how it was for another year or two," her dad said.

"It was leaking," Karen said.

"But not much. It could've waited until prices went down."

Karen focused her attention on her wineglass to keep from saying anything. If she'd waited for prices to go down, they would all be waiting until hell froze over. Her dad just couldn't wrap his mind around the idea that prices weren't what they were in 1975 and they never would be again. While he waited to save a few dollars, mold would've grown in the ceiling and Karen would've had to take care of that, too. Or wait until her dad hired a mold remediation company. The chances of her penny-pinching father hiring a contractor were about the same as Karen being crowned Queen of England.

"Speaking of, did you see the Hargroves put in a new slate roof?" Her father turned excitedly to Derek. "It's this gorgeous blue and it really makes the new siding pop. I wonder how much they paid for it."

"Well, don't interrogate them about it while we're out on the boat tomorrow. They'll think it's why we invited them," her mother said.

This was the first Karen had heard that their wealthiest neighbors were coming over the next day. She wasn't a fan of the Hargroves with their designer clothes and holier-than-thou attitudes, but her parents certainly enjoyed their company. Talk of their slate roof and their opulent house dominated the rest of dinner. Just a few minutes after Karen set down her fork, Derek declared his intention of heading to bed.

"You, too, boys. We have to be at the dock at sunrise for our catfishing adventure with Poppa Art."

The boys grumbled, but not nearly as loud as her parents groaned as they pushed up out of their chairs. Karen was exhausted from her day in the sun and the two glasses of wine, but she managed to stand and start collecting plates.

"Let me help you with that, dear," her mother said through a jaw-cracking yawn.

Karen took one look at the exhaustion blanketing her mother's movements and waved her off. "No, it's okay. You had a long day. I'll take care of it."

"Are you sure?" Her mother's voice was laced with obvious relief.

Karen had difficulty hiding her own relief that her mother gave in. Attention to detail wasn't exactly her mother's forte. When she helped wash up, Karen found half-clean dishes tucked precariously into the wrong cabinets. She always had to backtrack and redo everything her mother did, and that was on the lucky days when her haphazard stacking didn't cause a plate or two to fall, smashing into a million pieces. Normally, Karen would willingly do the extra work, but she was too tired tonight.

"Of course. Good night, Mom. Good night, Dad."

Her father's only acknowledgement was a grunt as he climbed the stairs, her mother following close on his heels. Before she knew it, she was alone in the dining room with a table full of dirty dishes and leftovers to box up.

She sighed and drained her glass before carrying the first few plates back to the kitchen.

CHAPTER TWO

Karen stood, staring into the vanity mirror, a toothbrush loaded with toothpaste hovering halfway to her mouth. Washing the dinner dishes had given her a second wind, but it was fading quickly. She squinted and scrunched her face, fixating on the lines around her eyes. When had those appeared? Maybe it was the deep tan she'd picked up in the last couple weeks? Surely thirty-two wasn't old enough for this many wrinkles? She wasn't old enough for crow's feet, was she?

Since she'd begun the examination, she took in the rest of her body. She was average height but with a muscular build that would make her look like a soccer player if it wasn't for the several extra pounds she also carried. She'd always liked both the muscles and the extra pounds since it filled out her frame nicely and gave her physique the masculine-of-center look she craved. It didn't hurt that she had a wide, almost square jaw. Her high cheekbones and prominent brow had a tendency to shadow her green eyes, giving her a studious look that could be sharpened to intimidate or softened to encourage her students. All in all, she liked how she looked. She just didn't like adding wrinkles to the equation. Fortunately, there were no gray hairs in amongst the brunette.

Finally putting brush to teeth, she let her mind turn to more mundane matters than her impending middle age. There were still a thousand little projects that needed doing around her parents' house. The landscaping timbers that formed a retaining wall around the old oak tree were starting to rot and would need to be replaced. Then there was the vinyl siding that could do with a power wash. The kitchen faucet in her brother's cottage was dripping and little Mason said it was keeping him up nights.

Any or all those projects could fill the rest of her summer with hard-earned sweat and a sense of accomplishment, but she wasn't all that interested. Even though she should be taking the summer off mentally as well as physically, all she could think about was her kids back in Bucks Mill.

Karen had grown up among the moderately wealthy elite in the Washington, DC, suburbs. She'd done her driving test on the Beltway and was part of a graduating class of two thousand students. Nothing could be more different from her childhood than the little town of Bucks Mill, Virginia.

Bucks Mill was the sort of sleepy town that most people knew nothing about, even if they'd passed through. Tucked into the base of the Appalachian Mountains near Charlottesville and the University of Virginia, Bucks Mill could have become one of a million anonymous bedroom communities across America. Instead, it was a place where people loved their neighbors and took pride in their community. Where everyone not only knew your name, but your brother's name and how many kids he had and what he did for a living over in the big city. The sort of place where the local coffee shop and bakery was the heartbeat of the town. Where the mom-and-pop hardware store delivered same day but Amazon rarely showed up. In short, it was the kind of town that made an elementary school teacher fresh out of college want to put down roots.

It was the kids of Bucks Mill who had put down roots—right in her heart. Here she was, surrounded by her own family, but all she could think about was Chloe Wentworth, whose father had a heart attack late last year, scaring her far too much for her age. And Noah Miller who had swapped T-ball for basketball in the spring and was flourishing. Then there was Liam, the youngest of the Sanderson kids who went off to middle school last year but came back after school sometimes to see her rather than going home. Karen was pretty sure his parents were fighting even though Becky Sanderson was good at keeping up appearances.

Of course, there was a huge place Karen set aside in her heart for Lily Hanson and her all-too-obvious crush on Tinley Bamford.

Lily reminded Karen of herself at that age, aware but not aware of her sexuality. The glow in her eyes last Halloween when she told Karen that her aunt, Nicki, and her girlfriend, Carter, had gotten engaged was just a little too familiar. When Karen was eleven just the whisper of something gay would have made her explode with joy in the same way.

Even though Karen had really hoped there might be something between her and Nicki, Carter was clearly the better fit. The same was true of her best friend and fellow third grade Bucks Mill Elementary teacher, Jessica. At least she had agreed to a second date with Karen, but by the third they were both more interested in being besties than lovers. Then Jessica had gone and met the man of her dreams and had plans for raising a brood of mini versions of herself. Even Jessica would joke that she could do without mini versions of Brandon. He was sweet and caring, but also loud and forthright enough to leave little space for anyone else. A perfect complement for her confident but quiet best friend.

Everyone in Karen's life seemed to have that person who was their ideal fit. Her mother and father, for all their deficiencies as parents, had been the model couple for thirty-six years. Hell, even her stupid older brother seemed to have a perfect marriage with his vapid, chronically absent wife.

Everyone had their match. Everyone had that one person who was the center of their world. Who put them first and cared about them more than anyone else on the planet. Everyone except Karen.

Before she could get too downtrodden, Karen swapped her toothbrush for her phone. Surely a dive into the tangled web of social media would distract her. Unfortunately, her Instagram was full of more happy people, arms wrapped around their person.

"I should've known better."

She grumbled and threw herself back onto her fully made bed, burrowing into a mountain of pillows. Her email seemed a safer app, so she switched to it as she wiggled into her nest. After sorting through a dozen or so emails from mailing lists she couldn't remember signing up for, she was left with a bill from her credit card company, a reminder from her OB/GYN's office to schedule her pap smear, and an email from her principal. Okay, so this haul was only slightly less depressing than social media, but she was one of the rare workers who actually liked her boss.

Hi Karen,

How's beach life treating you? Have you throttled your brother yet? I won't even ask if you've spent the last few weeks relaxing. I know you haven't.

That brings me to my reason for emailing. As requested, I had the county team clean your classroom first. They just finished the HVAC renovation today. You'll notice brand new air vents in your classroom, which will be ready for you to set up for the new year tomorrow. I'm going to remind you that you don't have to come in yet. Classes start the third week of August. Returning teachers are required on the second week of August. New teachers, of which we have two this year (!), will arrive the first week of August. Of note, the school board has chosen Bucks Mill Elementary for new teacher orientation this year, so our new teachers plus a handful of others from the rest of the county will be taking over the cafetorium that week, but the rest of the school will be open and accessible to everyone.

This schedule means you don't have to be here for another month. I'm sure it's fruitless to try convincing you to stay with your family and the salt air for four more weeks, but here's my best attempt:

Please have some fun. Swim in the ocean. Play with your nephews. Get drunk with your dad. Maybe even, and I know this is a wild notion, leave the state for a real vacation?

Hope that worked. Talk to you soon,

Roger

Karen couldn't help smiling at Roger's kindness and the resigned way he always tried to convince her to enjoy her full summer vacation. He was probably right. She'd shown some restraint her first two years at Bucks Mill Elementary, but for the last six years she had been the first teacher to return. She saw no reason to break the streak now.

From her nest of pillows, Karen surveyed her sterile if familiar surroundings. Her cottage needed the most work. But if she had to choose between fresh paint in her parents' guest cottage or ensuring the kids in Bucks Mill had someone to confide in when they couldn't confide in their families, there was no debate. She would pick her kids every day and twice on Sunday. Part of being that teacher was making sure both she and the kids were comfortable in her space. Somewhere her students wanted to spend time. Somewhere they would find a sympathetic ear. She'd had a teacher like that once. Someone who let her be herself when her parents were doting on her older brother.

Karen dropped her phone on the bedside table and switched off the light. She couldn't go home just yet, since her father was far too cheap to hire a plumber for the boys' cottage. Her last project would be replacing that faucet so Mason could sleep. She would leave on Saturday to head back to Bucks Mill. That would give her two days to wrap up here and maybe even spend a couple hours swimming off the pier, just to tell Roger she had. Her parents clearly didn't need her, but her kids did.

Gulls screeched overhead and waves crashed on the shore beside Karen as she strolled along the beach. Her camera was slung bandolier-style across her chest, waiting for the golden hour, and her linen pants were rolled up to a cuff at mid-calf. Grains of damp sand squished pleasantly between her toes with each step.

Karen took in a deep, cleansing breath and allowed herself a smile. She hadn't spent much time with her camera this summer and she quietly chastised herself for it. Her brother loved the roar of a boat engine and her mother loved the scent of salt, but this is what Karen loved. The tranquility of nature undisturbed. Even more, she loved capturing it with a lens.

As she had planned, she arrived at her spot just as the sun was peeking over the horizon. This spot was ideal for sunrise photos, since the beach curved gracefully out into the bay and the sun would throw the perfect golden hue over the waves.

She stopped and knelt, scanning the tumbled assortment of broken shells and smooth stones. Every now and then she found one that was captivating, but today it was more the jumble of them all together that made the perfect image. She trained her lens on the pile, taking shot after shot as she adjusted to slightly different angles and compositions.

She got so lost in the shells that she nearly missed the perfect sunrise shot of the beach and waves. Fortunately, that innate sense she'd developed as a photographer kicked in at the right moment and she lifted her camera, adjusted her focus, and rattled off a dozen shots. As she walked back to her parents' house, she scrolled through the images on the display screen, satisfied with her morning's work.

Karen was lounging on the sofa in the main house, nursing her second cup of coffee and reading a book by the diffuse morning sunlight through the bay windows when her family came in through the back door. They brought with them the scents and sounds of a morning on the Chesapeake Bay. Sea air and the brackish, murky smells of bottom dweller fish mingling with the cawing of water birds and the laughter of children who didn't have to go to school. Her father shuffled the boys to the back deck to clean their catch and her mother disappeared upstairs for a shower. Derek poured himself a cup of coffee and dropped into the armchair across from her, propping massive feet wrapped in dingy socks on the coffee table a little too close to Karen's mug. She thought she hid her cringe, but his booming laugh proved her wrong.

"Are you sure you weren't switched at birth?" Derek asked. "You're the only indoor cat in the family."

He smiled when he said it, but Karen couldn't keep the bite from her voice. "I'm not an indoor cat. I spent the entire day outside yesterday, busting my butt to keep a roof over our heads."

She chose not to mention her pre-dawn trip down the beach for photographs. She knew from experience he would not be impressed.

"Cats get stuck on roofs all the time. You aren't winning this argument."

Karen didn't have a comeback, so she stuck her tongue out at him. Sure, it was childish, but he was her older brother and it felt right. He flicked her off in response, but he did it with a laugh.

"I'm glad I caught you relaxing finally. We haven't had a chance to catch up. How's life? Do you have a girlfriend yet?"

That little flicker of hope lit in Karen's chest. Her brother asked more about her life than their parents did, but his interest was usually short-lived. Maybe this time things would be different? "Life's good. I'm heading back tomorrow to set up my classroom."

He didn't mention how she ignored the girlfriend question, instead shaking his head in disbelief. "I don't understand why you'd waste the one benefit of being a teacher—summers off—to go back to work just as the weather's heating up. Do you get paid overtime for going back early?"

"There are more benefits to being a teacher than having summers off."

"Oh yeah? Name one."

"Come on, Derek, you're a father. Watching the kids learn and grow. Don't you see the power in that? The joy in their eyes when they walk away, smarter than they were an hour ago?"

"I'm raising boys. They don't get smarter and certainly not in an hour."

"Charlie and Mason are smart as whips."

Derek set his coffee cup down and leaned forward. "Mason doesn't look up from his phone unless someone in the room farts and he can laugh at them. The boy will not be a Rhodes Scholar."

Karen had long experience holding back both her laughter and her eye rolls, but she let loose with both at her brother.

"You don't get it. Half my students come back to visit me even after they've gone off to middle school. They tell me how much they're thriving and how I helped them succeed. Nothing could be better than that," Karen said.

"You know what's better than that? A big 401(k) and a house you own. I just don't get why you're still at that backwater school even after you did your time to get your loans paid off."

"Because it isn't about student loan forgiveness. You know that. At Bucks Mill I make a difference. Poor country kids deserve a good education even if their parents can't afford private school."

Derek bristled and snatched his coffee cup off the table. "I know there's nothing wrong with public schools. I went to public schools."

"But your kids don't."

"That's Angela's choice. She insisted, so she's paying that tuition, not me."

"And she doesn't get to spend time with her family so she can afford it."

That was a low blow, but Karen was offended Angela didn't value the public school system that she worked in. If wealthy families always pulled their children from schools, they wouldn't have the support to hire the best teachers or the resources to supplement the students' educations.

"At least Angela gets paid overtime and big fat bonuses when she works through what was supposed to be her vacation. You don't, do you?"

Before Karen could protest, her mother leaned over the back of the couch, bringing the scent of lavender shampoo and clean cotton.

"What does he mean by that, Karen? You aren't leaving your vacation early?"

"Of course she is," Derek said. "Her classroom's ready so she's going back to the mountains to work twelve-hour days."

"Ten-hour days," Karen said.

"That's not any better, dear," her mother said. "You spend too much time working and not enough time finding a girlfriend."

"Mom, we've talked about this."

Her mother didn't listen. She was already in the kitchen, banging pans around to prepare breakfast. The nagging wasn't done, though. It rarely ever was.

"Maybe you can find someone at your ex-girlfriend's wedding. When is that again?" her mother asked.

"Nicki is not my ex-girlfriend, Mom. We only went on one date. Besides, there won't be any more lesbians at this wedding than a straight wedding, so my chances aren't any higher."

"But there is a chance."

Not really. She didn't want to say it out loud, but neither Bucks Mill nor Charlottesville were teaming with romantic options for her, especially at her age. Honesty was the best option here, but it pained her to admit it.

"There aren't a lot of lesbians out there."

"I'm not picky." Her mother cracked eggs into a bowl two at a time. "I'd love a bisexual daughter-in-law as long as she's a good cook."

"Who's this potential daughter-in-law?" her father asked as he came in from the porch.

Karen had had enough. She couldn't really tell if it was anger or embarrassment that made her face burn. She'd wanted this sort of undivided attention from her family for weeks and now she was getting it for all the wrong reasons. To her horror, tears prickled her eyes and the last thing she wanted was to cry right now. Desperate to change the subject, she said, "There is no potential daughter-in-law, but I do have a lot of great upgrades to my classroom coming this year."

"Oh, are you getting a Smartboard? Mason's teacher got one last year," Derek said.

"No. The county doesn't have that kind of money. But I'm in line to get a new whiteboard."

Derek didn't respond. His eyebrows did a little dance that looked a lot like a shrug, then he focused on his phone screen. Her father silently fought a fishing reel with a bird's nest of knotted line and her mother was rinsing out the coffee pot. She deflated with the reminder that no one in this family got her. More than that, in the face of her obvious excitement, they couldn't muster a response. Would they ever be happy for her? Maybe if she brought home that daughter-in-law who could cook, but then it still wouldn't be about her. They didn't know how much she craved finding her person because they never engaged. Why did they always have to do this? Remind her that she was alone and she had nothing more in her life than a handful of children who weren't her own and zero romantic prospects.

"I should go pack," Karen said.

When no one responded, she hustled around the couch and toward the kitchen door. She whipped through the door, careful not to yank it too hard behind her. The last thing she wanted was to slam the door like a teenager fleeing a temper tantrum. As she pulled the door slowly closed, she heard her family talking about her, not even bothering to whisper.

Chapter Three

The summer sun blazed hot and bright directly above her as Karen chewed up miles of blacktop in her ancient Honda Civic. She was nearing the boundaries of the Northern Neck, the air whipping through her windows rapidly losing its briny bite. Soon she'd be enveloped by the green scents of alfalfa fields and kudzu-lined highways. Then the warm slate of the Appalachian Mountains and she would be home. Her blood thrummed with anticipation at the thought.

Of course, all these smells would be offset by her own sweat. The heat and humidity of a July afternoon in Virginia was nothing to be trifled with, but the air conditioning in her tragically old car was dodgy at best. She was almost as hot as she had been two days ago on the roof. She rolled the window down as far as it would go, far more effective than the vents.

It wasn't just the AC that was pathetic in this old heap. She'd been lucky to find a used model without all the expensive bells and whistles, but that had been fifteen years before. Now she was living in a different century from everyone else. She still had to turn a key in the ignition and manually roll down her windows. Then again, since most of the electronics were failing, it was probably a good thing how many parts of this old car were manual.

The first thing to go had been the CD player, a relic in its own right. Six months before she'd had a bout of nostalgia and popped an old Tori Amos CD in the player. That was when the ejector broke. Now she was stuck with that one disc. Everyone loved "Cornflake

Girl," but not that much. As she drove into the radio dead zone that blanketed much of her drive, she started up the CD with a sigh. She hated her family's insistence on making money over everything else, but you bet your life this crappy old car had her understanding their point of view a little bit more.

She pulled off the interstate an hour later. The sun dropped lower and Bucks Mill was over the next hill. The proximity to home brought her back to her senses. Her brother was completely wrong. This town wasn't a backwater and nothing in the world would ever make her leave.

Bucks Mill was the jewel of Virginia's rugged western border. Snuggled into the foothills of lush, green mountains and rolling countryside, it was the quintessential small town. The kind of town where Main Street was the heartbeat and folks who had been born and raised here for generations were the life's blood. Growing up gay in the busy suburbs of Washington, DC, Karen had once thought that small towns were enclaves of prejudice where she'd never be safe or accepted. Certainly there were small towns like that, but Bucks Mill wasn't one of them.

As she pulled onto Main Street, the twenty-five-mile-per-hour limit gave her a chance to take in her favorite places and people. The stately Victorian homes of Old Town gave way to businesses only slightly more modern and certainly just as homey. There was Main Street Café, where she met her best friend for drinks and gossip. They'd put the festive purple-and-yellow umbrellas up over the outdoor tables, most of which were full of laughing, smiling families. A block further on was the brick and glass storefront of Brubaker's Pharmacy. The vertical sign on the corner of the building was ornately lettered, a perfect reproduction of the original that could be seen in a photograph dated 1911 hanging in the public library.

A gaggle of parents including the self-appointed queen of town, Meaghan Bamford, waved at Karen as she passed Sallie Bell's Coffee Shop. What she wouldn't give for one of Sallie Bell's famous iced salted caramel lattes, but no way she was stopping with Mrs. Bamford and her posse lurking outside. She had enough veiled criticisms and backhanded compliments from her mother over the last month, she didn't need any more. Next door, Todd Bailey sat on a rocking chair outside his hardware store, gossiping with a few of his friends. The way the group of older men mirrored the middle-aged moms, all gossiping and enjoying the late afternoon sunshine, was comical. The pace of life here was different. A person could build something meaningful with the people they cared about. When she found her person to build something with, everything would be perfect.

Karen pulled off Main Street into the little alley beside the Bamford Insurance Agency. She claimed her assigned spot in the tiny parking lot behind the building and grinned like an idiot at the blue door in the back of building marked "Private." It wasn't what most people would call idyllic, but warmth spread through her chest. Her parents' bay-front compound would never compare. Her tiny apartment up a creaky staircase above a life insurance office was her favorite place in the world after her classroom. Her sanctuary.

She had carried both her suitcases up to her apartment and was on her last trip to her car to collect her backpack when the patter of tennis shoes and an excited squeal interrupted her.

"Ms. Peterson! You're back."

She barely had time to register Lily's voice before all four feet and eighty pounds of her slammed into Karen. A second, slightly taller projectile hit her a heartbeat later. Karen threw her arms around the two best friends, as much to keep herself from falling backward as to hug them.

"Hey, Lily. Hey, Tinley. How are you?" Karen asked.

"We're so happy to see you," Tinley said.

"We've been hanging out with Tinley's dad while he works, but it's been really boring." Lily's voice was slightly muffled, smooshed as it was into Karen's middle. "I can't believe you're back already. We missed you so much."

"I was only gone a month."

Karen laughed it off, but a bubble of joy filled her insides. After her family's well-meaning indifference, she really needed this. Bucks Mill and her kids. This day couldn't get any better.

"Yeah, but we had to suffer through fourth grade with Mrs. Shelton last year," Lily said.

"We hated every minute of it. Why couldn't you switch to teaching fourth grade so we could stay with you?" Tinley said.

"Maybe you can teach fifth grade this year?" There was an adorable plea in Lily's voice that made the bubble of joy in Karen's chest expand another few inches.

Karen was used to this reaction about Margaret Shelton, especially from the students who had her as a teacher the year before. Margie was in her late sixties and raised in an educational environment that emphasized discipline and tough love. She didn't connect well with the kids, but that didn't mean she didn't care just as deeply.

"You know Mrs. Shelton's bark is worse than her bite." Karen toed the line between making them feel heard but not bashing a fellow teacher. "I bet you learned a ton. I bet you can multiply fractions in your sleep."

"Tinley can. I liked the history lessons, even though Mrs. Shelton totally brushed over the treatment of Native Americans," Lily said.

Lily's adoring look at her best friend made warning bells go off in Karen's brain. It was clear she had a massive crush, but Karen wasn't sure Tinley noticed or returned the feelings. Her focus was entirely on Karen.

"Who are we getting for fifth grade, Ms. Peterson?" Tinley asked.

Karen put an arm around each of their shoulders as they walked out of the parking lot toward the building.

"I don't know who you'll get, but it won't be me. I'm sticking with third grade."

"Can't you change for just this one year? Please?"

The whine Lily put on the please was actually really cute. Too bad she had no idea how different it was teaching fifth grade than third. Even if there were an opening for a higher-grade position, which there hadn't been for a decade, she was perfectly happy where she was.

"Sorry, girls. I'm locked in, but whoever you get will be awesome. You know my door's always open to chat if you need help with your homework."

"Thanks, Ms. Peterson." Tinley released her and skipped over to the sidewalk.

"You're the best, Ms. Peterson. I love your new haircut." Lily sprinted off to join her best friend.

Karen gave them a last wave as they turned the corner, then trotted up the stairs to her apartment. She loaded her tiny stackable washer-dryer unit with some clothes, then dropped onto her couch and pulled out her phone.

She'd missed a text from her own best friend while she was chatting with the girls.

The Stalk My Best Friend app says you're back in town.

Karen laughed at Jessica's name for the app on her phone that let her find the location of her family and friends.

I should revoke my permission, but yep, just arrived.

Meet me at Main Street Café for beers and gossip? Jessica asked.

It would be the perfect way to cap off the best day of her whole summer. She responded with an emphatic agreement and grabbed her wallet. Karen checked her hair and clothes in the mirror before she left, smiling genuinely for the first time all month.

Karen pulled into the parking lot of Bucks Mill Elementary School on Monday morning at eight o'clock sharp. That was an hour later than she would be arriving when the kids came back, but during the summer Roger wouldn't arrive to unlock the school that early and he would scowl something terrible if she was there waiting for him.

A single set in the line of double doors at the entrance was unlocked during the summer. Karen pushed through them, a blueberry muffin from Sallie Bell's balanced on top of her travel coffee mug. Her worn leather messenger bag banged against the door as it closed faster than she expected, nearly disrupting her breakfast's balance. A soft chuckle greeted her as the door fell shut and clicked closed.

Doug Green, the retired police officer turned school security guard, said, "The county finally coughed up the money to replace the air hinge this summer."

"I didn't think it would ever happen," Karen said.

"Only took them five years. Can I carry something for you?"

Doug was old enough to be her father, and he coddled her in that fatherly way that bordered on sweet and annoying. Was it her gender or her age that made him think she was incapable of carrying a muffin and a cup of coffee? Doug's generation considered such moments of chivalry polite, however, so she let it go.

"I can manage. How's the summer been?"

"Quiet as usual, but it isn't half over. You're supposed to be on vacation still."

Karen shrugged as he turned to follow her toward the wall of windows that was the office. "I like the quiet and I didn't have much to do at my parents' place anyway."

"Managed to get a tan, at least. I suppose you spent a lot of time on the beach?" Doug said, a hint of envy coloring his tone.

"I spent a lot of time outside, yes."

No need to share the real details of her break. Doug could stretch a single sentence response into a three-hour conversation. She waved a congenial goodbye as she slipped inside the office, this time managing not to get whacked by the closing door.

"I knew I shouldn't have sent that email." Roger's voice proceeded him as he emerged from his office. "Had a feeling I'd see you this morning."

Roger Hart was a tall, slender man in his early fifties with the pale, unlined face of a scholar and the receding hairline to match. He had been principal at Bucks Mill Elementary for ten years and, like Karen, was still considered one of the new kids on the block. He was beloved by all his teachers and most of the students, but somehow managed to command everyone's respect. He was also a silly, sweet man whose summer uniform consisted of pressed khakis and garish Hawaiian shirts.

"You know there's nowhere else I'd rather be," Karen said.

Roger shook his head but tossed her the room key he'd been dangling in front of him. She caught it with the grace of the decent softball player she'd been in high school.

"How are Arthur and Sue?"

"Same as always." Karen gave him this response about her parents every year. He never asked what it meant. "Have a good June?"

"Decent. The county approved a lot of new projects around here. School board is up for election and they're pandering, but I'll happily take their money."

"So I got my new whiteboard and shelves?" Karen asked.

"Yes to the whiteboard. The shelves didn't make the cut. The project was…shelved."

Roger emphasized his pun by mimicking a rim shot on air drums and Karen laughed even as she rolled her eyes. She was as much under his spell as everyone else in town. She couldn't help it. He was infinitely charming.

"Keith wants to have an end-of-summer barbecue at our house, so keep an eye out for the invitation," Roger said.

"Your husband's parties are always the best."

"Hey, it's my party, too. I've noticed you've missed the last few."

Karen forced her grin to stay put as she scrambled for a response. She still vividly remembered the last mixer she'd attended. A playful wrestling match ended with two of her colleagues falling into the pool. She wasn't the type for those kind of shenanigans, so she'd avoided a return visit.

"I'll definitely think about coming this time," she said as she backed out of the office. And she probably would. She did miss chatting with Keith.

He waved her off with a grin and she happily bolted down the hall. As much as she enjoyed Roger's company, she was itching to get to her room.

Bucks Mill Elementary was laid out like a large tree, with the office and library in the center forming the trunk, the cafetorium and gym off to the left forming the roots, and the classrooms branching off to the right. Karen slipped through the double doors leading to the academic section. The long hallway had open windows on one side showing row after row of bookshelves. The librarian, Sheila Washington, wouldn't be back this early. Karen would probably see her next week though, furiously cataloging the new books donated and purchased over the summer.

After the library, the hallway branched off in three directions. To her left were the LAMP classrooms. Students in every grade spent one section per week in each of the non-academic lessons: library, art, music, and physical education. Escorting her classes to these lessons was always a bright spot in her day, because it meant that Karen would have an hour to herself. Tucked away in that hallway were also the kindergarten classrooms. The youngest students benefited from a little bit of seclusion and less noise.

The central hallway led to the first and second grade classrooms and the special education wing. Right at the mouth of that hallway was the entrance to the teachers' lounge, an area where Karen spent very little time. As much as she got along with her colleagues, apart from Jessica, she didn't have much in common with them. They were more like acquaintances than friends. She would much rather eat her lunch in her classroom in comfortable silence or with the rare visit from Jessica to fill her in on all the other happenings at the school.

The final hallway, the one Karen practically skipped down now, held the classrooms for third, fourth, and fifth grades. Fifth grade students switched to different teachers three times a day for different subjects, so they were relegated to the front of the hallway where they would disrupt the fewest students with noisy shuffling. Fourth grade was the middle child, and third grade, Karen's domain, was tucked away at the quiet back of the hallway, isolated on the farthest tip of the farthest branch of the Bucks Mill Elementary tree.

This was one of Karen's favorite moments as a teacher. Walking through empty halls, occasionally brushing her fingertips against cinderblock walls covered in many inches of paint. The hall smelled like floor wax and industrial cleaner and something indescribable that reminded her of the infinite possibilities of childhood. On days like this she couldn't help but remember her own elementary school years. She was loved at home, but she felt like an alien. She never fit in and she didn't know why. But when she came to school and the teachers talked to her like her words mattered, she fit in.

School was where every knowable thing lived. In textbooks and the library and the minds of her heroes—the teachers who nurtured her desire to know and understand. That's why she came back here. That's why she didn't care about money or a car with satellite radio. Nothing had changed in the long decades since she was a student in a school like this one. This was still where she fit in.

When she reached the end of the hallway, Karen slipped the key into the lock of her classroom door. She closed her eyes as she stepped through the door, took a deep breath, and opened them as she flipped on the lights.

She saw the same four walls, single window looking out over the monkey bars, and heavy wooden door with a single side light, but it felt fresh and new. The thick layer of white paint on the cinderblock walls was the same, but there was a new thin layer of wax on the speckled epoxy floors. The air vents with caked-on dust that had rimmed the bent metal for her entire tenure was gone, replaced by shiny new ones. Karen took a deep breath and was surprised that the air felt cleaner now. Her old whiteboard was no more, swapped for one that wasn't chipped and stained. Even without the new shelves in the supply closet, it felt like a brand-new room, all set to welcome a brand-new set of young minds.

Karen set her bag on her desk and took in the glorious sight, excited as always to discover what this new school year had to offer.

Chapter Four

After a solid week of work, Karen had finally made enough headway on her classroom setup to dive into fine-tuning her lesson plans. Each year of teaching gave her a little more insight into what worked for her classes and what areas needed tweaking before she could really expect her students to engage. Some subjects were harder than others, but she loved the challenge of getting them excited about multiplication tables and the periodic table.

Right as she was getting into a groove, Karen's door swung open. She jumped at the burst of noise, but didn't even have to look up to know it was Jessica. Her best friend was fun and sweet and perfectly embodied the phrase "bull in a china shop." Jessica hopped up onto the teacher's desk, knocking over the stack of posters Karen was planning to hang after lunch.

"How's lesson planning going?" Jessica asked.

"Depends. Are kids still playing *Minecraft*?"

"I think so."

"Then it's going great. How about you?" Karen asked.

"Oh, I haven't started yet."

"Color me shocked."

Jessica stuck out her tongue, but then leaned in conspiratorially. "The new teachers started orientation this morning. Did you sneak a peek yet?"

Karen closed her laptop. Jessica wouldn't let her get any work done any time soon. She didn't mind. After all, Jessica was the one who kept her from falling into the all-work-no-play version of herself.

"I've been too busy," Karen said.

"I figured. Don't worry, I worked up a full gossip report for you."

"You know what goes super well with gossip?" Karen asked with a grin.

Jessica produced two cans of orange soda from her bag and waggled them in the air. Karen's whole body relaxed with the warmth of their shared guilty pleasure. Jessica hopped back off the desk and hurried over to the reading area in the corner, Karen on her heels. Jessica curled her legs beneath her on the armchair while Karen stretched out on the padded bench. The snap of cans opening and carbonation escaping filled their little alcove.

Jessica scrunched her eyebrows. "They didn't have Sallie Bell's for breakfast, which is a sacrilege. Imagine bringing in a new group of teachers and serving them last year's frozen cinnamon rolls thawed in cafeteria ovens."

"Our salaries are flirting with the poverty line. Free food is free food."

"Yeah, well, it's a disgrace that we treat our teachers like that. I told Roger as much while he was kicking me out."

"You got kicked out?" Karen asked.

"Yeah, the event was for new staff only."

"Wait, so you don't actually have any gossip to pass on?"

Karen's lip pout had always been effective with Jessica, and this was no exception. She sat up straighter in her chair and rushed to defend her snooping skills. "Of course I do. The high school chemistry teacher looks like a dweeb."

"Harsh."

"He was wearing a bow tie."

"Bow ties are cute," Karen said.

"Not on this guy. Trust me, he irons his underwear."

"Do you have any gossip that isn't mean-spirited?" Karen punctuated her teasing with a wink.

"I am not mean. I'm the sweet friend, remember? You better remember or you won't get to hear about our two new teachers."

Karen stretched her toes and pretended to contemplate for a moment, but they both knew she'd give in. Karen needed Jessica in her life. The person who ensured she had fun and took herself less seriously. Karen rolled onto her side, then settled her weight onto her elbow and gave her most winning smile.

"You are the sweet friend and you have the best gossip, so lay it on me."

"The new second grade teacher is from the Midwest. He sounds like the folks from that show. What's it called?"

"*Fargo*?"

"Yeah, that's the one," Jessica said.

"What's his name?"

"You know I'm terrible with adult names."

Karen laughed and shook her head. "I'll ask him when we meet."

"You won't because you'll be super distracted by the new art teacher." Jessica's sly smile was almost too obvious.

"Oh yeah, why's that?"

"She's really cute and I'm pretty sure she's queer."

Karen had been down this road more times than she could count and she had the scars to prove it, so she didn't want to get her hopes up. Still, her heart beat a little faster without her permission. She tried to be casual when she asked, "Why do you think she's queer?"

"She has orange hair."

There was the letdown Karen had been expecting. At least it was early this time. She rolled her eyes and slumped back against the painted cinderblock wall. "You're ridiculous."

"No, seriously. It's very queer hair. Not Prince Harry orange, more like traffic cone orange. You should check her out."

"What would make you think I'd be attracted to a traffic cone?" Karen's incredulity definitely colored her tone, but really, what a ridiculous thing to say.

"Sweetie, if I had a dry streak as long as yours, I'd be jumping on a traffic cone in more ways than one. Come with me to check her out."

Jessica's response was teasing, but with that gentle kindness that defined her so completely. Karen wanted to be upset, but she didn't have nearly enough rechargeable C batteries to keep living like this. When Jessica hopped up and told Karen to follow her to the cafetorium to spy on the cute new art teacher, Karen followed with only a little bit of grumbling.

They made sure to use the middle door that led from the atrium to the cafetorium because that was the only one that didn't currently squeak from years of neglect. The insider knowledge served them well because they made it in without being spotted by the presenter, the school district's human resource representative. It helped that the lights were dimmed for what was no doubt a riveting PowerPoint presentation.

Jessica leaned close to whisper in Karen's ear. "That's her in the second row on the end."

Karen didn't need the direction. She had spotted the new art teacher the moment she scanned the room. Karen could only see her profile, but she thought Jessica was right, she was probably queer. That assumption might have been because of her bearing, but Karen prayed to every god who had ever been worshiped Jessica was right because the new art teacher was absolutely captivating.

As though she could feel eyes on her, she turned and her eyes locked on Karen's. The buzz of the monotone presentation faded away and Karen swore she could hear the woman's breath catch. Or maybe that was her own gasp she heard because, God, those eyes. They were fathomless and dark, maybe from the subdued light of the room or maybe from nature. But mostly it was the way they seemed to pierce all the way to Karen's soul. She didn't look away like people normally would either. She stared at Karen unashamedly and unnervingly.

Karen stared back as long as she could, but all of a sudden, the intensity of that eye contact was too much and she had to look away. Breaking the eye contact didn't stop the flood of excitement-laced panic pouring through Karen's veins. She bolted before she could stop herself. She didn't even realize it until she was back in the atrium where the light was too bright and the sounds too sharp.

"Hey, you okay?" Jessica asked.

Karen hadn't realized she'd followed. She kept moving, staring straight ahead because she knew her best friend would know something was up if she could see her face right now.

"Fine. I just have work to do."

"She's cute, right?" Jessica asked.

"I couldn't really tell. It was dark in there."

Jessica didn't buy it, but Karen's fast pace had already carried them back to her classroom door. She rushed inside to hide behind her desk and mercifully Jessica stayed in the hall. She did lean in to fire one last parting shot, though.

"You'll get a better look soon and then I know you'll agree with me."

❖

Karen couldn't keep her mind on her task as she decorated her classroom. The new art teacher's shockingly dark eyes distracted her. And the way she unabashedly stared? Karen's stomach fluttered and she accidentally taped her thumb to the poster she was hanging. Too bad she'd been too far away to discern the actual color, but she couldn't forget the challenge in that stare. Confidence that was as terrifying as it was sexy.

She released her thumb and tried again. Why had that woman been staring at her with such confidence anyway? It wasn't like gorgeous women often went around staring at strangers. Especially her.

"Get it together," she growled.

Karen finally managed to hang the poster, but when she stepped back to examine her work, something caught her eye. The poster's border was orange, just like the new art teacher's hair. Jessica was wrong, though. It wasn't traffic-cone orange at all. The color was obviously fake, and not the best dye job at that, but it was more the golden orange of a setting sun than the blaze orange of a traffic cone. The wild color didn't make her queer, though. Did it?

What did it matter? Even if this woman was queer, it didn't mean she would like Karen any more than any other woman had in her life. Just look at Nicki, who had been more interested in spending three years single than going on a second date with Karen. She shouldn't get her hopes up. Hope didn't have a place in Karen's love life, and she shouldn't torture herself with it. Still, she kept seeing those eyes in her mind's eye and letting her stomach do their somersaults unchecked.

"Good afternoon, Karen."

Roger's voice unexpectedly booming out behind her made Karen jump, squeak, and drop the roll of tape. She spun to see a crowd gathered in the doorway.

"I didn't mean to startle you," Roger said. "The new teachers are on break from their orientation and I thought I'd show them around. Introduce them to the members of their new family."

Roger had always talked about the staff like that—like a family. Honestly, it was pretty accurate. They spent more time in these halls than they spent at home. There were folks here with friendships so close they might've been kin. Plus, just like her own family, Karen was the teacher all the other teachers were happy to see, but no one remembered to talk to, to paraphrase Jane Austen. Still, no matter how surface their relationships were destined to be, Karen was interested to meet them. Okay, she was mostly interested to meet the new art teacher who'd been haunting her thoughts all afternoon.

And there she was, just as confident and captivating as ever and staring at Karen like she was a butterfly pinned to a board. To save her sanity, Karen quickly looked away to the other new teacher, a young man who was so young he looked like he'd just graduated high school. He also looked like he was nearly bursting with fear in this new place. The contrast between them made Karen swallow a laugh and turn it into a smile. She was just like him once, so she didn't want to make him any more self-conscious, but it was still funny to see.

"This is our new second grade teacher, Ethan Fitzhugh," Roger said.

Karen shook the sweaty palm shoved toward her and tried the gentle smile she used on her shier students. "Hi, Ethan. It's nice to meet you."

He stuttered out his thanks—sounding exactly like the characters in *Fargo* as advertised—and then shuffled around to allow the new art teacher to the front. Roger didn't have a chance to introduce her before she took Karen's hand in a decidedly less sweaty, more tantalizing grip.

"Hello, I'm Bianca."

"Karen."

God, had she really introduced herself with a single word like a caveman? Had she even spoken out loud? Her blood was thudding so loud in her ears she could barely hear her own voice. Bianca was breathtaking in a way Karen had not experienced in a very long time, and she spent a long moment taking in all her details.

That golden orange hair fell in messy waves past her shoulders. Her eyebrows were a deep, luxurious brown and the visible hair on her arms was the same shade. Her eyes were finally discernible as a warm, fathomless brown. They were bold in a way that had nothing to do with the color and everything to do with the way she shamelessly examined Karen. Her gaze on Karen felt like a physical touch, leaving her exposed and raw.

Bianca's face was round with big cheeks and a high forehead accentuated by eyeglasses with chunky, black frames. The rest of her body was lost within endless folds of a flowing dress. That was most definitely a good thing since Karen really shouldn't be checking her out any more thoroughly than she already had.

Bianca held her gaze and her hand just a little too long for a new coworker and Karen found herself just as nervous as Ethan. Once she released it, however, Karen was able to remember her manners.

"Welcome to Bucks Mill Elementary. If you need anything or have any questions as you settle in, please don't hesitate to ask."

"Thanks, Karen. You're so sweet," Bianca said.

Hearing Bianca say her name did wonderful and terrible things to Karen's insides. Fireworks burst in her chest at the slight praise. A mild sense of fear swept over her, knowing she would do just about anything to get more.

Ethan didn't acknowledge the offer, maybe because he knew it wasn't exactly directed at him and maybe because he was too overwhelmed by the new environment to speak. The kid was hiding behind his new boss, and Karen felt an overwhelming desire to dive under her desk until the whole group left. When Bianca's gaze finally left her, Karen was lightheaded and didn't hear much of Roger's goodbyes.

Before she knew it, the little group had moved on, leaving her standing alone in the doorway like an idiot with only her water-logged brain and the lingering scent of Bianca's perfume.

CHAPTER FIVE

Bucks Mill Elementary was a whole new place the following Monday. It was a week before classes started and the first day that all teachers and staff were required to be on campus. While Karen preferred all the time she could get to set up her classroom and prepare for the coming school year, most of her colleagues could prepare in just five days. In all fairness, the turnover rate at Bucks Mill Elementary was very low and most teachers had been there for decades. In fact, before this year's two new hires, Karen's eight years of service put her last in line for seniority. The school district might've been poor and rural and it wasn't the most glamorous place to work, but this town was special and when people got there, they didn't want to leave.

When she arrived at the bank of front doors this time, all of them were unlocked and Doug was in conversation with a pair of kindergarten teachers. Since talking to Doug could make an entire morning disappear, Karen hurried toward her classroom. As she was passing the glass wall of the front office, Karen noted the school's secretary, Dana, was already hard at work helping a parent fill out paperwork. Unflappable as always, Dana spared a cheery wave for Karen before returning her full attention to her decidedly frazzled new parent.

"Hi, Karen. How was your summer?" Sheila Washington asked from the doorway of her library.

"Short as always. How about yours?"

Sheila's smile lit up her eyes and spread across her thin cheeks. Sheila's flawless skin was a dark, rich brown like fine mahogany and her long locs were liberally studded with silver. Her gentle voice and measured cadence gave her an air of authority that made students and teachers alike acknowledge her as the de facto grandmother of Bucks Mill Elementary.

"Glorious. My daughter took me and my grandkids to Bermuda for vacation."

"Sounds wonderful."

With parents who lived on the Bay, beach vacations had lost their shine for Karen, but she accepted that she was in the minority in that view. Besides, she loved hearing the exploits of Sheila's plastic surgeon daughter and her precocious twins. When the music teacher, Mary, joined them, however, Karen took the opportunity to make her exit.

"Oh, Karen," Sheila called as she walked away. "Congratulations on not being the new kid on the block anymore."

Karen laughed and waved, but how could anyone still think of her as the new kid after eight years? To her surprise, though, the sentiment was repeated by three other teachers on her journey back to her hallway. Nearly everyone she saw stopped her for warm, if surface, conversations. Karen tried to prolong them since she was feeling mildly extroverted that day, but everyone was so busy they didn't have time for much more than a recap of their summer and speculation on how long Ethan would make it before a student made him cry.

It took her longer than usual to get to her classroom door, but she arrived with warmth in her heart to see the halls brimming with life again. She was so thrilled to see all the classroom doors open and lights blazing. It would be even better in a week's time when the kids brought their own unique energy into the place. Karen was so distracted by the joy of fresh energy in the halls that the sight that greeted her in her classroom caught her completely off guard. Her metal travel coffee mug clattered to the floor before she even realized her fingers had lost their grip.

Bianca was sitting cross-legged on the edge of her desk, her flowy, diaphanous skirt brushing lazily against her nicely shaped calf. She had been staring intently at the posters on Karen's classroom wall, though surely she wasn't that interested in the different states of matter. At the noisy clatter of Karen's entrance, Bianca turned an absolutely bone-melting smile on her and hopped off the desk to cross the room. She marched over until she was right in Karen's personal space, then leaned over to retrieve the miraculously unspilled coffee.

"Sorry to barge right in. I thought I'd stop by to chat. We didn't get the most personal introduction the other day," Bianca said.

Karen couldn't quite corral her tongue. It seemed less interested in articulating words and more interested in lolling out of her mouth in drooling admiration of the woman inches away from her. Instead of talking, she forced a smile onto her numb lips and scuttled behind her desk. Breathing and moving her limbs was easier with some distance between her and Bianca, but it didn't last. As soon as she turned around, she found Bianca beside her, sliding back onto the top of her desk, this time with her long legs nearly touching Karen's chair.

"Sorry to pounce on you first thing this morning. I'd just love to get to know you better," Bianca said.

Her brain and tongue still weren't syncing the way they should. Karen blurted out, "Why?"

The question sounded a little rude, but Bianca seemed unfazed. "You did offer to answer my questions. I have tons."

Karen finally relaxed in the realization that this was a completely professional visit. She might be doused in hormones, acting like an idiot around a beautiful woman, but Bianca was scrambling to get her feet under her at a new job.

Karen laughed. "Don't worry, I won't tell Roger his orientation wasn't thorough."

Bianca joined her with a laugh that sent another shiver through Karen's body, but she waved her hand dismissively. "Oh, I've been teaching long enough that I can find my way around any classroom. No, I'm more interested in the students and the staff."

"If you're looking for gossip, I'm probably not your girl."

"No, no. I'm wondering who I should look out for. You know, which of the kids needs a little extra attention."

"Now that I can help you with," Karen said.

"I had a feeling. See, you are my girl."

Karen worked hard to swallow, but there wasn't any moisture in her mouth. She tried to tell herself Bianca hadn't meant it the way it sounded, but her racing heart wasn't getting the message. It seemed wiser to run away again, so she grabbed her coffee and made for the reading corner at the back of the classroom, barely remembering to wave Bianca after her.

Bianca settled into the teacher's armchair, pulling her knees up to her chest and sitting sideways like a teenager. She carefully tucked her feet beneath her and adjusted her skirt in practiced movements that told Karen she often sat this way. She hadn't been able to sit like that in ages without a dozen different aches and pains, but Bianca moved so gracefully. Karen forced herself not to dwell on how flexible Bianca was. Thoughts like that would not lead to a professional conversation.

In her khakis and loafers, Karen was able to sit on the padded bench without worrying about her wide stance. She dropped her elbows to her knees and contemplated who to discuss. No one had ever asked about this before, and she was impressed that a new teacher was more interested in her students' comfort than her own.

"Chloe Wentworth is a fourth grader who will probably be very quiet and withdrawn. I haven't seen her this summer, but she lost her father last year and took it very hard."

"Poor thing. What a huge loss so young." Bianca's eyes filled with sadness and maybe even a tear.

"She has a lot of support at home. She and her mother are both seeing a therapist, so hopefully she's healing, but be gentle with her."

"Of course."

"There's a pair of fifth graders, Tinley Bamford and Lily Hanson. They're very close and it will probably seem like they aren't paying attention, but they are. Most teachers try to split them up, but don't do it. They function better as a unit and they'll be your best students if you let them be," Karen said.

Bianca shook her head, her expression thoughtful. She might have been insulted about another teacher giving her classroom management advice.

Karen said, "Sorry. I just told you how to handle discipline in your own classroom. Forgive my rudeness. I just really like those kids."

Bianca waved off her protest. "I don't like to split up friends, even if they're a little chatty. It feels too much like punishing girls who take up the same space as boys."

"Wow. That's how I feel, too."

Karen looked at Bianca again, this time without lust clouding her view. Bianca was maybe a few years older than her, in her late thirties or early forties, and Karen hadn't really expected such a modern approach to gendered discipline. Maybe this was another point in the column of Bianca being queer? But it might just be that she was an artist.

"How long have you been teaching?" Karen asked.

"Fourteen years."

"Have you always taught art in elementary schools?"

"Oh, yes. I love kids this age. Their tiny little minds just bursting with all sorts of new ideas. They'll try styles and techniques the older kids wouldn't touch. They're just wonderful."

"I couldn't agree more," Karen said.

"So you've always taught this age. What year do you teach? I'm afraid I didn't do any research before I dropped in on you."

"Third grade. And yes, I've always taught third. Always taught third here, in fact."

Bianca leaned forward, a pair of dangling necklaces swinging free of her shirt in her interest. Before she could say anything else, however, the speakers overhead crackled and Dana's voice blared into the room.

"All staff, please make your way to the cafetorium for the welcome assembly."

Dana repeated the request twice before signing off. By the time the speaker had gone silent, Bianca had unfolded herself from the chair. She held out her hand to shake, and the contact sent a fresh jolt of electricity through Karen.

"Thanks for your time. We'll have to catch up more later," Bianca said.

As soon as Bianca walked out of her orbit, the light in the room dimmed. There had been an energy in her presence and Karen had basked in it. Part of her wanted to chase after Bianca just to recapture it. The rest of her recognized that would be super unprofessional.

Bianca was nearly out the door before Karen remembered her manners and said goodbye. Then she was alone in her classroom, her head still spinning.

❖

The first day of school was Karen's favorite day of the year, even better than Christmas. When she was a kid, she'd loved the smell of fresh pencils and the crinkle of unopened spiral notebooks. As an adult, she loved the energy. All the kids and parents in town had been on edge for weeks, waiting for their whole world to shift focus. Now the tension had snapped and the brand-new feeling rushed through everyone's veins like a drug.

The scene at Bucks Mill Elementary was pandemonium. Kindergarteners nervously excited and most of their parents simply excited to have a little time to themselves during the day. Eager fifth graders on the precipice of a new phase in their lives, but with one more year in their safety net. Everyone in between showing varying levels of nerves and elation.

Elementary school was a magical place. Teachers strived to ease a new generation into learning without ripping them out of their childhood. High school existed to do that damage. Elementary school was all about finding the joy in knowledge and new friends. There was no place like it and it was the energy Karen wanted permanently in her life.

Karen arrived at school ridiculously early—in fact, she was there before Roger as usual. She wanted to be the one to unlock her classroom on a new school year. By the time the roar of bus engines rattled her classroom window, she had already laid out a blank name tag and school calendar on each desk and written her name neatly on the whiteboard.

A burst of adult laughter filled in the halls and Karen fought the urge to scuttle over and peek through the sidelight of her classroom door. Despite Bianca's promise they catch up more last week, Karen hadn't seen her since the opening assembly. She'd tried not to get her hopes up, but disappointment flooded through her, a feeling Karen was intimately familiar with after years of romantic disappointment, but she still hated how quickly it had come this time around.

Bianca had been onstage for the welcome assembly that had broken up their meeting last week and Karen couldn't keep her eyes off her. Jessica had teased her mercilessly for the intensity of her interest. Right up until the point Roger had introduced her to the staff as Mrs. Bianca Harper. Had it been Karen's imagination that he'd put extra emphasis on the "Mrs." part? Jessica had given her that sad, apologetic look she got every time a new romance opportunity fell through.

Karen had been so embarrassed by the pity that she'd hidden in her classroom all week. She just needed time for Jessica to forget that she was hopeless. Jessica had been kind enough to play along. The crush, like all her others, had died an early death to be replaced with a determination for friendship. That had always worked for Karen in the past, and the last thing she needed was to pine after a married woman. Unfortunately, it was hard to make friends with someone she rarely saw, and Karen spent very little time in the common areas of the school.

Fortunately, the calendar she'd just deposited on every student's desk informed her that tomorrow morning at eleven a.m. she'd be dropping her students off at Bianca's classroom for their first art class. That would be her first chance to kindle a friendly vibe.

The first bell rang through the speakers overhead, pushing all thoughts of Bianca away. Her love life, or lack thereof, would never be enough to distract her from her duty to these kids. She yanked down on the points of her navy-blue vest, making sure they lined up with the crease on her khakis, and walked to her assigned spot in front of her classroom, ready to meet her new students.

CHAPTER SIX

The scratch of pencils on paper nearly lulled Karen into a stupor. She scanned the class, most of whom had their heads down, though a few stared blankly at the sample equation she'd drawn on the whiteboard. She checked her watch, then gave them another minute before rising to her feet.

"Okay, class, finish up your assignment and tidy your desks." She steeled herself for the next part. "It's time to take you to your first art class."

She'd barely gotten a chance to learn their names, much less their personalities in just one day, so she watched their reactions. They'd had art classes over the last two years, but they all knew a new teacher was waiting for them in the sprawling studio across the school. A few students beamed at each other, a few more bounced in their chairs.

Carly Simpson, who had practically run into the classroom the day before, was among the most excited. Art was a popular subject, of course, but Karen suspected she was equally excited for the adventure of a new teacher. Benji Brown was less enthused. He would probably be more excited for library day Wednesday, just like his older brother. But all the kids were too well behaved to make a fuss just yet.

At their age—mostly eight with a few nine-year-olds sprinkled in depending on their birthdays—most of Karen's students were pretty good. They didn't need to challenge authority like teenagers and the toddler-esque inattentiveness of the younger students had been worked out of them over the previous two years. Maybe later in the year some of them would test boundaries, but most would wait until fifth grade. She liked the ability to nurture her students and that was harder with troublemakers in the group. Troublemakers at this age were most likely in need of attention or affirmation, and Karen could give those in equal measure when needed.

"Okay, let's line up next to the door. Slowly please." Karen lifted her voice over the scraping of chairs and scuttle of sneakers.

They were lined up and almost still within a few minutes. Karen waited until the bell sounded to open the door and lead them down the hall. As they passed the library, she peeked over at Benji. He was, indeed, staring longingly through the plate glass windows displaying rows and rows of short bookshelves.

"Let's wait here for Mr. Fitzhugh's class."

The group stopped haphazardly, a few students bumping into each other as Ethan's second graders scuttled across the hall. He gave her a weak wave as his students lined up in front of the library, giving her a view of the sweat stains on his shirt. Karen gave him an extra warm smile, and he seemed to stand a little taller.

Karen leaned over to whisper in Benji's ear. "If I get a good report from Mrs. Harper after your art class, tomorrow I'll show you the new batch of books we got in over the summer."

There was extra bounce to Benji's step as they continued toward the art classroom. Karen couldn't help mimicking his excited walk as they neared the bathrooms. She was eager to take her first bathroom break of the day since her body had instantly remembered the more rigid school year schedule. The time between first bell and this eleven a.m. break felt longer than ever.

Not even her swollen bladder could distract her from the thought of seeing Bianca for the first time in a week, though. Despite her best attempts to see her only as a potential new friend, Karen had a hard time shaking the excitement her first glimpse of Bianca had brought. She just had to think of her as Mrs. Harper. It was easier that way, especially with an emphasis on the title. That would settle her firmly into friend territory in Karen's mind.

Karen turned the last corner just in time to see Bianca sweep out of her open classroom door. It had been foolish to think she could have gotten over her burgeoning crush so quickly. Bianca was stunning and somehow more so each time Karen saw her. Today she was wearing her bright hair partially pulled back by a pair of ornamental bronze hair pins, twisted in an intricate knot. Her normal thick-framed glasses swung in front of her on a beaded chain that disappeared in the flowing peasant top she wore over another loose skirt in a dizzying pattern. After greeting the first student and telling everyone to go inside, Bianca looked up and caught Karen's eye, showering her with one of those earth-shattering smiles.

"Ouch." Benji squeaked as he walked directly into Karen, then bounced off the cinderblock wall beside him.

"Oh, Benji. I'm sorry."

Karen felt the heat on her cheeks as she bent over to check on her student. She hadn't realized until he'd plowed into her that Bianca's smile had brought her to a dead stop in the middle of the hall.

"Uh, it's okay."

Karen picked up her pace and Benji trotted after her, rubbing the side of his head.

"Welcome, everyone. Head inside and grab any seat you want," Bianca said as the students filed past her.

Karen fiddled with the attendance sheet as Bianca greeted every second or third child exuberantly. Her heart beat extra fast. Why wouldn't her body cooperate? Bianca was a married woman. Her mind knew it was inexcusable to feel this way about her, but her body had not gotten the memo. It didn't help that the kids seemed drawn to her as well. Every movement Bianca made had the grace of a dancer and every child she made eye contact with walked away grinning from ear to ear. At least Karen wasn't the only one dazzled by her presence.

Once the last student was inside, Bianca turned back to Karen with that unflinching attention. "Nice to see you again. How's the first week going?"

"Good. Everything's good. The students are...good." Could she have said good anymore often? What was wrong with her today? "How's your day?"

"Good."

Bianca gave a little wink that made Karen want to melt into the floor. To cover the awkward moment, she held out the attendance sheet. "No absences today."

"I'd hope so. It's only day two." Bianca took the paper but didn't look at it. She kept those remarkably brown eyes trained on Karen. "See you at the end of class then."

Karen nodded and Bianca gave her one last smile before sweeping into the classroom and pulling the door closed. Karen stood there, staring at the closed door for a long moment before she remembered her full bladder and the forty-five glorious minutes of quiet before she had to collect the kids for lunch. She hurried back in the direction of the bathrooms. Why had she been so awkward on this first encounter? It wasn't like her to be so flustered. Apparently, the crush on Bianca had been stronger than she'd originally thought, but that was okay. Surely it would only get easier from here.

Karen walked down the blissfully quiet hall toward her classroom on Friday afternoon, leaving the muted roar of the cafetorium behind her. She loved her students, but she cherished this break in the middle of the day when she could shed the teacher persona and just be Karen. She didn't have to school her features or watch her words. She didn't have to prioritize the needs of a whole class of kids staring up at her. She could put her feet up on her desk, look out the window, and eat her homemade chicken salad.

As she entered the main hallway, the sound of sandals smacking against tile made her look to her left. Bianca strode purposefully down the hall, lunch box in hand and a series of long necklaces swinging. Karen hadn't seen her since their brief interaction Tuesday morning outside the art classroom, and she thrilled at this ships crossing in the night moment.

"Hi there." Bianca waved, her warm smile brightening the plain walls and scuffed floor.

Karen stopped, waiting for Bianca to join her. "How's your first week going?"

"Wonderful. The kids are sweet and my classroom is enormous compared to my last school."

"Happy to hear it." Karen squirmed as she ran out of pleasantries. "Well, enjoy your lunch."

Karen started back toward her classroom, expecting to hear Bianca's sandals slap off into the distance. Instead, Bianca fell into step beside her as she turned down the third-grade hallway.

"I noticed you haven't been eating in the teachers' lounge this week. Is that your normal habit?" Bianca asked.

"I like peace and quiet so I stick to my classroom." She didn't want to come across as antisocial, so she added, "Besides, I'd never get in a mouthful. My best friend is a teacher here, too, and she likes to chat with everyone."

Bianca laughed a musical, tinkling sound that sent a pang of regret through Karen's chest. She was fine with being just friends, but Bianca was far more enticing than her other failed romantic interests. Time and familiarity would dull that pang though, maybe it was time to get to know Bianca better.

"Where was your last school with the tiny classroom?" she asked.

"A Boston suburb called Waltham. It was nice enough but maybe a little too big for me."

"You definitely won't find Bucks Mill too big. Hopefully it isn't too small for you?" Karen asked.

"Not at all. I've had my fill of big cities. I'm looking forward to the slower pace."

Karen was going to ask Bianca why she'd had her fill of big cities, but they were close enough to her classroom to see Jessica waiting outside, her nose buried in her phone.

In fact, she was so focused on her phone that she didn't look up before saying, "Took you long enough."

"That's my fault for waylaying her on the way here," Bianca said.

Since Karen had known it would happen, she got to witness every hilarious moment of Jessica's reaction. She jerked her head up so fast at the unexpected voice that she nearly cracked the back of her head on the doorframe. Her wide eyes dropped to spot Bianca's lunch box, and one eyebrow shot up.

It took Jessica several long seconds to collect herself. "Oh, hi. Sorry to interrupt. I was just checking in on Karen, but it can wait. I'll go to the teachers' lounge."

"No, no. Stay. I was just heading to that charming little picnic table in the courtyard to eat my lunch alone," Bianca said.

"You don't have to do that," Jessica said.

"I'm feeling the need for some fresh air and the last of the summer heat. Enjoy your lunch," Bianca said.

Bianca wasn't even halfway to the courtyard door when Jessica opened her mouth, so Karen yanked her into the classroom by her wrist and shut the door.

The door barely shut behind them before Jessica burst out, "What the hell is going on?"

"Nothing." Karen marched to her desk and dropped into her chair.

"Bullshit. Why didn't you tell me you had a lunch date with the hot new art teacher?"

"I didn't have a lunch date with the married new art teacher." She put the same heavy emphasis on married that Jessica had put on hot. "We just ran into each other in the hall."

Jessica unzipped her lunch bag while leveling a distinctly skeptical look on Karen. She chose to ignore it, collecting her own lunch from her bottom drawer and taking her time setting out the different items. She knew Jessica wouldn't last long, and she wasn't disappointed.

"Everyone's been trying to get the scoop on her, but she doesn't share much," Jessica said around a mouthful of turkey on wheat.

"It's only been a week."

"That's usually plenty of time for the busybodies in this school. How long did it take you to spill your life story?"

Karen peeled the top off her salad and leaned back in her chair. The memory of her first year at Bucks Mill Elementary wasn't her favorite. She'd felt like a fish out of water and the constant interrogations from the rest of the staff didn't help.

"Three days," Karen said.

"I barely made it the first afternoon."

"And you wonder why I don't like eating in the teachers' lounge."

"They mean well, even if they are a little pushy. Anyway, I don't care about them. Tell me everything you know about Bianca."

"I don't know anything." Karen squirmed the same way she did on the rare occasions she went to the lounge.

"Oh come on, she must have told you something."

"All she said was that she used to teach outside of Boston and that she had a tiny classroom there."

Jessica's face twisted into a disappointed frown. "That's it?"

"She said she's had her fill of big cities and is looking forward to a slower pace in Bucks Mill."

That hadn't satisfied Jessica's thirst for gossip, but Karen had already shared too much. Since Bianca hadn't shared even those small bits of information with anyone else, she probably shouldn't have told anyone, even her best friend.

"Aren't you at least interested in why she doesn't share much?"

"Maybe y'all are coming on too strong," Karen said.

"Hey, don't include me in that y'all. I haven't been hounding her for details. I just get the secondhand gossip."

Karen chose not to point out the hypocrisy of that, especially when Jessica changed the subject to first impressions of their students. This was much safer ground for Karen. She didn't want to dissect why Bianca was comfortable sharing with her and not the other teachers. She just wanted to ease into a friendship with her.

CHAPTER SEVEN

K aren was up early on Saturday, just like it was any other school day. She didn't linger in bed or fight for more sleep. The work week was over, but that only made her more eager to be up and moving. This morning was just as much a part of the first week of school excitement as the classes.

Today she and Jessica were headed to the annual Sunflower Festival at a farm an hour outside town. They'd started the tradition not long after they'd moved from dating to best friends and it was one of Karen's favorite days of the year. It got them out of town and let them decompress after a hectic first week, and this was the first time she would have to take photographs since coming back to Bucks Mill. The sunflowers photographed beautifully, and images from previous festivals took up much of the limited wall space in her apartment. It didn't hurt that the farm also played host to one of their favorite local breweries.

Jessica was the type who liked to vent about every little misfortune and frustration, but it was in a kind-hearted way. Less complaining and more bonding over their shared experiences. Brandon was a fix it kind of guy, inclined to offer his opinions rather than be the vessel Jessica needed. Karen loved to sit back, bask in the sun, and revel in knowing she was exactly where she wanted to be in life.

Okay, not exactly where she wanted to be. Karen loved having someone to do fun things with on the weekends. She wanted it to be a partner, but a friend was good too. Of course, the more time she spent out and about, the more chance she had of finding someone compatible and single to try dating.

Her bag loaded down with her digital camera rather than her usual laptop, Karen stepped out of her front door into an overcast morning. The local weatherman promised it would turn into a perfectly clear day, and the sun was already starting to cut through the clouds. There was nothing like early fall in the mountains, with the leaves still green but a crisp note in the air. That change from summer to fall was such a magical feeling. Karen had always hated summer. Not just because of the oppressive heat and humidity, but because it took her away from school. Both as a student and a teacher, she hated those breaks. She wanted to be doing and learning. She much preferred the freshness of autumn and the endless possibilities that a new school year brought.

She took exactly one step down the sidewalk before her phone rang in her pocket. She laughed and continued her course toward Sallie Bell's Bakery as she answered.

"Just how late are you going to be?" Karen asked. "I was expecting fifteen minutes, but it must be even later than that if you're calling to warn me."

"Please don't hate me," Jessica said, that adorable whine in her voice.

"If I hated you every time you were late, we'd never get along."

"What about when I cancel?"

Karen came to a stop in the middle of the sidewalk. "What?"

"I'm really sorry, but Brandon had a horrendous week at work and needs some cheering up. I promised to take him to a movie and feed him more pizza than is good for him."

Karen shuffled out of the center of the sidewalk even though there was no other foot traffic this early on a Saturday morning. She leaned against the brick facade of the nearest building and squeezed her eyes shut, willing the stinging in her eyes not to turn into tears. The last thing she wanted was for Jessica to know how hurt she was. She didn't want Jessica's guilt to make it worse.

"Oh no, I completely understand."

"Are you sure? You're not upset?" The relief in Jessica's voice proved she'd done her job well.

"I'm bummed I won't see you, but no, I'm not upset." She swallowed hard around the lump in her throat. "Take care of that husband of yours and tell him to eat an extra slice of pepperoni for me."

"Thanks. Take some cool pictures and we'll do something next weekend, okay?"

"Sure. See you Monday."

Karen hung up and let her head fall back against the wall. She pushed against the full weight of her disappointment. After all, she didn't want to be that unhinged woman who cried on the street, especially since there was every chance a parent would see her.

Why did she let something like this affect her so much? She should expect it. Things like this happened to her all the time. On dark days she worried there was something wrong with her. No one ever seemed to want to spend as much time with her as she wanted to spend with them. Today seemed destined to be one of those dark days.

She closed her eyes and did the breathing exercise her therapist taught her for when she was starting to spiral. She focused on the air entering her lungs, bringing oxygen to the farthest reaches of her fingertips and toes. Then she focused on breathing out a lungful of carbon dioxide, thinking of the waste gas like the waste thoughts, both intent on sucking the life from her. It connected her to the rudimentary science lessons she taught her students and centered her.

Trying to shake the negative feelings before they settled too deep, she looked down the street toward the next corner where Sallie Bell's waited. She was about to head that way in search of sugary, buttery therapy, when the door swung open. Nicki and Carter stepped out onto the sidewalk, swinging Lily between them on every other step. Their laughter rattled off the windows and bricks of downtown.

A wave of humiliation washed through Karen. Why had it been so easy for Nicki to fall in love with Carter but not her? What did Carter have that she didn't? And what about Jessica? What did Brandon have that she didn't? Why couldn't anyone look at her the way Nicki was looking at Carter right now? The only saving grace was that they crossed the street, so they couldn't see her, standing alone on the sidewalk, just like she always did.

The tears were getting harder to hold back. Time to give up and go back home. Despite Jessica's assumption she would go to the sunflower festival alone, nothing would depress Karen more. She spun on her heel to hurry back to her apartment on what was supposed to be an empty sidewalk. Unfortunately, there was something very solid and very close behind her.

"Oh no, watch out," cried a voice in her ear.

The next few moments were a blur of color and flashing sunlight. Karen hopped somewhat gracefully to the side, back into the safe space she'd been occupying, but her balance didn't act as quickly as her legs. She teetered one way and the large, brightly colored blur teetered in the same direction. Karen threw her arms out to stop both their descents and ended up tangled inelegantly in yards of fabric and silky hair.

"Sorry," Karen said.

"Oof," said the blur.

Just as quickly as the collision had started, it was over. Her right arm gripped the rubber and metal of a bicycle handlebar. That seemed good. She was holding up the bicycle so it didn't crash to the sidewalk, taking its rider with it.

Her left arm was wrapped tightly around a soft object, her hand splayed across something both soft and firm. It took her a moment to realize her arm was wrapped around a person and her hand was pressed against their back. The person seemed enveloped in more fabric than was usual, and they smelled absolutely divine. Like rosemary and flowers with the warm undertones of citrus.

The person she'd collided with was holding her, too. One arm was wrapped around her back and the other hand on her shoulder, like they were holding a partner in a slow dance. Was her heart racing from the adrenaline of the collision or the aching intimacy of the moment? A few heartbeats later, she realized who she was holding. And she'd thought the day couldn't get any worse.

"That was kind of a disaster, wasn't it?" Bianca laughed.

"I'm sorry." Karen tried to disentangle herself, but her arms didn't seem to want to let go.

"It was completely my fault. I shouldn't have been riding my bike on the sidewalk. I just saw you over here and wanted to come say hello. You turned around at exactly the wrong moment."

Karen finally managed to take a few steps back from Bianca, who clearly was not as embarrassed as she was. In fact, Bianca looked happier than anyone who had just been clobbered by a pedestrian had any right to look. Her long, orange-gold hair was tied back in a ponytail, but otherwise she looked exactly the same as any other day at school. Her peasant top was overflowing with folds that danced in the morning breeze and her linen pants were rolled up past her ankles.

The embarrassment of their collision hadn't quite blown the storm clouds of Karen's dark day away, but it had distracted her. Why was Bianca alone on a weekend? She decided against asking where her spouse was. She didn't want the heartache just then.

"Well, enjoy your Saturday," Karen said.

When Karen tried to step around her, Bianca moved to block her path. "I've heard really good things about the coffee shop. It's just down the street, right?"

"Sallie Bell's. Yeah, it's the yellow building right on the corner. You won't be disappointed for sure."

"Excellent. Why don't you join me? Unless you're meeting someone else?"

"I was, but my friend canceled on me." Karen chided herself for the pout in her voice, but it was too late to take it back.

"I'm sorry to hear that. Lucky for me though. It means you're free to advise me on the best pastries."

Karen wanted to refuse, but there was such expectation in Bianca's smile she couldn't bring herself to do it. She couldn't do the same thing to Bianca that Jessica had done to her.

"Okay. Sure."

For all Jessica and the other teachers complained about Bianca being closed-lipped, Karen found her full of conversation. Sure, it was light and not overly personal, but she filled the time they spent crossing the street, locking up Bianca's bike, and waiting behind a handful of customers with easy, friendly chatter. Once they stepped up to be next in line, though, she was all business.

"Okay, what should I get?" Bianca asked.

"What do you like?"

"Everything. Breads, sweets, chocolate, fruit, cream, butter. Give me all of it by the bucket load."

Karen was surprised how quick her laughter came. "Sounds like you should get one of everything on the menu."

"I'm game if you promise to split them all with me."

"I don't know if I'd survive that much food this early in the morning," Karen said.

"Okay, we'll get half the menu this time and you'll just have to commit to another trip soon to try the rest."

"I might need more trips than that. There are at least twenty pastries in that case. Plus, she has seasonal specials."

Bianca gave her an exaggerated eye roll followed by another enticing laugh. "Fine, if you want to spoil my fun, I suppose we can take it slow. Will you at least split three with me?"

Karen's smile made her cheeks ache and chased away a little more of her gloom. "I think we can arrange that."

Sallie Bell chatted Karen's ear off while Bianca pored over the pastry case like a kid on Christmas morning. Then, of course, Sallie had to chat Bianca's ear off. She was possibly the sweetest of Bucks Mill's residents and definitely the chattiest. No one, Karen included, was immune to her charms. It wasn't until the customer behind them cleared his throat for the third time that Sallie finally released them.

"Have a seat, dears, and we'll bring everything to your table. And if you cough at me one more time, Frank Winchester, I'll drag you down to Becky's clinic myself to get you a flu shot," Sallie said.

Bianca laughed all the way to the rickety little table in the corner. She settled into her chair, leaned her elbows on the table, wrapped her hands around her mug of dark roast coffee with two creamers and three sugars, and directed her penetrating gaze on Karen. It was equal parts unsettling and energizing to be the focus of those deep brown eyes.

"So what's in the bag?" Bianca asked, her voice rich and sweet as her coffee.

Karen perched on the edge of her stool. Why did she feel like a child who was in trouble but didn't know what she'd done wrong? "Um…what?"

Bianca wiggled her fingers at the messenger bag settled onto the extra chair. The many rings clicked and clacked with the movement.

"You treated that bag like it might shatter when you set it down. What's in there?"

"Oh, just my camera." Bianca's gaze didn't waver. Apparently, she hadn't fully answered the question. "I was supposed to go to the Sunflower Festival at Three Lakes Farm. I like to take photos of the flowers."

Bianca's face lit up. "Nature photographer, huh? Unexpected depths. I love it."

The words felt too much like praise or interest or something Karen didn't want to internalize, so she focused her attention on the three plates between them. She carefully sliced the bear claw into two even pieces. "It's not that big a deal, just a hobby. Not like your art."

When Karen tried to set the knife down, Bianca intercepted her. There was a brief, confusing dance that left their fingers momentarily entwined. The contact was so warm and unexpected that Karen froze, unsure of what was happening. Was Bianca trying to hold her hand? Should she return the embrace? She decided it would be more embarrassing not to, so she turned her palm over to fit into the touch at the exact moment Bianca gained control of the knife. Karen wanted to melt into a puddle of embarrassment, but Bianca apparently hadn't noticed her awkwardness. Instead, she deftly sliced both the raspberry Danish and apricot orange cream scone in half. As nonchalantly as possible, Karen retracted her hand, trying to casually slide it off the table, still palm up.

"Why do you think photography isn't art?" Bianca asked, oblivious to Karen's mortification.

"Oh, well, it isn't. I mean, I don't create anything. I just take pictures of stuff that's already there."

Well, this was going swimmingly. Stuff. Every time she was around Bianca, she had the vocabulary of one of her students. Awkward and articulate. Why hadn't she just gone home?

Bianca took a bite of bear claw and let out a groan of pleasure. Karen's eyes darted around the room, and, as she suspected, noted at least three people turn toward their table. Bianca, who had rolled her eyes shut and let her head tip back as she chewed, didn't seem to notice the attention.

Once she'd swallowed and dabbed a bit of glaze off her lip with a paper napkin, she turned back to Karen. "First, that was amazing. You should have warned me. Second, and most respectfully, I have to disagree. Photography is absolutely art."

Karen was on a subway car that had started to move unexpectedly. Bianca always seemed to throw her slightly off balance. Most people saw her photography as nothing more than a cute hobby, so she'd expected the same reaction from an honest-to-goodness artist.

"Oh, well, I mean, it isn't anything special. Anyone could do it."

"Anyone can be an artist. Most people are, they just don't embrace it. Your photographs—no one else could take exactly the same one as you. Your perspective makes it art. A well-lit, well-framed photograph can be far more evocative than a painting," Bianca said.

A burst of warmth in Karen's chest made a verbal reply impossible. She settled for blushing furiously and shoving far too large a bite of bear claw into her mouth. It really was incredible. All flaky, buttery pastry and smooth almond. While she chewed, she tried to think of something, anything, to deflect from the conversation. Why did it feel so good for Bianca to say those things about something that truly did have meaning to her?

Once they'd finished their first pastry, Bianca asked, "Have you had enough sugar yet for me to ask a personal question?"

Karen had her coffee mug halfway to her mouth. Rather than risk a wobble, she set it down. "Depends on how personal."

Bianca's smile was far too wicked to be allowed. "As personal as they come."

"I might need to fortify with some scone first."

"I'll allow it."

Bianca's reaction to the scone was slightly more subdued than to the bear claw, but still deeply sensual. There was a sensuality to every movement that made her impossible to ignore. Karen tried not to stare, but it was hard.

"You have to forgive me," Bianca said. "It's the Italian in me. Loving food, especially rich, indulgent food, is genetic."

Karen's laughter caught her off guard, but the little moment of humor helped settle her nerves. Maybe she could survive this breakfast without making a fool of herself after all. "So you're Italian?"

"Yep. And I live up to all the stereotypes. I love red wine, I'm loud, I talk with my hands, and I have a huge family."

"Not all of them. Isn't the stereotype New York? You're from Boston, right?"

Bianca said, "That's right, but my uncle's side of the family is in New York."

"Your uncle's side? How many sides are there?"

"Just the two. My dad's side and my uncle's. We're the bigger branch of the family. I have two older brothers, two older sisters, then me and my younger sister. The older ones all have kids. I have seven nieces and three nephews."

"Okay, you weren't kidding. You do have a big family. Are you close?"

The light dimmed a little in Bianca's eyes. She started fiddling with one of her necklaces as she said, "Some tighter than others. It's hard to be close with that many siblings. I do miss them, though. We don't get to see them much."

Karen was about to ask who she meant by "we" when she remembered Bianca was married. With the coffee and the getting-to-know-you chatting, this morning had started to feel like a date. It had been easy for her to forget.

"Okay, the scone is finished. Ready for the super personal question?" Bianca asked.

Between the returned teasing grin and the reminder that Bianca was married, Karen felt far less nervous. "I'm ready. Lay it on me."

"Why did you become a teacher?"

Karen laughed and snatched up her half of the raspberry Danish. "That's not super personal."

"Again, I respectfully disagree." Bianca cradled her coffee cup in her hands and peered over it at Karen. "Teaching is your passion."

It wasn't a question and Karen couldn't and wouldn't deny it. "True."

"Then you have a deeply personal reason for teaching."

"That is sound logic."

"Even more evidence. You're stalling."

"I'm not stalling. I'm thinking."

"Liar." Bianca grinned, then reached down to tap a fingertip lightly on the knuckles of Karen's hand to the cadence of her words. "Quit stalling and spill."

Karen laughed but looked away. She'd told this story a few times, but no one ever seemed to see the gravity of it. Maybe she put too much pressure on other people's reactions. After all, no one else could know what defining moments for others felt like. Based off her reactions to other comments, however, Bianca might just be the one to see why this was meaningful.

"When I was a kid, I didn't really fit in with my family. They're very different from me and I always felt...I don't know if this will make sense."

Bianca said, "Try me."

"I always knew my parents loved me, but there was a sense of expectation from them in everything. We always had to be the best at things. We couldn't just do things because we enjoyed them. There had to be some benefit. Some job down the road that this activity would help with. Some competition to win."

"And you aren't ambitious in that way."

Bianca had a way of speaking in declarations rather than questions and so far all of them had been correct. Was Karen so easy to read? No one had been so good at it before. "With Mrs. Thomasson, there wasn't expectation, only encouragement. It made all the difference and it saved me. I think if it weren't for her, my personality, my sense of self, everything would have been crushed under those expectations. She gave me a chance to just be okay with being me."

"And you want to be that person for others."

"I do, yeah," Karen said.

"I think that's really lovely."

Had she felt warmth when Bianca declared her photography art? It was nothing compared to the heat in her soul now. If she could form a friendship with Bianca, she might have to get used to that warmth.

"What about you? Why did you become a teacher?" Karen asked.

Bianca let out a long breath and reached for her Danish. "Are you sure you want to hear this? It's not uplifting like your story."

"Hang on. Sounds like we'll need more coffee for this," Karen said.

Bianca's sweet laughter followed her all the way to the coffee station at the front of the shop. She rushed through filling their mugs and doctoring Bianca's into a beverage that could have been labeled a dessert all on its own. When she returned, she slid the steaming mug across the table.

"Okay, I think I'm ready now," Karen said.

Bianca's laughter didn't waver, even as she started the story. "When I was little, maybe six or seven, I had one great hero in my life."

"Your dad? No, your mom."

"The school bus driver." She paused while they both laughed, then dove right back in. "He was this sweet older man with a huge mustache, but really he was the hero because driving a bus that big made him a superhero. I would sit in the seat right behind his every day and talk his ear off. He told me all about his three dogs and his son the lawyer."

"Sounds like a nice guy."

"I thought so. He listened to me, and I talked a lot, so not many people listened to me. I should have realized he literally couldn't get away from me like my siblings could. One day after a snowy weekend I found this huge icicle hanging off our roof and I thought it was the coolest thing ever. I ran with it up to the bus and gave it to my hero because I just knew he would think it was as cool as I thought it was."

Karen cringed. "I don't think I like where this story is going."

"Nope, not at all. He did not think it was cool. He threw it into the trash can next to his seat without a word."

"Oh, Bianca. That would be heartbreaking."

"It was. I was absolutely crushed. For the first time in my life, an adult treated something I loved like it was stupid. It broke something in me." Karen expected tears or a frown or something to mimic the heartbreak little Bianca had felt. Instead, she was met with a determined, unfazed smile. "So that's why I teach. I want to be the adult who preserves the magic of childhood for my students."

Blood thrummed in Karen's veins. It wasn't exactly her story, but in a way, she and Bianca had the same reason for teaching. The same passion. It was about putting their students first and recognizing that there was power in kindness. She'd never met anyone who aligned with her worldview the way Bianca did.

"I should probably get home," Bianca said.

Karen agreed and they gathered their things. Stepping onto the sidewalk outside felt like waking from a daze.

"Thanks for sharing pastries with me. You were right, I was not disappointed."

"Of course. It was fun." Karen was shocked to discover that was true.

"It was fun. Hopefully we can do it again sometime."

Karen left her to fight with her bike lock and headed back toward her apartment. In the end, she was happy she hadn't gone straight back home earlier. She might not have what Jessica and Brandon or Nicki and Carter had, but at least she was making a new friend in Bianca.

CHAPTER EIGHT

The weekly staff meetings usually held on Thursday afternoons had been skipped for the first couple weeks while everyone settled in. That led to general rejoicing among most of the teachers, so Roger's announcement that they would resume wasn't well received. A few of the usual suspects found ways to buy themselves one more week's reprieve. Sheila gleefully informed Jessica and Karen that she had a doctor's appointment and requested a full report.

"She totally did that on purpose," Jessica said as they left the library on the way to the dreaded meeting.

"No way. I'm sure it was a coincidence."

"It wasn't. I tried scheduling a checkup with Dr. Sanderson this afternoon and she said Sheila had just called to take the last appointment."

They were among the first to arrive in the teachers' lounge, so they were able to snag a table in the back. Unfortunately, this put them close to a refrigerator that rattled, leaked, and smelled like it hadn't been cleaned in at least a decade. Clearly, their inexperience with the environs of the room showed. They hustled to secure a less odorous table but were waylaid by the arrival of the other third grade teacher. Detaching themselves was a chore, and they ended up having to settle for a table near the front of the room.

Karen leaned close to Jessica's ear. "This is what happens when you talk to people. Now Roger will try and volunteer us for everything."

Jessica could only shrug and give her an apologetic look since at that moment they were joined by Mary Jefferson and Bianca. Karen smiled and greeted them with a decent facsimile of casualness, but she was immediately captured by Bianca's eyes. She was trapped like a fly in honey. It had been the same each time their paths had crossed, and it was becoming distracting. Bianca had a way of smiling and looking at her that made Karen feel like a teenager with a crush.

"Okay, settle down, everyone. Let's get started."

Roger's voice barely cut through the chatter, but it gave Karen an excuse to break eye contact. She studied him straightening his papers with far more interest than the movement deserved. She glanced back once or twice to Bianca's side of the table and, although her body was turned to their principal, her gaze kept flicking back in Karen's direction.

Roger started into his agenda, giving a long speech about how proud he was of all the staff and how the parents had nothing but praise for how smoothly the school year had started. This was one of his stock speeches Karen had heard a million times. She let her mind wander with the drone of his voice.

He wasn't wrong when he sang the praises of their team. All the teachers here were top rate educators, and while they didn't all share Karen's style or her single-minded focus on their students, they were a wonderful team. Even the new teachers seemed to fit in well. Ethan still looked spooked most days, but he hadn't run out screaming. Sheila said his students were engaged and happy when they came to the library.

Then, of course, there was Bianca. Karen had seen with her own eyes how good she was with the kids. Everything from her manner to tone of voice was designed to make the students thrive. Not to mention there was her unique personal style. While most teachers wore the same bland khakis Karen favored or subdued dresses like Jessica, Bianca had a bit more freedom given her subject matter. The fact that she wasn't buttoned up and dignified was a point in her favor as an art teacher. That lightheartedness gave the kids space for creativity. She couldn't help but remember Bianca's impassioned speech at Sallie Bell's about keeping the magic of childhood alive for her students. She certainly looked the part of a whimsical keeper of childhood magic.

Of course, thinking about Bucks Mill's most distracting teacher made it hard to keep her eyes off her. She was focused on Roger, thank goodness, and didn't notice. Jessica, however, certainly did.

"She's not wearing a wedding ring," Jessica whispered.

Karen shushed her to avoid being caught by Roger, but then she looked back across the table. She'd been staring, but not at Bianca's hands. Now she took the time to notice Bianca's left hand, which was resting on table, picking at the corner of the legal pad she'd taken a few notes on. While there were several chunky rings on her forefinger, pinky, and thumb, her ring finger was naked. She hadn't noticed before. What did that mean? Maybe Bianca wasn't married after all? Before she could stop it, a flicker of hope bloomed in Karen's chest.

More than one of Bianca's rings was colored with tiny speckles of paint or smudged and darkened. The broad metal band on her thumb was green with tarnish and scratched. More than that, she couldn't help taking note of the thumb ring. Wasn't wearing a thumb ring a thing for queer women? She was pretty sure it was. Most of the women she'd dated in college wore thumb rings. Then there was also the fact that all of Bianca's nails were short and there was no hint of polish on them.

Maybe Bianca felt Karen's eyes on her or maybe she wanted to take some notes about whatever subject Roger was lecturing on now. Whatever the reason, Bianca turned back toward the table and totally caught Karen staring at her. Heat suffused her cheeks as she gave an awkward smile, and there seemed to be the twinkle of laughter in Bianca's answering smile. Karen turned her attention to her own hands. Why hadn't she thought to bring something to take notes with? Or at least a pen to fidget with until her embarrassment cooled.

"Moving on to the school events for the fall semester."

Roger made pointed eye contact with Karen as he spoke and she cursed under her breath. Not this again. When Karen arrived at Bucks Mill, she'd been determined to be fully engaged with her new career, so she had volunteered for just about every project on the calendar. She'd assumed she would join a group of eager and experienced staff members, but had been sorely mistaken. None of the old guard had joined her and she had spent years running herself ragged because it made the kids happy.

A couple of years earlier, Jessica had finally convinced her to take a step back. The timing had been perfect since her ex, Nicki, had stepped in as a parental volunteer for the Halloween festival that year. Of course, that's where Nicki had met her soon-to-be wife, Carter. When the Halloween festival was again under threat of cancellation last year, Karen had agreed to save it. That meant weekly trips to the local pumpkin patch to watch Carter and Nicki flirt incessantly. Karen had cried on Jessica's shoulder more than once. Worse, the project that truly captured her heart, the winter talent show, had suffered from Karen's lack of time and attention.

Roger gave her his expectant stare. "We're asking for staff volunteers for the autumn events. Karen?"

Karen gritted her teeth. Of course, he didn't even bother to ask anyone else. "I'm happy to do the winter talent show again this year."

He didn't even crack a smile, just stared at her and waited.

"Don't give in," Jessica said quietly.

Roger might've heard that, since he cut a look at Jessica. "And the Halloween festival?"

The rest of the room went quiet, and all faces turned to look at Karen. She could feel Bianca's eyes on her, too. She wanted to say no. Her brain played her images of the disappointed looks Lily and Tinley and half a dozen other students gave her every year when one of their favorite events was in the balance. It also reminded her of the bone-deep weariness she had lived through until winter break. All the late nights and weekends and the agony of two happy lesbians on display while she was single and lonely. She couldn't do it. She just couldn't.

Karen turned a pleading look on the only person she could count on. Jessica avoided her eye at first. She was not the volunteering type. She wanted to come to work on time and leave on time and spend as little of her summer on campus as possible. Still, she knew better than anyone what the Halloween festival had done to Karen. She might not care about volunteer projects, but she did care about Karen. After a long moment, she met Karen's stare with a resigned sigh.

"I volunteer," Jessica said with all the enthusiasm of a *Hunger Games* tribute.

Roger's eyes went wide. "You do? I mean, um, excellent. That's the spirit."

Karen's whole body slumped in relief, and she gave Jessica a grateful smile. With the fun over, the rest of the staff went back to watching Roger with professional disinterest. Bianca was still watching her, though, and she was pretty sure she'd picked up on the silent exchange with Jessica. What would she think of the whole thing? Would she think less of Karen for not volunteering for both events? An unexpected pang shot through her chest.

"Okay, moving on to—"

Bianca spoke up, cutting Roger off. "Before we move on. Can I ask a question?"

Now Bianca was the center of attention. Not just for Karen but for the rest of the staff as well. Very few people had the temerity to interrupt Roger once he was on a roll.

"Yes, Mrs. Harper?"

"What about Thanksgiving?"

"What about it?" Roger asked.

"Don't we have a school-wide event for Thanksgiving?"

Roger narrowed his eyes as though he thought Bianca might be fomenting a coup. "Not traditionally. What did you have in mind?"

"Nothing so exciting as a talent show." She turned a beaming smile on Karen that made her brain short circuit for a moment. "But something to acknowledge the holiday. It's such a wonderful time of year, but it's always overlooked with Christmas and Halloween so close."

"We don't actually celebrate Christmas, for the record. It's a nondenominational winter celebration," Roger said with the air of a lawyer protecting himself from litigation.

"Of course. I just hate to be dismissive of such a beautiful holiday. It feels like an injustice, doesn't it?"

Bianca looked across the table encouragingly and Karen was quick to mumble something she hoped sounded like agreement. In truth, she was struck by Bianca's conviction. She should have expected it. Bianca had shown herself to be a woman who saw things other people didn't. Even sitting here in this group, she noticed the exchange with Jessica when Roger didn't. Considering how overlooked Karen felt in her family and most of the relationships in her life, it was hard not to connect to that impulse in Bianca. Especially since her feeble agreement earned her another of those radiant smiles.

In fact, that smile might have been enough to get Karen through the rest of that long, boring meeting. Unfortunately, when Bianca broke eye contact and leaned over to jot a few notes on her legal pad, one necklace swung forward out of the tangle around her neck. The sight hit Karen like a punch to the gut. It was the simple, thin gold chain, and swinging from the end was a dazzling diamond solitaire and a delicate gold wedding band.

So that explained the lack of a ring on her left hand. A diamond that stunning should never be subjected to the hazards of an art teacher's daily work. It would be ruined if she wore it on her finger, so she kept it on a chain, close to her heart. Her spouse must adore her to buy her a ring like that. That thoroughly doused the flicker of happiness Bianca's dazzling smiles had lit.

Clearly, Jessica had seen it, too, because no sooner had realization hit Karen than Jessica's elbow dug into her ribs. She didn't even bother to share a knowing look with her. Karen gave the tiniest of nods and focused her attention back on Roger. She even managed not to glance over at Bianca every few minutes for the rest of the meeting.

CHAPTER NINE

"Once more, Maria closed her eyes. She im…im…"

Karen smiled down at Carly from the big armchair. She watched closely as she tried to sound out the word, careful to ride that fine line between letting Carly try long enough to succeed, but not so long she was embarrassed. She also kept an eye on Benji, who was positively radiating enthusiasm to pronounce the word for his classmate. Benji's strength was reading and vocabulary, while Carly excelled at math. Soon Karen would pair some students together so they could help each other, but it was too early for that now.

"That was really close, Carly. You did an excellent job sounding it out, but 'i' can be a tricky letter. It's pronounced imagine. Let's all say it together."

The whole class chanted the word with her three times, with pronunciations still all over the place. Each year, vocabulary got a little more complex and third grade was the biggest leap in complexity they'd had so far. She would start to see some separation throughout the year as some of her students fell behind. She'd keep an eagle eye out for it so she could give extra help where needed.

"Ava, why don't you pick up the next paragraph?" Karen said.

Ava launched into the story with the same eagerness some students showed running out to the playground. "'You'll have to climb up to get her,' Travis said. 'Why me?' 'Because you're taller.'"

"Just a little bit slower, Ava. Make sure to take a breath between the lines so we know someone new is speaking, okay?"

"Yes, Ms. Peterson." Ava took a deep breath and concentrated hard on the page in her hand. "'But I'm afraid of heights.'"

After Ava finished, it was time to let Benji read. She wanted to make sure he understood he had to share the spotlight time with his fellow students, but he would be so hurt and disappointed if he didn't get a chance to read to the class. As expected, he pronounced all his words correctly, even though Karen gave him the most challenging section with the newest words they'd learned. He wasn't the most encouraging of Jacob, who struggled the most, but Karen was extra supportive to make up for it.

After a few questions about the story and the new words they'd read, Karen could see at least half the class fidgeting. She checked her watch to discover they'd made good time on completing this lesson, but they were due in the library in fifteen minutes, and the last thing she needed was to deliver Sheila a class who couldn't sit still and be quiet in the library.

"Who wants a brain break?"

Karen's question was met with a resounding cheer, even from the quiet students. Brain breaks made them sound like learning, but they were essentially games and all the kids loved games. She couldn't help but laugh as she went to her desk to retrieve her stack of cards.

"Line up in two lines at the front of the class."

Students scrambled up from the reading area and hustled to the whiteboard, many holding the hands of their friends so they were in the same line. She knew they wouldn't end up teamed together as they thought, but the mild embarrassment on the faces of the students who didn't have friends clamoring to partner up with them relieved the sting. She had to shuffle a few people from one line to another to make sure the lines were even, but they settled down eventually.

"This group, you're my group A, and the group closer to the whiteboard, you're group B," Karen said.

She handed a colorful index card to everyone in group A, telling them not to look at it until she told them to. Then she had them form two circles, with group A on the outside, facing group B on the inside. She allowed them to stand there for a moment, smiling awkwardly at each other as they shuffled in anticipation.

"Group B, you're going to walk to your right when the music starts. When it stops, turn to the person across from you in Group

A and ask them to read their card. When you know the answer, both team members raise your hands. Everyone ready?"

Karen's question was met by an enthusiastic cheer, so she pushed play on her speakers. She'd chosen a music track that was a sampling of all the most popular cartoon show theme songs from the last few years. She loved seeing the kids perk up when they heard something familiar out of context and tried to match the music to the memory. She hoped they would react the same when they read their cards.

Though they'd only been in class together for three weeks, they had enough subjects to cover that she was able to create quiz questions enough for the whole class. As the year progressed and they learned more, the questions would get harder. For now, she wanted them to have fun and work together.

They made it through nearly all the cards before Karen had to call off the game so they could make it to their library time slot. The only student who seemed excited to end the quiz game/musical chairs mashup activity was Benji. She suspected this had as much to do with his rough performance at the activity as it did his excitement for the library.

Benji had been randomly paired with several science and math cards, and those were his weakest subjects. He hadn't gotten an answer right in the whole activity and not even his excellence in the reading that morning could lift his spirits. As she walked them down the hall toward the library, she focused on how she could utilize his love of reading to help him in other subjects. He was a smart kid, so the usual short stories about counting and states of matter wouldn't catch his attention. He saw them for what they were—transparent attempts to engage on a difficult subject. That only reminded him that everyone knew where his weaknesses were, and if Karen had learned anything from teaching his brother, showing weakness was the greatest sin in their household.

Karen was still mulling over what to do about Benji and whether she should step in to cool down the shoving match between a pair of students near the front of the line when she turned the corner to the main branch of the school. As expected, Sheila was waiting outside her library, ready to welcome Karen's class. Less expected was seeing Bianca beside her, chatting animatedly.

The difference was astounding. Karen hadn't thought Bianca was short, but standing next to the much taller Sheila made her average height more apparent. But more than the height, it was their demeanor and presence that made them an odd pair. Sheila was composed to the point of looking regal with her high-waisted, wide-leg royal blue slacks and simple burnt orange blouse. Bianca wore her usual mishmash of textures and prints with enough fabric to cover her frame at least twice. Her hair was distinctly frizzy in the late summer heat and pinned back haphazardly in a half-updo while Sheila's long locs were neatly tied at the base of her neck, the few silver strands catching the fluorescent light as she moved. Essentially, they looked exactly like an art teacher and a librarian, comfortable in their respective skins and comfortable in each other's presence.

As the class approached, they turned to the sound and both gave Karen and her students wide, beaming smiles. Karen was glad that she and Bianca were becoming friends. That smile had all the potential to make Karen's knees wobble. Instead, she felt the surge of happiness one always feels when they see a new friend and are eager to know them better.

"Welcome, students." Sheila's rich voice filled the hall. "Are we all ready to do some reading?"

The class nodded in response, some more enthusiastically than others. Following Karen's instructions, they lined up against the wall while Sheila propped open the library door and marked them off her attendance list. With her responsibility relinquished, Karen allowed her attention to wander.

"What brings you to the library this morning?" she asked as Bianca stepped to her side.

"I'm actually here for Benji."

The line had progressed far enough into the library for him to be right beside them. Benji looked up at them with obvious fear in his features. Karen kept an eye out for tears. He was a sensitive kid, and if he were to be reprimanded for some assignment failure here in the hall, he would likely crumble.

"For me?" Benji asked, his voice squeaking.

Bianca held out a slip of paper to him. "I promised to show you a book about Kandinsky."

The fear melted from Benji's face, replaced with a smile that showed all his slightly crooked teeth. He snatched the slip of paper from her hand a little too fast and muttered a barely audible apology, but held the paper close to his eyes without shame.

"That's the title of the book and its Dewey Decimal number. Do you think you can find it yourself or do you need Mrs. Washington's help?" Bianca asked.

"I can find it." Benji straightened to his full height and threw his shoulders back, a posture Karen had never seen from him before this moment.

"Benji is a whiz with Dewey, aren't you?" Sheila dropped a hand on his shoulder like she was showing off her favorite grandchild.

Benji nodded his head so vigorously it might've fallen right off his neck and hustled inside, for once the last student of his class into the library. Sheila gave Bianca the slightest of winks before following him and pulling the door closed. Karen could just hear her voice boom out a reminder to the class to be quiet while others were reading before she was swallowed by the stacks.

"He was having a tough time in our last class." Bianca walked so close Karen could feel the feather-light touch of fabric as she passed. "We were painting Kandinsky's circles in squares and Benji wasn't connecting with the lesson. I thought using his love of books to help him understand would boost his confidence."

"I was thinking of doing the same thing with his academic struggles," Karen said.

Bianca leaned in a little closer and whispered, "I won't tell anyone you copied off my paper if it works."

Warmth spread through Karen at Bianca's conspiratorial smile and wink just before she slipped into the library herself. How was it possible they were so often on the same wavelength? This new friendship already felt right in a way few had. She barely felt the steps back to her classroom, she was so focused on the memory of Bianca's smile.

CHAPTER TEN

Karen stood near the hostess stand at Main Street Café. There were about two dozen Formica-topped tables and half as many booths crammed between the long stretch of plate glass windows and the hulking bar. The wooden chairs creaked whenever their occupants moved and most of the booths sported cracked vinyl, but the wear and tear only added to the charm. There was no restaurant in town like the Café.

It was six p.m. on a Thursday and nearly every table was full. The menu hadn't changed in fifteen years and none of the dishes would win awards for creativity, but there wasn't a better place for good old-fashioned, home-cooked Southern food in the whole county. In fact, there wasn't a better place in the whole world. Thursday's special was the cheeseburger and fries for five dollars, and happy hour pricing on beer and wine lasted all night for teachers, fire fighters, and paramedics.

Annabelle Green shuffled up to the hostess stand, her girth and her bad knee equally to blame for her gait and her labored breathing. Annabelle had been manager of Main Street Café most of her life, but had retired and sold before Karen had moved to town. Like her husband, Doug, however, she couldn't stand to be idle and had taken on some part-time work. They were the best-informed couple in all of Bucks Mill. He picked up all the gossip from the school and the hospital where he also filled in as a security guard, and Annabelle got the rest here at the Café.

"Evening, Karen. How are the students this year?" Annabelle parked herself behind the hostess stand.

"Wonderful as always. Bucks Mill kids are the best."

"That's just what Jessica said. She's in the last booth facing the windows."

Now that she knew where to look, Karen could see her, slouched in the best booth in the house, peeling the label off her bottle of beer. Karen considered holding back a little longer, just to make Jessica sweat after bailing on their return-to-school outing, but peeling the label off her beer was Jessica's nervous habit and clear evidence that she was feeling guilty. Karen couldn't twist the knife any more than Jessica was doing to herself. She thanked Annabelle and hurried across the busy dining room.

"Is this seat taken?" Karen leaned against the booth and gave Jessica a cheeky wink.

"There you are. I thought you were so mad at me you wouldn't show." Jessica jumped out of the booth and pulled Karen into a tight hug. She was several inches shorter, so had to hop up on her tiptoes to wrap her arms around Karen's neck. It was adorable and sweet but also very public, which made heat bloom across Karen's cheeks and ears.

"Oh, come on. You know I'd never stand you up. I know you have a life apart from me," Karen said.

Jessica pulled back from the hug only far enough to look Karen in the eye. "I'm still really sorry. I want to make it up to you."

The embrace felt a little too intimate and people were starting to stare, which made it even worse. She wasn't so reserved that she couldn't hug her best friend in public, but she hated being the center of strangers' attention. "Just sit down and buy me a beer and we'll be square, okay?"

"Two beers and also a burger."

"Fine. Just sit down, you goof."

Jessica finally released her and dropped back into the booth looking distinctly more comfortable. The same could not be said for Karen. There were lots of eyes still on her, including several of her past students' parents. Since they hadn't done Back to School Night yet, she couldn't be sure whether any of the gawkers were parents of her current students. Just in case, she slipped into her side of the booth as quickly as possible.

"You sure you're not mad at me? I mean, it's been two weeks and we haven't talked."

"What do you mean? We talk every day."

"About school stuff. It's always like a couple quick sentences and we're off again. We haven't had any good gossip sessions. It's weird," Jessica said.

Karen was tempted to lie just to smooth everything over, but her therapist had challenged her to be more honest with the people she loved. Maybe this was a good time to start. "I was hurt, but it's not your fault. Your husband comes first." Karen picked at her fingernails for a moment while nerves twinged in her stomach. "You know you can always bring Brandon along when we hang out. I wouldn't mind."

Karen held her breath while she waited for Jessica to answer. She'd been flaking out on Karen more than usual recently and a niggling anxiety had been plaguing her. What if Brandon didn't like her? Lots of best friendships withered when one half got married and the other didn't. There was also the fact that Karen and Jessica had dated, albeit briefly. What if Brandon didn't want Jessica hanging out with Karen as much as she did? She couldn't bear the thought of coming between the two of them any more than she could bear the thought of losing her friendship with Jessica over a misunderstanding.

It might've been Karen's imagination, but she thought Jessica's grin looked a little forced. "Are you getting bored of me, old pal? You don't have to drag my husband in as a buffer if you are. You could just tell it to me straight."

"No, of course not. Besides, you know me. I can't do anything straight."

"Then we're good. We don't need to drag Brandon into girls' night and you can just forgive me for standing you up."

It sounded sincere, and Karen chose to believe it was. "Of course I forgive you. I actually had a nice breakfast with Bianca Harper that morning."

Karen had timed the comment for right when she saw their waiter headed over. As she suspected, Jessica stared at her while she ordered her own beer and a second for Jessica. The moment he was gone, Jessica pounced.

"You had breakfast with her? How? Where?"

"At Sallie Bell's. I was almost there when I got your call and she saw me on the sidewalk. She wanted to try all the pastries Sallie had, but we ended up splitting three of them. Have you had her bear claw before? It's amazing. I've never tried that one."

"Yeah, they're Brandon's favorite. How come you didn't tell me this sooner?"

Karen didn't miss the flicker of hurt that flittered across Jessica's features. Why hadn't she told Jessica about it? That didn't take a lot of introspection, actually. The breakfast had felt private—intimate—like a date. If she'd admitted that to Jessica, she would have seen that same pity Jessica had shown at the welcome assembly. She couldn't stand that, but she also couldn't stand hurting her best friend.

Karen reached out and squeezed Jessica's hand. "I'm sorry I didn't tell you. I should have."

And just like that, the light was back in Jessica's eyes. "I forgive you."

"Now we're even," Karen said.

The waiter returned with their beers and took their dinner order. Once he was gone, a parent stopped by to say hello and by the time they were alone again, Karen had lost the thread of their conversation. Honestly, she didn't care. She just wanted to spend time with her best friend exactly like this, chatting away about their days and all the trivial things in life.

"Okay, what did we miss out on chatting about at the sunflower festival? Any challenging students this year?" Jessica asked.

"No troublemakers yet. You?"

"None, thank God. Last year about did me in. I have a few struggling academically, though."

"Me too. Benji Brown is having the hardest time with the math this year. I think I know what to do about it, just need time to do some research," Karen said.

"Research?"

"I want to figure out a way to leverage his love of reading to get him interested in the other subjects. Actually, it's funny. Bianca had the same thought. I ran into her at the library this week. She had Benji go find a book on an artist they were working on to get him engaged."

"That's smart," Jessica said.

"Yeah, I thought so. She joked about how she won't turn me in for copying off her test paper if I do the same thing. It was pretty funny."

"Sounds like it. Can't do that too much or he might catch on, though."

"True. He's a smart kid and he'll figure it out eventually, but it should take a while."

"Why do you say that?"

"Well, I think he'll cut Bianca some slack. He was kind of swooning over her in the library."

Jessica's laughter was a little too knowing as she leaned across the table. "He's not the only one."

"What do you mean?"

"I mean you haven't stopped talking about her since you sat down. Benji's not the only one with a crush."

"No way. She's married. We're just friends."

"Sure. You always talk nonstop about your friends." Jessica gave her a wink that made the heat come back into Karen's cheeks.

"You're just jealous that I'm talking more about her than you, aren't you?"

"Me? Jealous? As if."

"Gosh, you're so needy. I don't know how Brandon puts up with you."

Jessica laughed again and this time it was clearly her laughing at herself. "I am needy, aren't I?"

"The neediest." They laughed together and it filled Karen's chest with warmth. This was what she thrived on. A little one-on-one time with her nearest and dearest. "You're right, though. I do talk about her a lot. I really respect her and I'm excited to have another friend. She isn't as cool as you, of course."

Jessica raised her bottle to tap against Karen's. "Of course."

"But seriously, I need to make more friends. I can't expect you to be everything to me. You've got your own life and soon you're going to start popping out babies left and right. I need a respectable stand-in for my bestie for those times when you can't be there to entertain me."

"You know I always have time for you."

Jessica slid her hand on top of Karen's when she said it, but far from the comforting gesture she clearly meant it as, the weight of her hand was oppressive. That's what Karen was for everyone—someone people had time for, not someone they really wanted to be with. Her family, her coworkers, even her best friend. They didn't think of Karen first.

The depressing thought made Karen angry at herself. She didn't want this night to dissolve into self-pity. She'd wasted so much time on that already in her life. If she wasn't careful, she would end up bitter and only alienate herself further from the people around her. Besides, she was putting too much pressure on everyone, including herself. She needed to relax into friendships. Relax into romantic relationships. Maybe she should even relax into her family dynamic. It would be so much healthier than whatever this was.

Fortunately, the waiter arrived with their burgers and another round to break the tension. They busied themselves with mayonnaise, mustard, and stealing fries off each other's plates. Once the first pangs of hunger were sated by perfectly grilled burgers covered in an excessive amount of melted cheese, Karen was able to mull over her social life again with a little more optimism.

"Speaking of me making more friends, I was thinking about actually going to some of Roger's staff mixers this year," Karen said.

"Mmm. Then you'd get to sample Keith's incredible cocktails."

"He is an amazing bartender."

"There's also the option of, you know, making friends who aren't teachers at Bucks Mill Elementary," Jessica said.

"He has the middle school teachers over sometimes, too."

Jessica rolled her eyes. "You know what I mean. Go out into the wild. Find friends who aren't coworkers."

Karen thought for a moment. "How?"

Jessica's eyebrows crunched together as she thought. They were both silent for a long time, trying to brainstorm through the slight buzz of alcohol.

Jessica gave up first with a shrug. "I have no idea."

"Making friends as an adult is hard."

"It sure is, bestie. It sure is."

❖

A week later, Karen initiated the soft launch of making friends with her coworkers. After dropping her class off in the cafetorium, she went back to her classroom and collected her lunch cooler. Instead of spreading the contents on her desk as usual, she rushed out her classroom door and down the hall to the teachers' lounge before she chickened out.

She regretted her bravery the moment she stepped through the door. The room was about the size of one of their classrooms, but instead of being packed to the gills with desks, it was stuffed with small bistro tables, mismatched plastic chairs, a very suspect microwave, and a few ancient, rattling copiers for ambiance. Nothing like the smell of melting toner to enhance the culinary experience.

The problem with all those small tables was that they forced small groups to engage in conversation. Did she take the empty seat at the new moms table and make small talk about breast feeding and diapers? She'd probably fit in at the table for the male teachers. They were less chatty than some of the other groups, but there were exactly four male teachers at the school and four chairs at their table. The table next to the older of the copiers was mostly empty, but that was only because the copier was convulsing with the work of printing hundreds of quizzes.

Everyone had their own little cliques and there really wasn't a spot for Karen. It was her fault. After all, she rarely spent time in the lounge or engaging with teachers other than Jessica and now Bianca. Had she really expected to walk in and be welcomed with open arms? Prickling embarrassment washed over her skin. Could she scuttle back out of the room without anyone noticing her?

"Hey, Karen, why don't you join us?" Bianca's voice was a light in the darkness.

Karen rushed across the room to join her. She was at a table under the window with Sheila, the sunlight making Bianca's orange hair glow like a campfire at sunset. Sheila's smile was so warm and welcoming Karen felt foolish for wanting to run.

"How lovely and rare to see you in here," Sheila said. "I thought you and Jessica usually ate together in your classroom."

Karen felt even more foolish now, having to admit the truth. "We do some days, but I'm trying to be less introverted this year."

"You introverted? No way. You always open up with me," Bianca said.

"She does? You must tell me your secrets because our Karen is sweet, but I can rarely get her to chat with me," Sheila said.

"That's not true. We talk about your grandkids all the time."

"Well yes, but that's about me. I want to know everything there is to know about you," Sheila said.

It had never occurred to her that anyone would be interested in her life, but that seemed silly in the glow of Sheila's smile. Maybe she'd been missing out on a chance at real friendships by being aloof. Still, the spotlight of their attention felt too bright in this moment. She focused undue attention on straightening her containers of vegetables and hummus. "I don't have anything interesting to tell."

Out of nowhere, Bianca's hand slid onto Karen's forearm and gave her a supportive squeeze. It was clearly meant as a friendly, supportive gesture, but it made the skin on her arm tingle and her heart rate double.

"Don't sell yourself short, Karen. I think you're very interesting," Bianca said.

Bianca wore a smile just as friendly and warm as Sheila's. The sight relieved some of her embarrassment and she could even feel the corners of her own mouth turning up, though she couldn't remember telling them to do so.

"Karen, it's so great to see you in here. What a surprise." Roger's hand landed on her shoulder around the same time his words landed in her ears.

"Oh, well, I'm trying to get out more."

"I, for one, am thrilled. I love talking to Karen, don't you, Sheila?" Bianca asked.

"I surely do," Sheila said.

It was a little awkward to be encouraged by her colleagues like a shy student who spoke up in class for the first time, but it was also nice. Maybe she should make this a regular occurrence.

"Then you should come to our barbecue this weekend," Roger said.

"Oh, is it that time already?" Karen winced at how weak the response was. She had always declined the mid-month mixers with the excuse that she didn't want to spend time with her boss after work. The reflex was to decline, but she had told Jessica she was going to attend one of the parties. Plus, she did love Roger's husband's cocktails. "You know what, I'd love to come."

"I understand, but remember the invitation is always—Wait. Did you say yes?"

Karen couldn't help laughing at the confusion etched in the lines behind his wire-framed glasses. "I did say yes. Thank you for the invitation."

Roger's voice squeaked with surprise and she hoped just a dash of pleasure. "That's wonderful. Keith will be so thrilled. He's making sherry cobblers."

The same agreeable surprise lit Sheila's face. She, of course, knew Karen had been absent from their get-togethers for ages since she never missed one. Bianca's joy was uncut with shock. It lit the gentle curve of her cheek more effectively than the sunlight. That happiness made her even more confident in her choice.

Roger turned his attention to Bianca. "Are we going to see you and Alex at the cookout?"

"You most certainly will. We can't wait."

The full force of Bianca's smile remained fixed on Karen when she answered, but it somehow lost a little of its power. A cookout had less appeal now than it had a moment earlier, now that it meant finally meeting Bianca's husband. She shouldn't feel that way. After all, a good friendship meant knowing and celebrating all the good things in a friend's life and surely Bianca's husband fit the bill. Hadn't she just told Jessica she wanted to hang out with Brandon more? Still, as Roger moved to another table and Karen finally started eating her lunch, the food wasn't quite as delicious as she had expected.

CHAPTER ELEVEN

B ecause she ate lunch in the teachers' lounge rather than her classroom, Karen had not spent that hour catching up on the endless task of grading papers and preparing for the next day's lessons. Most of her workdays lasted long after her students boarded a bus, but today was longer than usual. Of course, it didn't help that she was distracted and moody thanks to her promise to waste her Saturday making small talk with her colleagues.

She had managed a quick chat with Jessica while they escorted students to the bus line, and she'd been just as shocked as everyone else that Karen had actually committed to the cookout. Jessica went to a few of the staff mixers, but only because Brandon was an investment banker and it was good for his career to be friendly with as many people as possible. She hadn't planned on going to this one since Brandon would be playing golf. Karen practically dropped to her knees begging Jessica to go with her.

Jessica pouted and even stomped her foot like a teenager on the brink of being grounded. "This was your project to make more friends and do more social things. Why am I getting dragged into it?"

"Because you need to make friends, too. Neither of us are social enough, you agreed on that."

"I'd already had two beers when I agreed. I cannot be held responsible for my actions."

"Come on, it'll be fun. You know it will. Keith is making cobbler," Karen said.

Jessica's eyebrow flew up a full inch and Karen knew she had her convinced. If there was one way to Jessica's heart, it was through her stomach. More specifically, through her sweet tooth.

"Fine. I'll go, but I do so under protest."

"Thanks, bestie," Karen said with a sigh of relief.

Was it fair to bribe and manipulate her best friend? No, of course not, but Karen was desperate. The barrage of emotions that had assaulted her at lunch had yet to dissipate. She could freely admit that Bianca was physically attractive, she'd known that since the moment they met. Now she was getting to know her better, she realized how synced their energies were. Not just their interests, but also their philosophies in teaching and their single-minded focus on prioritizing their students' needs. It was rare and compelling and it made everything different.

She'd never felt such an intense draw toward another person, and she absolutely could not deal with meeting Bianca's husband alone. Even knowing his name was a thorn in her brain she couldn't ignore. If Jessica wasn't there to support her on Saturday, she would crumble and probably make an ass of herself.

A gentle knock on her open classroom door dragged Karen from her thoughts. She managed to bite back her groan at the inevitable sight of Bianca standing in her doorway.

"Hi. Sorry to interrupt."

Bianca's voice held a note Karen hadn't heard there before. She was always so confident. So firm. But now she sounded almost sheepish.

"No problem. Is everything okay?" Karen asked.

Bianca's shoulders jumped up and down once in imitation of a laugh, but no sound came with it. "I guess I'm not very subtle, huh? I'm a little embarrassed. I need a favor."

Karen hopped up out of her chair and hurried around her desk. She may be wrestling with her own emotions, but she would never back down from helping a friend.

"Don't be embarrassed. What do you need?"

"My ride is caught at work and most of the others have left. We don't really know each other that well, but I don't know most of them at all. Is there any chance you could drive me home?"

It was foolish and reckless to spend more time alone with her and it wouldn't help stave off the disappointment she was destined for, but Karen stood a little taller. Bianca came to her when she'd needed a favor.

"Of course I'll give you a ride. The way you hesitated, I thought it was going to be something big like helping you hide a body," Karen said.

Bianca's eyes sparkled with that mixture of amusement and mischief that was so unique to her. "Not for the first favor. I have to earn your trust first. That's the third favor."

Karen realized too late that she was staring, maybe even drooling a little, but she recovered enough to turn around and hustle back to her desk. "Let me just grab my stuff and we can head out."

"I hate to take you from your work. I can wait. You're doing me the favor after all."

Karen definitely did have more work to do, but she slapped her laptop closed and shoved it into her messenger bag. She would hate herself tomorrow for not staying and finishing. There was no chance, however, that she would leave Bianca waiting and even less of a chance that she would get any work done with Bianca sitting there in the classroom with her.

"Nope." Karen hid the lie with extra cheeriness. "I'm all done. Let's go."

The sun was dipping low as they emerged from the school. The few scattered clouds glowed salmon and harvest gold and the mountains in the distance were shadowed into silhouettes against the deepening blue of the sky. Karen was so mesmerized by the beauty of the evening, she nearly missed Bianca's question.

"Have you always lived in Bucks Mill?"

"I wish. No, I grew up in the DC suburbs."

"That's a big change. What brought you out here?"

Karen weighed her response as she sorted through her keys. It was far too early to get into her family drama. As close as Bianca was with her family, Karen doubted she would appreciate her need to work as far from her parents and brother as possible. She went with a far more benign answer. "I got tired of concrete and pavement."

Bianca looked at her across the hood of the car for a few beats longer than was comfortable. "I can understand that. This is a far cry from Boston and I love that."

Karen let out a short breath, amazed that she'd been let off the hook. Bianca gave her a whole three minutes to collect herself and steer the car toward the exit before she spoke again.

"How long have you been teaching here?"

"Eight years. Bucks Mill was my one and only interview right out of college."

"And you've never wanted to leave?" Bianca asked.

"Not for a minute. I love it here. The people. The town. Bucks Mill has everything I've ever wanted."

A wave of loneliness washed over Karen. Everything except the one thing missing in her life—someone to share it with. When was the last time she drove with someone in the passenger seat? It was rare, to say the least, and it was wonderful. She got so lost in the warmth of another person in her space that it took her a long time to realize she hadn't asked Bianca where she lived.

Gliding to a stop at the next intersection, Karen asked, "So where are we headed?"

"Oh no, you're not getting off that easy," Bianca said with a laugh. "I don't know anything about this perfect little town and now I discover I'm in a car with the perfect tour guide."

Bianca had turned in her seat to the furthest extent her seat belt would allow, bringing her warmth even closer to Karen in the limited confines of her Honda. Suddenly the space seemed to hold less oxygen and Karen's quickened breathing couldn't catch any of it.

"I don't think I'd be the best tour guide. I've only lived here a few years. There are folks who've been here their whole lives."

"That's what makes you the perfect guide. They take this place for granted and for you…well, new love is always strongest."

Blood pounded in Karen's ears. They were probably glowing red. Why did Bianca have to say things like that? Why did she have to talk about love and make Karen feel like the world was melting around her? Before she could come up with a coherent response, a loud honk from behind them made Karen jump and speed away from the intersection. Without a clear destination, muscle memory took her toward Main Street.

"Take me to your favorite place in Bucks Mill." Bianca relaxed back into her seat.

"Well, you've already been to my favorite coffee shop, but they close at three. Do you mean my favorite restaurant or my favorite shop?"

"I mean your favorite place. The one you go to when you want to contemplate the world."

Karen immediately turned onto a side road so she could backtrack. She wasn't exactly surprised that Bianca would ask to go to a place like that, though no one else in her life had even considered Karen had a place she'd go to reflect. If she thought about it too much, Karen might decide it was too intimate to take Bianca there, so she didn't think about it, she just drove.

The sky was still ablaze with color but darkening fast when Karen parked her car at the spot closest to the split rail fence at the top of Jouett Hill south of town. Bianca was out of the car and hurrying to the overlook before Karen had a chance to kill the engine, and she followed a little slower, intrigued by Bianca's excitement.

"You can see the whole town from up here," Bianca said somewhat breathlessly.

"You wanted a tour, right? This is the best place to see the town."

Karen started with Main Street, obvious from the streetlights popping to life. From there she pointed out all the neighborhoods, radiating out from the center. Just visible beneath them was Old Town with its Victorian houses and wealthy inhabitants, stretching all the way to the edge of the businesses. The country club just east of Old Town was home to Bucks Mill's version of the nouveau riche. Continuing counterclockwise around the compass from there, Karen pointed out Ashcroft Court and its older and mostly modest homes, then Forest Lakes with its newer and more modest homes. From there it was farmland and single homes rather than entire neighborhoods, but the darkness was encroaching so much by then that Karen wouldn't have been able to give a good tour anyway. Plus, it wouldn't be wise to spend too much more time studying the way the sunset formed a halo around Bianca's profile.

"Which neighborhood is yours?" Bianca asked.

"The most modest of them all. I live in a little apartment over a business on Main Street."

Hopefully, the embarrassment didn't show too clearly on her cheeks with the chill of night descending, but she didn't need to worry. Bianca wouldn't think less of her for not having the finest house in town the way her parents did.

Bianca groaned. "Why do teachers get paid so little when our job is so important?"

Karen shrugged. "That's one I'll never figure out."

Bianca caught her eye and Karen couldn't look away. "It's worth it though, right?"

"Absolutely." Karen's voice was barely above a whisper.

Bianca didn't look away even as the moment stretched and solidified into something Karen chose not to name. She couldn't name it. Bianca might be intriguing and stunning and share all the ferocious dedication to their work that Karen had, but she was married and that was an impenetrable barrier.

"Which is your neighborhood?" Karen pushed herself off the barrier fence and turned back toward the parking lot. She was only slightly surprised when Bianca followed without protest.

"Ashcroft Court. In the decidedly modest home section."

They didn't say much as they drove the ten minutes to Bianca's neighborhood, but it was a comfortable silence. Karen pulled to a stop at the curb next to a mailbox painted with vivid flowers and a driveway with a hundred radiating, poorly-patched cracks.

"Thank you for the ride and the tour. I had a lovely time," Bianca said.

"I had a great time, too."

Before Karen could decide whether it would be more chivalrous than wise to walk her to the front door, Bianca pushed her car door open and popped out. "See you tomorrow."

Karen scrambled for something to say that would be witty or memorable, but was distracted by the wash of headlights flooding over them and then whipping into the driveway. The passenger side door closed and Bianca skipped up the driveway just as the pickup truck's engine died. A lanky woman with dark hair and a jaw chiseled by the gods hopped out. Her boots had barely hit the pavement when Bianca threw her arms around her, pulling her into a tight hug. The woman, who must have been Alex, laughed and hugged Bianca tight, then kissed her on the top of the head.

They walked arm-in-arm to the door, chatting and laughing, without once turning to acknowledge Karen. She dimly registered the pang of disappointment before she turned the key and navigated her ancient sedan out of the neighborhood in the tracks of Alex's brand-new truck.

So, Bianca was queer. Alex wasn't a husband, but a wife. Not just any wife, though, the type-specimen of butch lesbian with the pickup truck and the muscular arms and the gorgeous wife. Just like Carter.

At least they'd gone inside the house quickly. Karen escaped before having to witness them share a real kiss.

CHAPTER TWELVE

Roger's house was a twenty-minute drive from Bucks Mill in a swankier but far less charming neighboring town. The subdivision was built a decade after any home in Bucks Mill and had the fresh, young feel to match. All the front yards were vivid green, and all the fences were immaculately stained the same red-pink cedar.

Karen hated everything about it. The whole neighborhood reminded her of the ostentatious vanity of her childhood home in Northern Virginia. As much as she loved Roger and Keith, being here reminded her of weekends with her family where all they could discuss was the project they had planned with their upcoming bonus or their next lavish European vacation. She was an outsider here. Why did no one else feel the same way?

"Better get it over with," Karen mumbled to herself as she climbed from her car.

As she gathered the gift bag from the back seat, Jessica roared into the cul-de-sac in her shiny new SUV. She rolled the window down and shouted excited greetings at Karen before she'd even put the vehicle in park.

"Try not to ding my bumper, would you?" Karen faked a scowl.

"How would you even tell if I did?" Jessica pulled her into a tight hug. "Did you bring a gift? Were we supposed to? I never bring them anything."

Karen shrugged but a bubble of embarrassment stirred in her. "I have to bring a gift when I come to someone's house. My mom would never let me live it down if I didn't."

"Oh yeah, I keep forgetting you're the quintessential Southern lady," Jessica said.

As they neared the front door, Sheila joined them from the opposite sidewalk. "You're such a better guest than I am, Karen. I should bring them a gift."

Jessica said, "We can be shamed together by Karen's kindness."

The bubble of embarrassment burst into a flood of self-doubt. Now she was making her friends feel bad. She contemplated turning to toss the bag back in her car when the front door swung open and Keith threw his arms up in welcome. While Roger exuded middle-aged dad vibes, Keith was the prototypical boyish, skinny, hyper-feminine gay man. Karen could even detect a hint of blush and eyeliner.

"Karen, darling, it's been far too long. When Roger told me you were coming today I cried. I really did. I've never been so happy," Keith said.

"Oh. Thanks. You're so kind."

Sheila and Jessica shared a look, but Keith waved away their protests and pulled Karen in for air kisses on both cheeks. The sudden burst of energy made her head spin. She panicked and shoved the gift bag at him with such force a piece of tissue paper flitted out and plunked onto the entryway rug.

Keith squealed with joy and tore into the bag. "You shouldn't have."

Karen agreed, but it was too late. "Just a little something. Nothing special. Roger mentioned you remodeled the guest room and had a hard time picking the right shade of yellow."

"Sunflowers!" Keith squealed again and tossed the bag aside to admire the framed photograph.

"Is that from this year's festival?" Sheila asked.

Before Jessica's look of disappointment could penetrate, Karen said, "No. It's from last year's."

Keith's jaw dropped in exaggerated disbelief. "You took this? It's gorgeous and it will go so well in the new room. Come, all of you, and take a look."

Karen's steps were light as air as he dragged the three of them up the grand staircase to the second floor. Maybe the gift had been a good idea after all. He really seemed to like the photograph, and she'd managed to wriggle out of the awkward reminder that she and Jessica hadn't made it to this year's Sunflower Festival.

"This is the guest room? There isn't a bed," Sheila said.

"We finished the basement last winter and moved the guest suite down there. This is the dogs' bedroom. Isn't it perfect? It changes the entire vibe of the house," Keith said.

"It's stunning," Karen said.

"Since when do dogs need a bedroom?" Sheila whispered.

Fortunately, Keith hadn't heard. He was busy explaining every tiny detail of the room. The walls were a vivid shade of yellow that truly brightened the space. It looked like a sunny afternoon inside, even with the curtains drawn and just a pair of floor lamps.

"Roger wanted Classical Yellow, but he has no sense of style. I nearly went with Emberglow, but settled on Afternoon. It's perfect and these sunflowers will just make it pop. They'll go right here."

He left them to bask in the perfection of his design long enough to fetch a hammer and nail to hang Karen's photograph. The banging barely disturbed their ancient Pekinese, RuPaw Charles, but their pug, Porkchop, hopped down off his dog-sized chaise lounge and scurried from the room.

Once they'd had their fill of the glory that was the dogs' new bedroom and Karen's photograph, Keith escorted them to the backyard where the party was in full swing. Karen would have rather hurried back to snuggle with RuPaw over this boisterous group.

Jessica leaned over and whispered in her ear, "You could smile, you know."

"My face will crack if I try," Karen whispered back.

Fortunately, the two of them were too far from Keith for him to hear, but Sheila snickered. She leaned in to quietly ask, "Why do two middle-aged men with no human children needed a five-thousand-square-foot house with a three-car garage?"

Karen wondered the same thing, but since Brandon was far more successful than any of them, the opulence was not as big a shock to Jessica. That opulence certainly extended to the backyard. In fact, calling it merely a backyard seemed insufficient. It was an oasis, more lush and magical than some botanical gardens, and sporting a lagoon-style pool. There was also a lavish tiki bar on the edge of the patio, and this was where Keith installed himself, swiftly cutting two large oranges into wedges before dropping them into a glass pitcher.

When he produced a comically large muddler and several bottles, Karen asked, "Can I just have a beer?"

Keith was either too busy or too offended to answer, so it was down to Sheila to remind her. "There is a signature drink for every party. You have to try one."

When Keith dropped behind the bar to fill plastic wine tumblers with crushed ice, Jessica quietly said, "There's usually a cooler of beer near the pool for round two."

"What is today's signature drink, Keith?" Sheila asked.

"Today you're having sherry cobblers with a really nice little Amontillado sherry and my own little touch, a simple syrup with rhubarb from our own garden."

While Keith poured and mixed and explained how he had harvested the rhubarb back in June and frozen it for this very application, Jessica leaned over close to Karen's ear. "You promised me cherry cobbler. Dessert with delicious cherries, not a weird drink with sour celery for garnish."

Karen was equally disappointed by the confusion, so she took her lumps and tried to smile when Keith handed her a glass that was mercifully seventy-percent crushed ice. The three of them took their drinks to the shade of a perfectly trimmed white oak at the edge of the party and each took a tentative sip as they scanned the crowd.

"Wow, this is actually pretty good," Jessica said.

"You're right." Karen agreed with both the sentiment and the surprise. Despite her previous belief that sherry was only for cooking or the clandestine alcoholism of 1950s housewives, the drink was delicious. Light, refreshing, and just the tiniest bit nutty, there was a depth of flavor that surprised her. "I'm not likely to run away with Keith's pitcher or anything, but given the oppressive humidity, a fruity drink that isn't too sweet is actually perfect."

Sheila and Jessica fell into conversation as Karen scanned the crowd. Much like their little trio, most of the guests had clustered in small groups underneath trees or the many strategically placed umbrella-shaded tables. The older crowd stayed closer to the house on the gray-brick patio, but the younger teachers spread out more. No one had ventured into the pool, and Karen suspected most, like her, hadn't bothered to wear a bathing suit under their clothes. There was something distinctly odd about being so scantily clad in front of one's coworkers. Karen was especially glad of that social restriction when her gaze settled upon Bianca.

Bianca was standing in one of the larger groups and the only one not hiding from the punishing rays of the late summer sun. As always, she looked as though she had just stepped out of a new age yoga retreat. Today she could be a little less conservative, and she'd taken advantage by wearing a sleeveless sheer top that was blessedly darker in color and thus not fully see-through and a pair of beige linen pants with sandals. She was absolutely stunning, with the light breeze ruffling her pants and the loose strands of her hair glowing like a torch in the bright sun.

At her side, Alex looked equally at ease in a button-up shirt covered in palm trees over a tank top, both showed off muscular arms and a slim waist. Bianca had her arm around that waist and her head leaned against Alex's shoulder as they laughed together. Karen suddenly wanted very much to go home.

"You could at least try not to stare, you know," Jessica whispered into her ear.

"I'm not staring."

"True. You're just glancing over at them every three or four seconds. Your jealousy is showing. If you're not careful, Bianca's wife is gonna kick your ass."

Karen gave them one last look. "She looks too nice for that."

"Try not to test your theory," Jessica said.

Karen forced a smile, but her face felt like stone. Sheila was working very hard to pretend she hadn't noticed either the whispered conversation or Karen's discomfort. Heat crept up her cheeks. She was being ridiculous and making everyone else uncomfortable right along with her. Time to shake herself out of this and have a good time. It was surprisingly easy to do.

"How are things over at the library, Sheila? I saw you had a ton of new books donated this year," Karen said.

She brightened immediately and launched into a story about the moms' group who ran a fundraiser for her over the summer. To her delight, one of Karen's very first students at Bucks Mill Elementary had joined the initiative and even written a piece for the high school paper about it. She was so engaged in conversation with Sheila that she forgot about Bianca and Alex. It felt good—exactly what she had wanted from this social event. Maybe she could drown out her crush after all.

"Hey, everyone," said a smooth, husky voice from over Karen's shoulder. "I come bearing normal booze."

Karen somehow knew it would be Alex, so she steeled herself for the encounter before turning around. It didn't help. Alex stood there, gripping two beer bottles in each hand like the picture of butch lesbian coolness, Bianca at her side beaming with pride. Bianca smiled at Karen and all her organs melted into a watery slush and puddled in her tennis shoes.

"Thank God. I couldn't stand another one of these." Jessica eagerly abandoned her tumbler on a nearby table and snagged a bottle.

Karen's instinct was to say she loved the cocktail, as much out of a stubborn reluctance to take anything from Alex as loyalty to Keith. The problem was, as refreshing and summery as the drink was, it wasn't her style at all.

Alex turned her smile on Karen, holding out the bottle like an olive branch. "Hi. We haven't met yet. I'm Alex."

Karen noticed dimly that she and Bianca had the same smile, though hers came with twinkling green eyes rather than Bianca's rich mahogany. So they were one of those couples that started to look alike after so many years together. They probably wore matching pajamas in their Christmas card picture, too.

"Thanks. Nice to meet you. I'm Karen." She grabbed the bottle and tipped it to the sky. A little alcohol to dull the pain seemed in order.

"I'll pass. In fact, I'm going to get myself another one of these delicious sherry cobblers. Bianca, do you want one?" Sheila asked.

"Bianca is a beer girl, aren't you?" Alex handed her the extra bottle and they shared a look and a laugh that had inside joke written all over it. Karen couldn't get the beer down her throat fast enough.

"I would be embarrassed for her antics, but you've all heard about Alex," Bianca said with a heartbreakingly fond smile.

"Oh yes, the infamous Alex. Your reputation proceeds you," Sheila said.

While Sheila and Alex shook hands, Karen cut a look at Jessica. Her return eyebrow raise and tiny shoulder shrug communicated quite clearly that she hadn't heard any of the stories that made Alex so infamous either. Jessica faked a big laugh as she turned back to the conversation, making it clear she had no intention of owning up to her ignorance. She wasn't alone on that. Karen certainly didn't want to hear any of the stories that no doubt painted her as the perfect, charming hero of their real-life rom-com. She would much rather wallow in her self-pity, but that wouldn't win her any points in therapy, so she tuned back into the conversation, too.

"I can't believe I had to miss the first staff meeting of the year. I hear you're taking over the Halloween festival this year, Jessica," Sheila said.

"Yep. Karen practically forced me to since she has her hands full with the winter talent show. Didn't you?"

"I wouldn't say forced exactly. Didn't you volunteer?" Karen asked.

"I was volun-told I think," Jessica said with a laugh.

"I hear we're actually doing something for Thanksgiving this year?" Sheila addressed the question to the whole group, but Karen couldn't help noticing Bianca never stopped looking her way.

"Yep. Bianca stepped up to honor the forgotten holiday," Jessica said.

"You know, I never realized that we haven't done anything before," Sheila said. "What a shame."

"It is a shame. I love Thanksgiving. We have a huge family and it's my favorite time of year. All the traditional decorations and foods," Bianca said.

Karen was too distracted by the disappointment of hearing the "we" about Bianca and Alex's family to chime in on the conversation that followed. Instead, she did her best to chase mental images out of her head. Bianca in a big, cable-knit sweater leaning over a cornucopia to plant a kiss on Alex's lips. The two of them snuggled up on a couch to watch the Macy's Thanksgiving Day Parade. All those little intimate moments people who love each other share with their family. She shook the thoughts out of her head before they could make her grumpy.

"I know Roger is thrilled for you to volunteer," Jessica said.

Karen snorted a laugh. "Roger would let you do just about anything as long as it doesn't cost the school anything and he doesn't have to do the work."

"I heard that," Roger said from over her shoulder. "And incidentally, Karen's right. Do anything you like as long as you handle all the logistics."

"My husband, the great delegator," Keith joked from his side.

Karen tried her best to engage in the conversation since Roger and Keith had arrived to enliven the group, but it took all her focus to keep from leaning into Bianca's familiar warmth at her shoulder.

"Alex is busy with some work thing all day next Saturday," Bianca said quietly enough that only Karen heard her. "Want to try some more pastries at Sallie Bell's?"

Surely it was Karen's imagination, but there seemed to be a flirtatious glint in Bianca's eye as she proposed the illicit date. Not date. Bianca didn't ask her on a date because Bianca was married. She just wanted to be friends and didn't realize Karen had a growing crush.

"Um, sure. If Alex won't mind, of course," Karen said.

"She won't mind. She doesn't like sweets the way you and I do."

That definitely sounded flirtatious. And was Bianca leaning really close to her or had Karen actually gone over the deep end? No, she was being ridiculous and she needed to get a grip. What better way than to use a little familiarity to douse her interest?

"Okay. I'll see you then." Karen's voice was croaking and breathy.

"I can't wait."

Bianca gave her a little wink before skipping happily back to Alex's side.

CHAPTER THIRTEEN

When Karen brought her class to the art room on Tuesday morning, Benji made a beeline for Bianca. He engaged her in an animated discussion that lasted well after the rest of the students filed into the classroom. His exuberance provided a reprieve for Karen, but it would be short-lived. After all, she had to be back in forty-five minutes to pick her kids up.

Karen tried focusing on work during her break, but she was too fidgety to concentrate. The warm, sunny weekend had bled into Monday, but today she had woken up to gray skies and drizzling rain. She felt the weight of the clouds against her back through the classroom window and couldn't stand it. After only a few minutes of work, she practically sprinted out of her classroom. She wandered the hall, but on her second pass she could see she was distracting Jessica. Still, the walking was helping and so she continued to wander and was unsurprised when her feet carried her back to the art classroom.

She shouldn't peep through the window and watch Bianca work. Friends didn't stare at each other like that. Still, she was drawn to the window like a moth to flame. How could she not be? Everything from Bianca's confident posture to the gentle smile that highlighted fine lines around her eyes and mouth was captivating. She moved from student to student, answering a question here and encouraging a hesitant artist there. She was a natural teacher. Bianca knelt next to Ava, putting them on the same level, and showed her a spot on her painting project that was thin. She didn't take the brush, didn't force her own agenda on the student. Surely it was a difficult line to walk— to be both teacher and artist—but Bianca walked it with a grace that left Karen's head spinning.

As though she felt the heat of Karen's gaze on her, Bianca looked up and met her stare. Had Bianca been smiling before? It was nothing to the way she beamed when she met Karen's eyes. Her face lit up in pure joy, and Karen's heart sank to the worn toes of her loafers. No wonder Alex fell in love with her. If Bianca looked at a friend like that, how must she look at her wife?

She didn't realize Bianca had stood and hurried to the door until it was too late to retreat. Peaking her head out, Bianca said, "Are you free? I could really use your help with this lesson."

"Me? I'm, um, not an artist."

Bianca closed the gap between them in three long strides and then suddenly her hand was in Karen's. "Come with me."

Karen's focus was entirely on Bianca's palm against hers, soft and firm and so incredibly warm. Then the warmth was gone and she was standing at the front of a classroom, staring at familiar faces in an unfamiliar space.

"Class, Ms. Petersen just told me she isn't an artist," Bianca said.

Benji's hand shot into the air, but he didn't wait for Bianca to call on him. He spoke in a singsong recitation. "Everyone is an artist in their own way. All we have to do is believe in our own creativity."

"Very good, Benji," Bianca said.

Heat filled Karen's cheeks, but also her chest. Bianca had insisted she was an artist before, and she wasn't sure she believed it. Clearly, however, this was a part of Bianca's philosophy. It was just like all the times Karen insisted to her struggling students that they were smart, they just needed confidence and practice.

"I asked Ms. Petersen to help us with today's project. Is that okay with everyone?" Bianca asked.

A sea of nodding heads emboldened her, and she turned another radiant smile on Karen.

"I guess I'm outnumbered," Karen said with a smile. "Today I'm an artist."

A smattering of cheers and clapping from her students sent a wave of giddiness through her. Was this how they felt when she praised them? She hoped so.

"Not just today, and that's why I need your help for this lesson. Class, did you know that Ms. Petersen is a photographer? She takes beautiful pictures of trees and flowers, just like the landscape we're painting today."

Bianca gestured to the whiteboard behind them, where she had projected a massive photograph of a woodland scene. It wasn't all that different from the view at the top of Jouett Hill, though the forest was pine trees rather than oaks. Vibrant flowers dotted the ground, which was grassy in some areas and rocky in others. The sky was full of puffy clouds and cut occasionally with far-off mountains.

"We're learning about perspective and focus today," Bianca said. "How we can make the mountains and clouds look far away and the flowers look close up. But also how we can choose to focus on one area to make a painting we like better than the whole."

Karen smiled and turned back to class. "That focus is important in the pictures I take. If I like this one purple flower here, I don't want to take a picture of the whole valley to capture it, I would make the flower the focus of my picture."

Ava jumped up and down on her stool, her little head poking out from behind the small easel on the desk in front of her. "I liked that flower, too. That's what I'm painting."

"Really? I'd love to see it."

Karen circled the desk and knelt down to examine Ava's painting. It was wonderfully charming and would no doubt earn a central spot on her home fridge. The flower was painted with a great deal of care, though the limited palette of colors meant the shade wasn't quite right. She hadn't done much on the background, but Karen could see where she'd started to paint the mountain before realizing the perspective was wrong. She'd covered it with white paint that wasn't quite up to the job.

"That's really pretty, Ava," Karen said.

"Did I get the focus right? Like you would with your camera?" she asked.

Karen crinkled her brow and rubbed her chin, her exaggerated movements earning a giggle from Ava. She held up her thumb and forefinger from both hands to make a box to peer through like movie directors did, studying the projection through it. Ava giggled again. Her playfulness was infectious, but Karen was determined to help her learn.

"Looks good to me. You see that one rock behind the flower? How would you paint that in to show the perspective?" Karen asked.

Bianca gave her an encouraging nod as Ava painted, explaining the process she'd learned to Karen. For the remaining class time, Karen and Bianca moved from student to student, helping them with their work. It didn't take long for Karen to realize that her photography experience did, in fact, help with this assignment.

When she chose the focus and framing of her photographs, most of the work was instinct. She had improved over the years mainly because she learned what worked from the happy accidents of the photos she liked. It hadn't occurred to her that she would ever be helpful in an art class, but Bianca had certainly proven it to her today. Or rather, Bianca had let Karen prove it to herself. Her head spun with the joy that lesson had brought her, but also with the beauty in Bianca's intense gaze on her.

Fortunately for Karen's sanity, the class bell rang and shattered the moment. Bianca sprang to her feet and started calling out instructions. Stools scraped on tile and the patter of little feet filled the room.

Karen took advantage of the melee to duck into the hallway and out of sight. She leaned back against the wall, the cool surface pleasant against her overheated skin. She closed her eyes and took several long breaths. She had an unrequited and inappropriate crush and she needed to rein it in before she made a fool of herself. Worse yet, if Bianca found out how she felt, Karen risked her job and reputation as well as putting a strain on a colleague's marriage. She didn't want to be that person. She would not be that person.

The door burst open beside her, bringing her back into the moment. She schooled her features into her sternly gentle teacher expression and directed the kids toward the classroom. They moved with the sluggish excitement of kids in need of a nutritious lunch and a break from learning.

Karen felt the warmth and electricity of Bianca walking up beside her before she spoke. "I'm starved. Aren't you?"

Karen watched her class's progress down the hall rather than look over at her. "Absolutely. I can't wait to drop them off in the cafeteria and dig in."

"Are you going to the teachers' lounge today?"

Karen cringed at the idea of another large social gathering so quickly after the last trip to the lounge and the weekend party. "As much as I enjoyed the pungent copier toner fumes, I think I'll stick to a quieter atmosphere today. Plus, I have spelling quizzes to grade."

"Would you like some quiet company? I'll even help you grade papers."

Karen should've said no, but the clear hint of longing in Bianca's tone pulled at her heartstrings. Maybe she was having trouble connecting with the other teachers, too. For someone new to the area that could be horrible. A good friend would invite Bianca to join her. It had nothing to do with her simmering crush, of course. She was just being polite.

"I'd love some quiet company, but I wouldn't dream of making you work during your lunch break," Karen said.

"If I don't work, then you can't either." Bianca gave her a little wink before turning back to her classroom. "I'll tidy up and meet you there."

The wink definitely didn't make Karen's heart simultaneously race and ache. She only hurried the kids along to collect their lunches and get to the cafetorium because they were hungry.

When Karen returned, Bianca was leaning against the wall outside her classroom, hands clasped around a bright pink, well-worn lunch cooler. She didn't see Karen's approach, her gaze fixed into the middle distance, a studious, serious expression painting her features. Somehow, she was even more beautiful in her seriousness than in her happiness. Was there anything about this woman that wouldn't enchant Karen?

"You could have gone inside to wait. I left the door unlocked," Karen said.

The smile reappeared in a flash. "I didn't want to invade your space without permission."

"It isn't my space exactly," Karen said, though she appreciated the thoughtfulness.

"Nonsense. I feel more at home in my classroom than anywhere else in the world. I get the feeling this is your happy place, too."

Karen loved how insightful Bianca was. How she seemed to know Karen from the inside out even though they'd shared so little. "Maybe so."

They settled down on either side of her desk without having to discuss the arrangement. There was an ease to Bianca's manner as she unpacked a sandwich wrapped in wax paper and a drink that looked like something out of a health food store. The juxtaposition of a bag of Doritos and a green smoothie amused Karen more than it should have.

"Thanks for helping with my lesson today," Bianca said.

"Of course. It was fun."

"Do you believe me when I say you're an artist now?"

There was an undercurrent of teasing in her words that Karen couldn't help matching. "I doubt it, but Benji was very convincing."

Bianca laughed. "I should have scolded him for not waiting until being called on to speak, but the look on your face was priceless."

"What look?"

"Like you really believed him. Out of the mouths of babes, as they say."

"Hmm. Maybe. But I'm pretty sure you taught him that."

Bianca smiled again and it nearly shattered her. "Maybe."

They ate in silence for a while. It was a chance to regroup, but Karen was having a hard time remembering how to be friends with someone when she was alone with Bianca.

"Do you have a lot of family in the area?" Bianca asked around a mouthful of bread.

"Nope. My parents live out on the Northern Neck and my brother is in DC."

"Where is the Northern Neck?"

"Oh sorry. I forgot you're not from Virginia. The Northern Neck is the coast around the Chesapeake Bay near the Maryland border. The rivers up there create this peninsula that people say is shaped like a neck," Karen said.

"Did they always have the beach house? Were you there a lot growing up?"

"Oh no. We rarely left DC when I was young. They spent that time making their money so they could retire early and pass along all those money-making opportunities to my brother."

Karen hadn't realized how bitter she sounded until Bianca's long pause was followed by an overly gentle question. "I'm guessing they love how he followed in their footsteps, but they don't have quite the same admiration for your chosen career?"

"You could say that." Karen set her fork down, her salad holding significantly less appeal while she discussed her family's shortcomings. "He's the golden son. I was the oops baby who came five years later and isn't interested in building a stock portfolio."

Karen wasn't sure why she was being so honest about the tension in her family. She rarely talked about how much her parents' disinterest hurt her, even to Jessica, but Bianca's openness made her want to bare all her wounds for inspection.

"Because you care about things far more important than stock portfolios. Like nurturing your students and making them excited to learn," Bianca said.

It was a blatant attempt to stem Karen's jealousy of her brother, but the obviousness didn't dull her pride that a woman like Bianca truly saw her. She shrugged off the compliment, but the heat on her cheeks belied the feigned nonchalance.

Karen shrugged and smiled, desperate to force the blush off her cheeks. "I was born to teach, not climb the corporate ladder. Besides, I could never pull off a power suit."

"Oh, I'm pretty sure you could pull off anything you wanted to wear," Bianca said with one of her dangerous smiles. "But I'm glad you aren't into making millions."

"Don't tell me you think rich people are terrible and should be flogged in the streets? I'm no fan of billionaires myself, but I'd take the money if someone offered it."

"You and me both. No, my reason is far more selfish. If you were into that corporate world, we never would have met and that would make me very sad."

So much for any chance of Karen getting rid of the embarrassing color in her cheeks. Even worse, her fingers chose that moment to go numb or spasm or something. Her salad fork clattered to the ground and she took the opportunity to dive out of the beam of Bianca's penetrating stare.

When she sat up straight again, it was to find Bianca's focus securely back on her lunch. That didn't mean the interview was over though, far from it.

"Is that why you ended up in Bucks Mill? To get as far from them as possible?" Bianca asked.

"No. I was just looking for a school system that offered student loan forgiveness. Bucks Mill is well below the poverty line, so my eight years here have been enough for full forgiveness."

Bianca smiled knowingly. "And you stayed because you love it."

It wasn't a question and Karen nodded in response. "I don't think many people could spend time in Bucks Mill and not love it."

"You're right about that."

"Wait, if your parents have that much money, why did you have student loans?" Bianca asked.

"Dad was a 'pull yourself up by your bootstraps' guy and wanted his kids to be, too."

Bianca rolled her eyes. "Bootstraps were a lot sturdier back in his day when college cost basically nothing and houses cost even less."

Karen's laughter was more bitter than she'd intended. "Try telling my dad that because he sure doesn't believe it when I tell him."

"He sounds like my dad."

"I hate to say it, but he might be right. I'm proud of what I've built. I don't know if I'd be as happy if I couldn't truly say it was all mine."

"You should be proud. You've done a lot here."

They ate in silence and Karen did a passable job of not staring. She was even starting to feel a tiny bit comfortable.

"So you aren't close with your brother at all? That's too bad. Siblings can be a pain in the neck, but that's a bond you can't have with anyone else," Bianca said.

"He probably tries harder than I do, but we're just built different. I spent some time with him and my nephews this summer and I couldn't have taken one more day if you'd paid me."

"How many nephews?"

"Two. They're five and eight and they're such..." Karen let her words trail off while she searched for the right word for that particular type of loud, obnoxious masculinity. "Boys."

Bianca burst into a fit of laughter and Karen's cheeks burned even hotter, though she wasn't entirely sure if her blush was from embarrassment or the captivating way Bianca's face lit up when she laughed.

"I know exactly what you mean by that, but you don't seem to mind the boys you have in your class. What's so different about your nephews?"

"Probably that they have my brother's face to go with their desperate need to be the center of attention," Karen said. "Well, not Mason. He looks like his mother."

"And you don't like your sister-in-law any more than your brother? Or are they separated?"

"No, they're still together. I don't really understand why. They both work seventy hours a week and never see each other."

"Maybe that's why they're still together. Nothing keeps a bad marriage going longer than a workaholic spouse."

A shadow crossed over Bianca's features as she spoke and then she fell into an uncharacteristic silence. Karen tried not to be too obvious about her staring. Bianca needed a ride home from school one night, and this coming weekend they would be getting pastries together for the second time because her wife was working. Was Alex making her miserable? An anger like nothing she'd ever felt before kindled in Karen's chest at the thought of Bianca in an unhappy marriage. It took everything in her to stamp that feeling down enough to hear Bianca's next question.

"But you don't have that worry, right? I mean I haven't noticed a wedding ring," Bianca asked, her words tripping all over themselves as they tumbled out.

"Me? No. I'm not married."

Bianca shook her head and leaned against her side of the desk. "Oh, come on. That was an obvious attempt for gossip. You've got to tell me more about your romantic life than that."

"Oh. Umm. I don't really have one. A romantic life that is. I'm single."

The roller coaster of this conversation was playing havoc with Karen's appetite. She picked at her salad and tried to ignore the way Bianca was watching her. When she finally braved a glance up, however, Bianca wasn't laughing at her for not having a girlfriend. She was studious again, looking at Karen like she was a puzzle on the verge of being solved.

"Is that intentional? It has to be. You're way too gorgeous to be single unless you want to be single," Bianca said.

"I, um, I…"

Karen couldn't manage anything articulate. Her face was too busy melting off her body with the heat of her blush. Bianca went back to her lunch as though she hadn't said anything amiss. Maybe she hadn't. Maybe she was the type of person who called her friends gorgeous all the time. Karen was definitely not that kind of friend and definitely not with a married woman who filled her mind morning, noon, and night.

Didn't Bianca realize how flirty that sounded? She probably didn't. She was just sitting there, searching through her bag of chips for the perfect one while Karen was having whatever happened before a mental breakdown.

"We're still on for pastries this weekend, right? I've been dreaming about those huge cinnamon rolls," Bianca said.

She'd been dreaming, too, but not about cinnamon rolls. The nagging guilt should have soured her mood, but it didn't stand a chance against Bianca's excitement. Obviously, this was an innocent outing for Bianca, but would Alex see it as innocent? Karen certainly wouldn't love the idea of her wife spending a lot of time with a single lesbian and calling her gorgeous. Then again, Bianca had hinted that she was in an unhappy marriage. Maybe she was looking for a way out. Maybe she was looking for a friend with a shoulder to cry on. One thing was certain, whatever Bianca was looking for, as long as it didn't involve cheating, Karen wanted to be it for her.

"Yes. Absolutely. I'm looking forward to it."

CHAPTER FOURTEEN

K aren woke up early Saturday morning, her body tangled in the sheets and her mind full of fading confusion from an intense dream. The pre-dawn sky filled her window with deep purples and deeper blues, the beautiful colors drawing her eye and chasing away any thought of falling back asleep. The colors lightened and coalesced into morning, her body and mind too exhausted to get out of bed but too wired to truly rest.

She couldn't believe that this school year was already a month old. It felt like just yesterday that she had sweated her way through that drive home from Kilmarnock. Then again, so much had happened since. Her new students were already so precious to her. Jacob had correctly answered every question in that week's spelling quiz. Ava wasn't just an eager reader, she turned out to be a natural at multiplication tables. Then there was Benji and the way both Karen and Bianca had been able to harness his love of books to improve his other subjects.

It was inevitable that Karen's mind would turn to Bianca, of course. Nothing about this year so far made half the impression on her as Bianca. Women had fascinated Karen before, but nothing like this. Not even her first crush way back in her own elementary school years. The crush had deepened in middle school and turned into a full-blown crisis in high school when Karen finally came to terms with what it meant right around the same time her crush started dating boys.

It had worked for her to curb her romantic inclinations with a heavy dose of friendship. And that strategy had served her well for another fifteen years. Right up until she met Bianca Harper. Now the more she got to know Bianca, the more she wanted her. And God, did she want Bianca. The number of times she had fallen asleep to fantasies of running her fingers through that golden-orange hair, pulling her in close, brushing her lips against Bianca's. What would her kiss taste like? Those lips were some of the most luscious Karen had ever seen. What would they feel like? What would they kiss like?

Bianca seemed the sort of woman to take charge of a kiss. To let her desire turn to greed. God, what Karen wouldn't give for just one kiss. But she knew with a bone-deep certainty that, if she kissed Bianca one time, she would tumble into a web of desire that would drag her so deep into Bianca's orbit she would never come out again.

"Okay, I need to stop this line of thought," Karen said to the empty room.

She popped out of bed, determined to find the energy her lazy morning had lacked. A cold shower and a hot cup of coffee had her mind back in appropriate places, and she focused on keeping it there. She hadn't checked in with her parents since she'd left their house in July, and that seemed a way to keep both her mind properly engaged and dispatch her daughterly duty. Despite their lukewarm relationship, she shared the guilt because of her lack of communication. It was just after eight a.m. She was meeting Bianca at Sallie Bell's in an hour, and her parents would have been awake for at least that long.

Her mom's phone rang twice before she answered, and she seemed genuinely happy to hear Karen's voice. "Good morning, sweetheart. How's school?"

There was a sweetness to the question that reminded Karen of being a kid, coming home from school, and hopping up on a stool at the kitchen counter to tell her mom all about what she'd learned that day.

"It's good. The kids this year are all really engaged and ready to learn," Karen said.

"That's nice, dear."

Karen could hear the rattle of dishes in the background. Or maybe it was the rigging on the boat. It was hard to tell. Whichever it was, it paired perfectly with the vague response to her excitement.

"There are a couple new teachers this year. First time we've had anyone new since I started."

"Oh really? That's nice."

"Bianca, the new art teacher, is gay."

Now her mother's voice perked up. "Oh really?"

"I met her wife at a barbecue last weekend."

"Oh? That's too bad."

The way her voice dropped from excitement down to disappointment would have been comical if it wasn't an exact replica of Karen's own feelings.

"She's becoming a good friend. We're going to have breakfast this morning."

"That's nice."

Her mother was starting to sound like a bored parrot with only one phrase to repeat, so she changed the subject. "How are you and Dad?"

"Oh, your father is in heaven. Did I tell you that the Hargroves bought the same model boat we have?"

Karen tried hard to inject some sort of interest into her voice. "Did they? I guess they really enjoyed their time on Dad's then?"

"They fell in love and your father is over the moon. They can't stop singing his praises around town."

Her mother prattled on at length about the way their star had risen amongst the elite of Kilmarnock. As disinterested as Karen was for that sort of social standing, it was everything to her parents and she was happy for them. Still there was only so much name-dropping she could handle before she started to sound like her mother, repeating "that's nice" endlessly.

Eventually, her mind started to wander, and that was Karen's cue to end the call. "I should probably get going. Send my love to Dad."

"I will. Try to have a good time."

Karen tossed the phone aside and looked over at the clock on her living room wall. That stilted conversation had burned less than ten minutes off her hour-long wait, but Karen couldn't stand the thought of puttering around her little apartment. She shoved her camera, book, and wallet into her messenger bag and hurried out into a glorious early autumn morning.

Bucks Mill in autumn was a sight to behold. The crisp air, the rattle of the first fallen leaves tumbling down the sidewalks, the thin sunlight on old brick and older clapboard. For a town of less than ten thousand residents, the sidewalks were rarely empty. Kids darted ahead of their parents in search of what little adventure they could scare up. Teenagers flirted and joked under the watchful eye of older residents and shopkeepers. It was a town out of another place and time, and for Karen, who grew up in the soulless concrete of commuter suburbs, it was heaven on earth.

Karen expected the two-block stroll to Sallie Bell's to be a solitary one. But as soon as she hit the sidewalk, she spotted Bianca standing at the corner where she'd nearly flattened Karen a few weeks before.

"You're early," Bianca said by way of greeting,

Karen shrugged, trying to force down the butterflies Bianca's presence kept spawning. "It's a beautiful morning. I didn't want to be cooped up any longer."

Bianca's smile lit the space between them more effectively than the early morning sun. "I was hoping you'd say that." She pointed to an overstuffed woven bag at her feet. "How would you feel about a breakfast picnic up on that hill you showed me?"

"That sounds perfect."

Coffee and pastries was becoming their thing. There was enough charged pressure in that without Sallie Bell's matchmaking. Besides, Karen couldn't stand hearing Bianca explain that they weren't an item in the face of Sallie's eager romantic encouragement. Plus, she hadn't taken pictures up on Jouett Hill since she'd returned to town and she was itching to get out there.

Fortunately, the café was far too busy to allow its owner to gossip too much. Bianca hurried straight for the pastry case and pressed both hands against the glass like a kid in a candy store. Her excitement was so adorable and Karen had to force herself to focus on having a normal conversation rather than swooning.

They settled on pumpkin spice cinnamon roll—it was the season after all—a cranberry scone, and pecan pie muffin. Sallie's nephew boxed them up and handed over a beverage tray for their coffees.

They had their breakfast secured and were out on the sidewalk again in no time.

"Shall I drive us up to the hill? It's walkable, but it's a long walk," Karen said.

"Sure. Then you can drive me home after. Alex dropped me off on her way to work, so I don't have my bike."

The drive through town was brief and uneventful, thanks to Karen's hyperfocus on avoiding brushing her hand against Bianca's arm. Her Civic never felt so small as when Bianca was sitting so close, smelling better than any pastry Sallie concocted. Then they were at the top of Jouett Hill and back into the crisp air.

Bianca's bag held a myriad of items. A huge blanket of woven wool in zigzags of mustard yellow and dark turquoise, a pair of small pillows that were equally useful as lumbar or head support, a well-worn sketchbook, and a tin with pastels and pencils. Karen appreciated her preparations, but equally appreciated her own hobby required her to move around. Sitting next to Bianca sketching would be far too distracting on such a small blanket.

"I figured you for a pumpkin spice latte kind of girl." Bianca handed Karen her black Americano.

"It's the name, isn't it? I've not had a moment's peace since the internet decided to crucify my name."

"I like your name. I don't know many Karens. Well, okay, I know a lot of 'Karens,' I just don't know any actual Karens. Am I making sense?"

"I know exactly what you mean. Hopefully, I only fall into one of those categories."

"You're the least 'Karen' Karen possible."

Heat suffused her body, so she tried to deflect from the compliment. "I'll never have the 'Karen' hair, that's for sure."

Bianca ran her fingertips across the short hair over Karen's ear, sending a shiver of delight though her body. "I'm happy to hear it. I love your hair."

"Thanks," Karen stuttered.

Thanks? That was the best she could do? Karen broke the corner off the scone and shoved it into her mouth to keep from saying anything else so milquetoast. Fortunately, Bianca took the cue to move into the pastry portion of their picnic. Unfortunately, Bianca had a tendency to moan in delight over pastries.

"There's more than just cranberry in here, isn't there?" Bianca examined the chunk of leftover scone in her hand.

Karen took a bite and examined the flavors mingling on her tongue. "Orange and something else. Cinnamon?"

"Nutmeg?"

Karen closed her eyes as she took her final bite. "I think you're right. I think it's nutmeg."

When she opened her eyes, she found Bianca's gaze lingering on her. Her heart skipped a beat and she tried not to read anything into it, but there was such an intensity to that stare. Surely she didn't look at everyone like that?

They decided that the pumpkin spice cinnamon roll was their favorite and that the pecan pie muffin was not to Sallie's usual standard.

"I can't believe I picked the one bad pastry. You'll have to make all the choices on our next trip. Clearly, I can't be trusted," Bianca said.

Again, Karen's stomach did flips of pleasure. Every time they saw each other, Bianca made it clear she wanted to see Karen more. It was hard not to read too much into that.

After finishing their pastries, Karen laid back on the blanket with her book to read while she digested and Bianca flipped open her sketchbook. A blissful half hour passed with Karen luxuriating in a fictional world with the sounds of birds chirping and scratch of Bianca's pastels across the page. Bianca looked over at her with a lazy smile and it felt too much like they had woken up next to each other in bed. Karen pushed herself upright to break out of the fantasy.

"Can I see your drawing?" Karen asked.

Bianca handed over the sketchbook without a moment of hesitation. Her unselfconsciousness was as unsettling as it was wonderful. Karen wasn't the kind of person who would so willingly make herself vulnerable, but maybe she should be. Maybe she could learn that confidence from Bianca if they continued to be friends.

The drawing was only an impression at the moment, but it was undoubtedly the landscape before them. Karen would have recognized the gentle slope of the hill in the foreground and the perfectly placed rooflines even if she couldn't see the real thing in front of her. Bianca had not only captured the shapes, she'd captured the feel of Bucks Mill. The colors were perfect and the gracefulness majestic.

"This is beautiful," she said.

"Thanks. I don't use pastels much, but this view seemed to call for it. I remembered how vibrant the colors were up here last time you brought me."

"What do you normally use?" Karen asked.

"I usually sketch in pencil." Bianca waved her hand encouragingly toward the sketchbook. "Flip through if you like."

The first few pages were tight with everyday images. A cardinal perched on a sliver of branch, a mailbox with ivy growing up the stand, a foot with dark painted nails. They looked like practice drawings, though she didn't know the process since she didn't draw. Next were more composed images. A brick house with a steep staircase to the entryway, a forest scene, and a small bistro table that Karen recognized from Main Street Café.

"These are incredible." Karen heard the breathlessness in her own voice.

"Thank you." Bianca's voice was low, almost husky.

The change in her voice made Karen look up. Was Bianca shy about her work? But she looked anything but shy. Bianca met her gaze with an intensity that set Karen's blood racing. She swore Bianca was leaning toward her. Leaning in for a kiss?

No. She wasn't. She couldn't. Bianca was married and, even though Karen had only seen them together a couple times, the affection between her and Alex was unmistakable. They had a connection. A love that Karen could never—would never—break. Bianca wouldn't either. Would she?

Karen focused back on the sketchbook, flipping to the next page. "I thought you were a painter, though. There are some paintings hanging in your classroom with your name on them, right?"

Bianca nodded and sat back.

"And didn't I hear you talking to Benji about pottery?" Karen asked.

"Ceramics were my first love. I've never really been able to give them up. I mostly draw these days because I haven't had time to set up my full studio. Before we moved, I was studying textiles."

"You're so talented and in so many disciplines. What led you to teaching? It certainly wasn't the old 'those who can, do, those who can't, teach.'"

"For me it's closer to 'those who can't do just one thing teach.' I can't make up my mind what medium I want to focus on. I like them all too much. Alex teases me that I'm pansexual and panartistic."

There was at least one point in Alex's favor. Karen couldn't abide queer people who looked down on other sexualities, and lesbians didn't have the best track record for accepting pan and bi women. At least Bianca was married to a woman who respected her that much.

"Well, I think it's amazing that you have such a big heart that makes room for everything," Karen said.

A smile grew on Bianca's lips and that mischievous glint was back in her eye. "Are you talking about my art or my sexuality?"

"Both."

"You aren't so very different, though. You teach every subject."

Bianca was leaning close again, even closer than she had before and Karen was lightheaded with longing. What would it hurt to play along just for a little while?

"I don't have to do any of them well. After all, I teach third graders, so I don't have to know advanced math." Bianca's laughter encouraged her and made her bold. She continued before she lost her nerve. "I don't have as much room in my heart for love, either. I only date women."

Bianca's smile was positively wicked. "How lucky for the women of Bucks Mill."

Heat rushed through Karen's face and her ears rang with the pounding of her heart. Still, she leaned back as Bianca leaned farther forward. Karen turned away, toward the view of the town she loved and the distant horizon. She wouldn't be that person. Even if Bianca knew her actions felt like flirting, which she probably didn't. Bianca couldn't be the one for her. She had to accept it. She dreamt of loving someone who would put her first, but Bianca never could. Not when she had Alex at home.

"I'm sorry," Bianca said. "I've always been a little too open."

"No. It's fine."

And maybe it would be. For someone else. For someone who didn't ache for Bianca. For someone who only felt friendship, Bianca's openness and tactile nature would be just fine. Karen wasn't that person though. Karen would walk across a mountain top barefoot for just one kiss from Bianca. She had to control herself or she would ruin everything.

Karen hopped to her feet and dug her camera out of her bag. "I'm just a little restless. Think I might take a walk around the hill."

Bianca rose to her feet. "Would it be okay if I join you? Unless you'd rather be alone?"

"No. I mean, yes, it would be okay if you join me. I wouldn't rather be alone."

Karen's forced smile must have convinced Bianca she was telling the truth. She wasn't entirely sure she was, but her need to process was much weaker than her desire to spend every minute she could with Bianca.

They walked slowly, comfortable silence interspersed with idle conversation and the occasional photograph. Soon enough the simple act of identifying local landmarks and discussing their shared students returned Karen's calm. She could still do this. She still wanted to do this. She wanted to be Bianca's friend and she could set aside her feelings to make that happen.

The cool morning had changed to muggy afternoon by the time Karen navigated the steep, unmarked road winding down Jouett Hill. Bianca cranked down the window and leaned her head against the headrest, her eyes closed and a contented smile on her lips. Karen watched from the corner of her eye because she loved to see her friend happy and not because Bianca's contentment made her neck stretch in a distractingly sexy way.

"Is it always this hot in the fall?" Bianca asked over the wind whipping through the vehicle.

"What do you mean? It's barely eighty degrees."

Bianca rolled her head on the seat. "It's the end of September."

"Yeah. So?"

"In Massachusetts it snows in October."

Karen looked both ways before pulling out onto the road leading into Ashcroft Court. "Seriously? That's way too early for snow."

"When do you normally get your first snow here?" Bianca asked.

"Depends. Last year it didn't snow at all."

Bianca sat bolt upright. "What do you mean? You didn't get any snow?"

"None that stuck. It snowed in January, but it was too warm for accumulation. It melted as soon as it hit the ground."

"Wow. No snow. I had no idea. I thought that would just be a Georgia and Florida thing."

"You didn't research the weather before you moved to Bucks Mill?" Karen asked.

"Nope. We threw darts at a map and ended up here."

The answer was so matter-of-fact that Karen couldn't help but laugh. It was so very Bianca. Maybe it was the stress of keeping her feelings to herself, maybe it was intoxication from a full afternoon with unfettered access to Bianca, but when Karen started to laugh, she couldn't stop. It started as giggles and turned into a burst of noise all the way from her chest. Distantly, she heard Bianca laughing along with her. Tears of mirth streamed down her face as she laughed and laughed and laughed.

The mirth ebbed away and her laughter subsided. Today was the most fun she'd had in a long time. If only she could feel this every day. If only she could live off a steady diet of the happiness being with Bianca provided. But she couldn't and she shouldn't hope for it. No matter how much this felt like driving Bianca home after a date, that was only Karen's wishful thinking and overactive libido.

At least there was no truck in the driveway as Karen parked at the curb. She didn't have to see Alex greet Bianca with a kiss.

"Would you like to come inside for a tour?" Bianca asked. "And maybe a cold drink? I don't want you suffering in this heat."

Karen ignored the warning bells going off in her head. "Sure. Thanks."

They walked up the driveway in silence, but Karen's mind was loud enough for both of them. Bianca didn't turn toward the steep staircase in front of the front door. She opened a keypad next to the garage and punched in a code that made the door rattle and shake its way open.

The garage was as tidy as any Karen had ever seen, with pegboard walls of tools hanging neatly in their place. The bike Bianca had nearly flattened her with weeks ago was parked off to one side, directly across from shelf after shelf of neatly stacked plastic bins labeled with different holidays or seasons. Bianca walked deliberately to a coat rack next to an interior door and hung her bag on the lone empty hook.

She turned to Karen and the earlier unexpected shyness was back. She gestured to the keypad lock on the door. "I lose keys all the time, but I'm good at memorizing combinations."

Karen smiled weakly as Bianca took a step or two toward her. Maybe it was more? Suddenly she was right in front of Karen, the scent of sun-warmed skin made her dizzy. All she could do was stare at Bianca's lips. They split and her tongue slid between them, wetting the ruby red flesh and making everything from Karen's arms to the very air around her heavy. And she hadn't stopped moving. Hadn't stopped gliding across the painted concrete until she was achingly close. Too close. How could Karen possibly resist?

Their kiss felt inevitable. Preordained. Bianca tilted her head a fraction and Karen's head tilted, too, quite unintentionally. She was closing her eyes when she heard the crack of hinges opening. Bianca wasn't so close anymore. She had stepped back and away, heading toward the exterior door on the other side of the garage and taking all the oxygen with her. Karen opened her mouth to take a breath but had to physically command her lungs to act.

Alex stepped into the garage, pulling the door to the backyard shut with a clatter, leaving a crushing silence in its wake.

Jesus. I almost kissed her right in front of her wife.

That wasn't quite right, of course. Bianca had been the one to almost kiss Karen. Perhaps that distinction didn't mean much to anyone else, but Karen had definite feelings about cheating. At least she thought she had until about fifteen seconds before. The realization of near disaster made her physically ill and she had to turn away until it passed.

When she had control of herself, she turned around and wished she hadn't. Alex had her arm casually draped over Bianca's shoulder like a teenage boy trying to cop a feel. Bianca wrapped both her arms around Alex's waist and hugged her tight, laughing at some comment Karen had missed. The way Bianca seamlessly shifted from nearly kissing someone else to cuddling with her wife made Karen's stomach roil. How could this be the woman Karen wanted? She wasn't the sweet, passionate woman Karen had imagined her to be. She was a liar and a cheat and Karen had to get out of there before she fell completely apart.

"I'm going to go," Karen said.

Bianca's laughter died in a heartbeat and she dropped her arms from Alex's waist. "What? I thought you were coming inside for a tour?"

The words were so innocent. Had Karen misread the situation entirely? The confused look Alex and Bianca shared seemed to confirm it. Bianca wasn't the terrible person here. Karen was. She had made up this whole thing in her head. She had allowed her crush to blossom and she had nearly tried to kiss a married woman. God, how fortunate was Alex's timing? It had saved Karen from making the biggest mistake of her life.

Karen ducked her head and hurried out of the garage. She couldn't bring herself to look at either of them after what she'd done. "Not now that Alex is home. I'm sure you have...couple things to do."

To her surprise, Bianca stepped in front of her, blocking her escape. Karen glanced up and saw confusion painted across her features. Bianca asked, "What do you mean?"

Before Karen could craft an answer, Alex burst into a torrent of laughter. That was unexpected and it kept Karen from dodging around Bianca and escaping. Alex slapped a hand to her belly and doubled over.

"What are you laughing at?" Bianca asked.

Alex collected herself enough to blurt out, "She thinks we're married, doofus." Alex dissolved back into laughter.

Bianca shook her head. "Why would she think that?" When Alex's laughter prevented her answer, Bianca turned to Karen. "Why would you think that?"

"I told you to drop the Mrs. and change your name back after you got divorced, idiot." Alex turned to Karen and held out her hand. "I clearly didn't make a complete introduction at the cookout. Let me try again. Hi, I'm Alex. The hot lesbian sister."

CHAPTER FIFTEEN

K aren had never been so confused in her life. The words rattled around her brain but didn't penetrate. Bianca didn't seem to have an answer either. In fact, the most adorable line appeared between her eyebrows and Karen could almost see her trying to work everything through. Her instinct of telling herself to ignore all the adorable or sexy or captivating things about Bianca arose, but maybe she didn't have to listen?

Because she couldn't think of anything else to do, Karen took Alex's hand and shook it. Everything seemed to slow down as she processed. Belatedly, she asked, "Sister?"

Alex laughed again and Karen realized the laugh sounded a lot like Bianca's. She also threw her head back in unashamed delight the same way Bianca did. When she looked back down, Karen noticed that, while she had green eyes rather than brown, they were the exact same shape as Bianca's. So was her mouth and there was a shadow of Bianca in the set of her jaw. As the dots lined up, a flicker of hope kindled in Karen's chest.

Bianca shoved Alex aside and Karen lost the grip on her hand. "You're not nearly as hot as you think you are." Bianca took the hand Karen still held stupidly out in front of her and yanked her toward the house. "Come on. We need to talk."

Karen didn't so much walk through the door from the garage to the house and down the hall as she was dragged. Honestly, it was a good thing that Bianca took a firm hold of her hand, entwining their fingers and keeping a firm tension. Karen's mind was numb, the single word "sister" zipping around it like a firefly trapped in a jar.

A few doorways passed by without grabbing Karen's attention, but she was pretty sure she saw an assortment of easels through one and a stackable washer/dryer through another. Bianca took a hard right to push through a half-open door and Karen's pulse thudded in her veins. It only took one glance to realize this was Bianca's bedroom.

The room had her same vibe. The walls were so thickly covered with canvases, picture frames, shelves full of pottery, and floor to ceiling tapestries that Karen couldn't see the wall paint. Furniture in all shapes and sizes littered the room in what appeared at first to be an unruly clutter. Upon further examination, however, Karen could see the order in the chaos. The clearly outlined paths from one carved end table to the vibrantly painted dresser and on to the tall, cushioned bed frame.

Karen's brain emptied at the sight of the bed. Then it filled with a hazy mental image of Bianca splayed across that bed. She probably slept as haphazardly as she lived, with sheets twisted around her ankles and acres of bare skin exposed.

Bianca pulled Karen down to sit beside her on the foot of the bed. "We should talk."

Karen attempted to kick-start her brain, but it was like a dodgy lawn mower that needed several pulls on the starter cord for the engine to come to life. "Right. Talk."

She agreed to the conversation assuming Bianca was fit to lead it, but when she made eye contact, Bianca just stared at her. There was a fondness in her gaze that had a storm of butterflies fluttering around Karen's stomach. She couldn't quite forget that they were in Bianca's bedroom and she was sitting on Bianca's bed.

"What do you think is going on here?" Bianca asked.

"Honestly? I have no idea."

Bianca's laugh soothed and ignited her, and Karen offered an apologetic smile. Bianca ran her thumb across Karen's knuckles, and that was how she realized Bianca was holding her hand.

"Let's start with some biographical information. I'm Bianca Cassani Harper. I'm thirty-eight years old. I've been divorced for five years. I moved to Bucks Mill in January with my sister when her divorce was finalized and we decided to start over in a new town."

Karen nodded as each new word spread across the surface of her brain and then slowly, ever so slowly, soaked in. She must have looked ridiculous, because Bianca gave her another radiant smile and reached up to run a thumb along her jawline.

"I've also been trying very hard to flirt with you for weeks now," Bianca said with a shy smile. "And, I flatter myself, I don't usually have to work this hard."

Karen's throat went dry as the desert and she couldn't seem to blink her eyes. "Roger introduced you as Mrs. Bianca Harper."

"Of course. I realize now why I had to work so hard. Most of our colleagues know my whole story, but you don't spend much time in the teachers' lounge," Bianca said.

"I had no idea."

"And you assumed Alex was my wife."

"I had no reason not to," Karen said.

"I don't wear a wedding ring, for one."

Karen reached out and touched the longest chain in the group around Bianca's neck. Her fingers shook but she managed to make contact with the diamond solitaire. "I thought you didn't want to get paint on them."

Bianca looked down. Oh God, Karen's hand was resting just between her breasts. She pulled away quickly and Bianca gave her another wicked smile. "They're my grandmother's. It was the only thing I wanted from her when she passed."

All these smiles and explanations. With each word the possibility of something truly special between them felt more real. "Oh. That makes sense."

"And now that I think about it, Jessica hasn't been around when I've talked about my ex-husband or my sister. You really ought to broaden your gossip circles. You could have asked, you know."

Honesty and vulnerability would have been terrifying a few minutes ago, but right now nothing could burst the bubble of pure joy in Karen's chest. "I guess I didn't really want to know the fairy tale story of how you met and fell in love with someone else."

"Because you like me?"

"Isn't that obvious?"

"I still want to hear it," Bianca said with a purr.

"Yes. I like you. Like a whole lot."

"The feeling is mutual."

Some of the tension was leaking out of Karen, replaced by possibilities. Possibilities she had been stuffing down for so long, but now didn't have to. Sweat broke out on her palms. She ran a shaky hand through her hair. All she could do was stare into the coffee-rich depths of Bianca's eyes.

"What are you thinking?" Bianca asked.

"I really want to talk all this out, but I've wanted to kiss you from the moment we met. It's all I can think about."

"Are you asking for permission to kiss me?"

A boldness crept into Karen she hadn't realized was there. She stared deep into Bianca's eyes. "Bianca, can I kiss you?"

"I thought you'd never ask."

She meant to lean in slowly, seductively even, but her need got the better of her. All her carefully stitched composure snapped like a dry twig underfoot. In the end she sort of launched herself at Bianca's lips instead. It shouldn't have been sexy, but the moment their lips touched, Bianca moaned into her mouth. It was everything she'd hoped for their first kiss and more. Their lips fused in a perfect, primal dance. Bianca's mouth was soft and burning hot, opening to Karen with the least provocation and inviting her deeper. The kiss was wild and wonderful and maybe a little too forward, but Karen had wanted her for so long she couldn't be restrained. Bianca certainly didn't seem to mind. She held Karen hard to her with fingertips wrapped around her neck. Every inch of her skin tingled.

When they finally broke apart, Karen was gasping for breath and Bianca's eyes flashed with hunger. Her stare was so intense, Karen was a little nervous to be sitting on the same bed with her. How could she possibly control herself now, knowing that Bianca was just as desperate for this, whatever this turned out to be? Did she really want to control herself, though? Sure, they had lots more talking to do and it would be beyond foolish to jump into bed. They were coworkers and they only just shared their first kiss, but Bianca's chest was rising and falling in a staccato rhythm. She was clearly just as caught up as Karen was.

Just as they both leaned in to see where another kiss would take them, a loud throat clearing from the hallway saved them from themselves. They jumped apart like a pair of teenagers caught by their parents. It would have been funny if it was happening to someone else.

"I'm going to the hardware store. The one in Charlottesville that's over an hour away, where I'm going to look at every single table saw they carry. Then I'm going to the good grocery store on the other side of town. You two should have plenty of time to, um, talk."

Alex shot a cheeky wink through the door and then hustled down the hallway. Karen kept staring at the blank wall until she heard a Hemi engine roar from somewhere in the backyard. She chanced a glance across the bed to see Bianca looking just as sheepish as Alex. It was so cute, but it shifted back to naked hunger on a dime.

Bianca grabbed a fistful of Karen's shirt and pulled her into a bruising kiss. Part of her wanted to be a lady and slow things down, but that part went silent when Bianca pulled the hem of her shirt free from her jeans. Her touch was pleasantly cool against Karen's quickly heating skin. She had dreamt of this touch so many times, but nothing lived up to the reality. Karen's flesh burned with the gentlest swipe of her fingertips. Bianca's hands circled to her back, and when her nails raked lines across Karen's back, she lost all control.

Karen pushed forward, harder into the kiss, needing to feel more of Bianca. Needing the solid press of her body. Rather than press against her, Bianca's body yielded and Karen found herself lying on top of Bianca, pressing her into the mattress.

"Oh, fuck. I'm sorry." Karen panted as she broke the kiss, trying to push herself off Bianca.

Bianca held her down. "Don't go."

"I don't want to get carried away. I mean—Jesus, I thought you were married until like ten minutes ago."

Despite her verbal protests, her body was reluctant to move from its position, slotted awkwardly between Bianca's legs. Clearly Bianca could read her like a book. She shifted beneath Karen, keeping her hands locked on her hips so she wouldn't leave, but helping them settle into a far more traditional position. Karen's mind swam. She was propped on her elbows, but the rest of her body, from her stomach to her aching core, was caged between Bianca's arms and legs.

Bianca slipped both hands back under Karen's shirt and caressed her sides. "You said you wanted to kiss me. I'm pretty sure you're interested in other things, too? Am I right?"

Karen nodded and a lock of hair came free from her top knot to dangle in the air between them. Bianca's hands crept a little higher on Karen's sides, grazing against her ribs.

"And what might those things be?" Bianca asked, a teasing note in her voice.

Karen's body trembled. No one had ever asked her to verbalize like this. Could she even do that? "I...um..."

Bianca ran her nose and then her lips along her neck, sending a pulse racing through her body. "Do you want to touch me?"

"God yes."

"Then touch me."

God, how Karen wanted to, but fear crept in around the edges. "Are you sure? I mean...I know you're sure. And I'm sure. I really am. I just...isn't it too quick?"

"We're both adults here and neither of us is exactly traditional. So if we're both comfortable with it, I think we can add sex into this equation. Are you comfortable with it?" Bianca asked.

Karen wanted to scream yes, especially as Bianca's nails scratched lightly against her lower back. It had been a really long time for her, and she was absolutely certain about her feelings for Bianca. And she was right. Tradition wasn't made for queer people. They could do whatever they wanted.

"We're talking a relationship here, right? Not just casual sex? Because I definitely want more than casual sex with you," Karen said.

A strange flicker of hesitation or maybe insecurity flashed across Bianca's face. "You do?"

"Yes, absolutely."

Relief washed away the hesitation. Of course she hesitated. She'd been throwing herself at Karen for weeks but gotten nothing back. No wonder she was nervous. A pang for what might have been guilt flared in Karen's chest, but Bianca seemed to recover quickly.

Bianca's wicked smile sent a surge through Karen's core. "Definitely more than casual." She pushed up off the bed to drag Karen into a slow, seductive kiss. "There's no way fucking you once will be enough for me."

Karen couldn't control herself any longer. Her hips bucked forward, slamming into Bianca's and earning her a gasp that Karen eagerly swallowed in another kiss. Bianca's nails dug into her back and Karen started pulling at clothing with reckless abandon. She needed them to both be naked. Now.

She could not for the life of her figure out how to remove Bianca's skirt, but she was far more successful with her flimsy blouse. Bianca pushed off the bed enough for Karen to pull it up over her breasts. As she had suspected, Bianca was not wearing a bra. Her bare breasts and pink-brown nipples were too much to bear. She dropped down and sucked one hardened nipple into her mouth.

"Oh God, yes. Karen, please."

The musky, salty taste of her flesh sent Karen into a state of bliss. She swirled her tongue around the hardened bud and sucked hard. Instinct told her Bianca wasn't a delicate flower in the bedroom, so she experimented with a graze of teeth across her nipple. Bianca arched into her and scratched her nails harder down her back. A burst of need coursed through Karen, but she wouldn't let it divert her. Yet. When she switched to the other nipple, Bianca groaned and slid her hands under Karen's jeans to grip her ass.

Karen took her time, lavishing attention on Bianca's breasts, stomach, and chest. At some point Bianca ripped her own blouse off, allowing Karen to transfer her light bites and eager tongue to her neck.

"Don't make me explain hickies or bite marks to the kids," Bianca whispered.

"Good point." Karen slid off the bed, settling on her knees beside the bed, Bianca's legs draped over her shoulders. "I'll leave my marks where only you will see them."

Bianca's mouth dropped open. A burst of pride spread though Karen at that look of shock. The heady, rich scent of Bianca's desire swept over her. She wanted nothing more than to taste it, but she was determined to take her time. To tease. To make her desperate the way these last few weeks had made Karen desperate.

Karen pushed Bianca's skirt up to bunch around her waist, then took in her conquest. The thrill of Bianca's already soaked panties made her breath catch, but she could do better.

Karen slid the flat of her tongue from Bianca's knee, down the inside of her thigh. When she reached the bunched muscle just above the apex of her thigh, Karen bit down. She was gentle at first, but Bianca cried out in obvious pleasure and Karen bit a little harder. Bianca's hips jerked up, obviously seeking pressure where she needed it most.

She switched her attention to Bianca's other thigh, repeating the long, steady lick from knee to inner thigh. This time she journeyed a little farther, flicking her tongue across the lace edge of her panties. Bianca groaned and squirmed, but Karen moved away, teasing without touching. Leaving Bianca wanting more.

"If you don't touch me soon, I'm going to scream," Bianca said.

"That's not much of a threat. I want you to scream."

"Karen, dammit, you're killing me."

Karen chuckled, but she needed to move along soon. Bianca wasn't the only one whose underwear was soaked. The pressure of denim against Karen's core was a constant torment. She spread Bianca's legs further apart and slid her hands across the smooth, warm skin of her thighs. When she reached her panties, Karen slipped her thumbs beneath the fabric. Her touch was teasing, barely grazing her folds, and Bianca squirmed, trying to direct her where she wanted her most.

Bianca whimpered and Karen's self-control snapped. Bianca's obvious desire was intoxicating. She ripped Bianca's panties off with less finesse than she had intended and buried her face between her thighs. Her first taste of Bianca was the start of an addiction. She would never get enough. Never get enough of the salty-sweetness of her. Never get enough of her cry of pleasure. Never get enough of Bianca burying her fingers into her hair to hold her close.

Karen slipped her tongue through Bianca's folds to gather her flavor, then went to work on her swollen clit. She kept firm, insistent pressure. Bianca's nails scraping along her scalp told her she was hitting the mark. Bianca ground her hips in time with Karen's tongue and she had to hold on with her arms wrapped around her thighs or risk being bucked right off her target.

Bianca's breathing turned into panting turned into keening. Karen took one last moment of teasing fun to wrestle back control and stopped dead. Bianca's scream this time was one of obvious frustration and she pushed her hips forward, begging Karen to continue.

"Please don't stop. God, Karen, please don't make me beg."

"'Please don't stop' already sounds like begging to me," Karen said.

Bianca whimpered, a lovely reward for Karen's moment of boldness. Karen had been a desperate, foolish mess for weeks. Maybe she could gain the upper hand between them if she made Bianca beg. How many nights had she lain in bed, imagining this moment while she brought herself to an unsatisfying peak? Bianca had wanted her all that time, too. Bianca had been just as desperate and just as big a mess. Now Karen could give her the release. She couldn't deny her another moment.

Karen pressed back in, licking harder and harder until she had Bianca panting again. This time, rather than pulling back, she moved faster, held Bianca's thighs tighter. Bianca's panting stopped and silence held for the space of two heartbeats before she screamed so loud it made Karen's ears ring. Her hips ground faster and Karen rode through pulse after pulse.

Just as Bianca was relaxing back into something close to calm, Karen slid two fingers inside her and plunged back in with her tongue. Bianca's breathing stuttered and her hips bucked harder than ever. Karen curled her fingers to press against her front wall, and a moment later Bianca was screaming again. She released a flood around Karen's fingers and over her chin.

Karen's jaw ached and her wrist was caught at an awkward angle, but Bianca's walls were still fluttering around her fingers. She couldn't stop now. This time her hips were more sluggish and her fingers stroked Karen's hair rather than gripped at it, but she wasn't quite done. Karen could wring just a little more out of this magnificent body.

As she had suspected, Bianca's third release was quick to come and earth-shatteringly loud. She drenched Karen again and her scream petered out slowly. Never in her life had Karen been with such an expressive lover. Bianca orgasmed the way she did everything, full-throated and without shame. It was incredible. Karen's desire nearly consumed her.

"I need a break." Bianca gasped. "Please come up here."

Karen eased her fingers out, trying to be as gentle as possible. She had maybe gotten a little carried away. Hopefully, between this and the biting she wouldn't leave Bianca sore. Uncertainty flashed through her like a wave of ice water. She was not ashamed to be a vigorous lover, but she hardly knew Bianca. She had assumed so much. What if she had assumed too much?

She climbed gingerly onto the mattress beside Bianca, her heart slamming against her ribs. Bianca's eyes were closed and her breathing slowed. She had always been able to read so much from that open, expressive face. Now she was lost. Not to mention, as she settled against Bianca's side, her body reminded her that she was still far from satisfied herself. Her usual feelings around Bianca—crushing need and overwhelming worry—came back in earnest. How strange to feel those now, with the musky taste of Bianca so present on her tongue.

Bianca's lids fluttered open and her gaze settled on Karen. The look in those earth-brown eyes stole her breath away. There was satisfaction and desire, but more than anything else, Bianca looked at Karen like she was the only person in the world. A lazy smile spread across her lips and she reached up to stroke Karen's cheek.

"Hey, you," Bianca whispered.

Karen's heart burst at the tenderness. All her worries fled and the throb in her core intensified under Bianca's fond gaze. This thing between them was so fresh and new, but it already felt precious.

"You're incredible," Karen said before she could stop herself.

Bianca purred like a contented kitten and her eyes rolled back. "You're not so bad yourself, tiger."

She could have stared into those sparkling brown eyes for eternity, but Bianca clearly had other ideas. She was already working at the button and zipper on Karen's jeans and the tug of her hands so close to Karen's throbbing clit was almost too much. Bianca's hands slid beneath the waistband of her boy shorts and she had to bite the side of her cheek to keep herself grounded in the moment. She was going to embarrass herself by coming ridiculously quickly, but she wanted to last as long as possible.

"Look at me," Bianca said.

When had she shut her eyes anyway? She forced them open and managed a single breath. Then Bianca's fingers found her clit and she lost the ability to breathe. She groaned and her vision swam, but she was able to focus on Bianca's eyes.

"That's it. Stay with me. I want you to watch me while I fuck you."

Karen's mouth went dry and her heart thudded ten times faster. How had she not known how sexy talking during sex could be?

"Is this good?" Bianca asked.

All Karen could do was whimper and nod. So much for her ability to participate in sexy talk. No way she could keep it up while Bianca touched her. Bianca pressed hard into her, drawing tight circles around her clit and slid her hand through the hair coming loose from Karen's top knot. Sweat beaded on her brow as Bianca stroked her agonizingly slowly, and her gentle fingers wiped the sweat away.

Pleasure coursed through her in time with Bianca's rhythmic touch, but her nerves were stretched too thin. Her need too raw. Karen groaned. "Faster. Please faster."

Bianca's smiled as if she'd been waiting for Karen to ask. Karen would beg. She would do anything for Bianca. She was lost and it had been foolish to think she could handle such intense sex with Bianca so soon, but she had been powerless and she always would be.

"Like that?"

"Yes. God yes…Bianca!"

Her orgasm surprised her and she was swept away in it. She probably screamed Bianca's name more than once, but her ears were ringing with the thud of her own blood as she came. Bianca's touch never wavered and Karen wasn't sure if she had a second orgasm or just a glorious extension of the first, but it felt like her pleasure lasted for hours.

When she calmed enough to become aware of her surroundings, her face was buried in Bianca's neck. She breathed deep the mingled smells of sex, sweat, and Bianca's flowery perfume. It was a cocoon she wanted to live inside for as long as humanly possible.

When Bianca started to pull her hand out of her pants, Karen grabbed her gently. "Wait. Can you just hold me for another minute?"

Bianca smiled against her neck. She cupped Karen and dropped a gentle kiss on her ear. "Anything you want, babe."

CHAPTER SIXTEEN

The tender moment didn't last nearly as long as Karen would have wished, but Alex could return at any moment. Maybe that was on Bianca's mind, too, because after just a few minutes of cuddling, she gave Karen's forehead a kiss with the air of finality.

"We should clean up a little before the tour," Bianca said.

Karen's shyness returned as she borrowed Bianca's face wash and toothbrush. Bianca swapped out the quilt, now distinctly ruffled and wet in suspicious places, for another, nearly identical one from her closet. It was so practical, such a letdown from the intensity of their intimacy. Still, Bianca was her usual attentive self, touching Karen on the shoulder or hip as they passed each other and smiling at her every time their eyes met.

Karen floated through her tour of the cute little split-level house. Bianca and Alex had set it up as a double primary, with Bianca living on the bottom floor with her own bedroom, living room, and office/art studio. She only had to go upstairs for the kitchen and Alex only had to come downstairs for the laundry, so they could spend most of their time in their own bubbles.

"Of course, my sister and I are super close, so we end up hanging out most of the time anyway." Bianca slid her fingertips up and down Karen's forearm as she spoke.

Karen managed to nod and make a sound in her throat that could be interpreted as understanding, but even that small task was a challenge. Bianca was a very tactile person, with an arm wrapped around her conversation partner's shoulder or sometimes holding their hand. She'd touched Karen's hand or arm a few times before Karen's growing attraction made her keep her distance. Now that they'd had sex, however, Bianca had barely stopped touching her.

Bianca had looped her arm around Karen's as soon as they began the tour and she hadn't released her since, opting to twist and turn through doorways or sharp corners rather than break contact. The warmth of Bianca so close beside her and the occasional gentle press of her breast against Karen's arm or side had done a number on her ability to form coherent thoughts, much less words.

The touch was distracting enough, but Karen's heart skipped a beat every time Bianca looked over at her. A little zing of energy shot through her when Bianca said "my sister." Alex wasn't a competitor for Bianca's affection. Bianca was a free agent and had made it clear she was solely interested in Karen. Was this real life?

The touch and the looks and the thrill of being wanted was overwhelming. Luxurious. So damn good. Probably too good since they hadn't really talked about what the sex meant. But why spoil this moment with practicalities? She wanted to be the center of Bianca's attention for as long as it lasted. Reality could wait.

"We've been renovating the house one room at a time as we have the money and the time, which isn't often now that the school year started." Bianca pulled Karen quickly through a thoroughly nineties-era kitchen.

"You've done a great job." Karen was proud of how normal her voice sounded since this was the first full sentence she'd managed.

"It's mostly Alex. I usually just do the finishing projects. I'm not even allowed to paint the walls. Can you believe that? I'm literally a painter and she kicks me out when the rollers come out."

"Why's that?"

Bianca pulled them down onto a deep, cozy couch under a bank of windows in need of recaulking. "Alex says I get too impatient and spray little dots of ceiling paint everywhere."

Another zing of happiness shot through Karen, making her smile. "Is she right?"

"Of course she's right. Painting rooms is boring, but she doesn't have to be all superior about it." Bianca tucked her feet underneath her legs as she laughed at her own joke. Enchanting lines popped out around her eyes and her throat bobbed.

How had Bianca taken such a deep hold on her already? She was in deep trouble. Karen always fell too hard, too fast, and she had the scars of untold failed love affairs as evidence, but she couldn't make herself put up those barriers and Bianca didn't seem likely to let her anyway.

Bianca cradled Karen's hand in both hers. "You look like you have questions."

"I guess I do, yeah."

"What's on the top of your mind? We'll work down from there."

Bianca emphasized the question by running the very edge of her fingertips across Karen's temple, then sliding them back into her hair. She had finger-combed her hair and pulled it back into her usual top knot, but Bianca's short nails found their way through, scratching lightly against Karen's scalp, reminding her of those nails scraping all over her body so recently. She stroked again and again, almost hypnotically while Karen tried to think.

"You can probably guess what's at the top of my mind," Karen said.

Bianca's eyebrow arched, making Karen's thoroughly satisfied body hum. "I'm going to need a little bit of a break before round two. I'm not as young as I used to be."

"That's not what I meant."

"No? Too bad."

"You're impossible," Karen said with a laugh.

"Yeah, but you like it."

"I really do." Bianca leaned in close and kissed her softly on the lips. The gentleness of the kiss pushed some of Karen's fears and insecurities away.

"I just want to be sure what it means. You're serious about us dating, right?" Karen asked.

"Of course. I really like you. I thought you knew that?"

"I do. You said you did. I just thought you weren't interested for so long. You were flirting with me all that time?"

Bianca smiled. "I thought I was being obvious, but I might be out of practice."

"No, I don't think you are. I just figured it was wishful thinking on my part."

Bianca leaned dangerously close into Karen's space, making her throat go dry. "So you're saying that you did want me to flirt with you?"

The words held a teasing lilt, but there was hesitation there, too. Just like when they were in bed together. Bianca had wanted her for a long time, too. Bianca thought she was being rejected, but she didn't give up. She'd been brave and strong and then she'd soothed Karen's fears, too. It was Karen's turn to be brave.

"I like you so much. More than I've liked anyone in a long time. Maybe ever? I'm just so excited about a relationship with you, but I'm scared, too."

"You don't need to be scared."

"Neither do you."

A flash of surprise lit Bianca's eyes and she laughed. "Have I been that obvious?"

"Not as obvious as I've been oblivious."

Bianca laughed again and Karen's heart fluttered in her chest. She really liked being the one to make Bianca laugh. She wanted to do that a lot more. "It's kind of a lesbian thing to be oblivious. Why do you think I kept flirting all these weeks without encouragement?"

Karen tried to respond with something witty or smooth, but Bianca's light, teasing touch slid through her hair to the back of her head. Her nails grazed Karen's skin through the shortest part of her hair and down to her neck. Rather than words, what escaped Karen was a groan laced with need, delight, and a heavy dose of desire. Bianca's throaty chuckle did nothing to douse the fire her touch had sparked. Heat bloomed up her neck and across her cheeks, but also in her belly. How could she possibly be so turned on again already?

"Do you like that?" Bianca whispered in her ear. "Do you want me to do it again?"

Karen swallowed hard and managed a nod, but she was pretty sure Bianca hadn't needed her reply. After all, her body was giving ample evidence of her approval. Bianca's lips pressed lightly against her neck, just over her throbbing pulse point. Karen squeezed her eyes shut, trying desperately not to make a fool of herself, but she was defenseless against the onslaught.

Bianca kissed her way up Karen's neck, lingering on each press of lips to skin. Karen's body took over for her brain. She leaned her head back to give Bianca better access. Bianca took the movement as the invitation it was, sliding closer on the cushion until their bodies were entwined. Karen slid a hand up Bianca's thigh to her hip, the warmth and softness of her body evident through the thin fabric of her skirt. She pressed a hand against Bianca's back and she couldn't help remembering the taste of Bianca's nipples. The taste of her release.

Bianca's teeth scraped against Karen's ear and her gasp was nearly as desperate as her earlier groan. A thousand possibilities exploded in her mind and the rush of need nearly overwhelmed her. Fortunately, it was enough to bring her to her senses.

Karen's voice cracked as she forced herself to say, "I thought you said you needed a break."

She couldn't be sure if she was more disappointed or impressed when Bianca immediately pulled away. It must have taken the same monumental effort Karen had expended in asking for the reprieve, because Bianca buried her face in the couch cushion and groaned.

Bianca's voice was muffled by the cushion. "I did. I do need a break. That doesn't mean I want one."

"You won't get one if you keep that up. I've wanted you for a long time. If you don't stop teasing me, I'll be ready to go again way too soon."

Bianca's lips were back on her neck. "I was just thinking the same thing. Maybe we should see just how close we are to ready again."

It was a tantalizing thought, especially with Bianca's hot breath and wet lips laying claim to her. Still, they needed to talk more. They'd already had sex once and she didn't want Bianca for just one afternoon, she wanted something real. They both had to walk in with eyes wide open and heads clear. Karen scooted farther away on the couch, earning another frustrated groan from Bianca.

Bianca flopped back on the couch but threw one alabaster leg over Karen's lap to keep some contact. "Okay. Okay. I'll be good, but I do so under protest, for the record."

Karen's laugh was unsteady and her hand shook as she stroked it across Bianca's leg, wishing she'd taken the moment to see if she'd left a bite mark earlier. "Believe me, my entire body and most of my mind is protesting, too. But we should probably get to know each other a little better first."

"Yeah, you're right. You're very smart, you know?"

There was still a flirtatious glint in her eye, but Bianca didn't make another move. She took in the moment. How had the whole world spun on its axis so quickly? She'd started this day pushing down her feelings because she didn't have a chance with Bianca. Now here she was, her body still pulsing from their shared orgasms. However she got here, it was an amazing place to be.

Karen focused on facts rather than feelings. "So, you're divorced."

"I am very much divorced."

"I think you said it has been five years, right?" Karen asked.

"Yep. We got married before we even graduated college. His name is Frank and he's an accountant."

"Can I ask what happened?"

"You can ask me anything." Bianca's smile was only a little bitter. "He was an overachiever. Graduated high school a year early and completed a double major in just four years. Opened his own firm at twenty-three when all his friends were still struggling to find a job working for someone else. I guess it shouldn't surprise me that he had his midlife crisis early, too. He went full bore on it. Sports car, hair plugs, taking up poker. He might've cheated, I don't know and I don't want to. He asked to open the marriage and I'm not that kind of person, so he left without a second thought after twelve years."

"I'm so sorry. That must've been painful."

"You'd think it would be, wouldn't you? Somehow it wasn't that much of a surprise. I think of him as my first husband even though I don't have a second. I really did love him early on, but eventually he was just an annoying slob of a roommate with a receding hairline and a crooked dick," Bianca said.

"Oh. Um…"

"I'm sorry. There I go being blunt and oversharing again. Alex tells me I shock people. Did I shock you?"

"Yeah, you did, but I like it."

"Really?"

"I mean, I could do without knowing about your ex-husband's genitals, but I like that you are open and honest," Karen said.

"What you see is what you get with me."

"I like what I see."

"Careful. Too many compliments and I'll start kissing you again."

Karen's heart rate picked up. Maybe they didn't need to talk that much.

"My turn," Bianca said.

"Ask away."

"You only date women, right?" When Karen nodded, Bianca asked, "Ever married any of them? Any kids?"

"No kids. I prefer to keep my parenting professional. No marriages either. Heck, I haven't even had a second date with anyone in years."

"I find that hard to believe."

"It's hard in a small town and work keeps me busy."

"I'm glad I won't have to fend off any broken-hearted exes."

Karen's laugh was laced with the bitterness she'd never been able to avoid. "Not at all. In fact, women tend to date me right before they find the love of their lives."

"I thought I heard you and Jessica had a history."

"Not much of one. It was always clear I liked her more than she liked me. That's pretty common, though, and we're much better as friends."

A wrinkle appeared between Bianca's eyebrows and Karen was dreading an explanation. She shouldn't have alluded to her disappointment with Jessica, but Bianca's oversharing was contagious. Karen was spared the conversation by the clomping of heavy boots on the stairs.

"Everyone has their shirts on, right? I do not want to ruin my weekend with seeing my sister naked," Alex called from the hall.

"Shut up and get in here," Bianca shouted back.

Alex bounded into the room with the energy of a caffeinated teenager, a lopsided smirk emphasizing her good looks. Now that she wasn't a threat, Karen could appreciate her charm. She flopped on a nearby armchair and rested her elbows on her knees.

"Everything good here?" Alex asked.

Bianca reached out and rubbed Karen's shoulder, sending another wave of electricity across her nerve endings. "Everything's great."

"Glad to hear it because I got three steaks at the grocery store. You're not a vegetarian, are you Karen?"

"No, I'm not, but I don't want to intrude on your dinner."

Alex hopped back up. "Don't be silly. Of course you're welcome. Besides, I need to interrogate you on your intentions with my sister. I know her intentions are definitely impure."

Bianca tossed a throw pillow at her that Alex caught. Karen laughed along with them. "Oh really? Good to know."

"Oh yeah. The way she's been talking about you nonstop for weeks, I'm surprised she hasn't chained you to her bed before this."

"I would if you'd leave us alone for two seconds," Bianca said.

"If you don't feel safe alone with her, you can come help me at the grill," Alex said to Karen.

"Would you stop it?" Bianca laughed.

"I think I can handle myself."

Karen did her best to mimic Alex's roguish grin, and it must've worked because Alex laughed and gave her an encouraging slap on the shoulder as she trotted out of the room. Bianca rolled her eyes as they laughed together. A moment of pure excitement shot through Karen. What were the chances she might end up with both a girlfriend and a new friend after today?

Karen could barely contain her excitement as she escorted her class to the art room on Tuesday morning. Every few steps she had to remind herself to keep her usual pace rather than sprinting down the hall. Anything that would get her to Bianca a second faster.

She and Bianca had texted or talked on the phone every night since dinner on Saturday, but they hadn't actually seen each other. In fact, most of their conversations had been pretty surface. During Monday's morning class, two fifth graders had fought and Bianca had struggled to break it up. It didn't end until one of the students banged into Bianca's desk, knocking over and destroying a vase she'd made in art school. It had been one of her favorite pieces and she had been heartbroken. Karen had offered to come over and talk, but Bianca turned her down, preferring to spend a quiet night at home with Alex. Karen had understood, of course, but her desire to see Bianca and give her a big hug had been almost overwhelming.

In truth, she was just as nervous as she was excited to see her today. This was the part where everything had gone wrong for her in the past. When the woman she was interested in lost interest in her. How would she bear it if she got to the art room and Bianca avoided her or looked through her? It might just be enough to destroy her entirely. She knew Bianca wouldn't hurt her intentionally, but it was far easier to believe the worst. History had a way of repeating itself when it came to her love life.

She turned the final corner, holding her breath and steeled for rejection, but when she looked up, Bianca was standing outside her classroom, leaning against the wall and looking like a vision of beauty. Those bewitching brown eyes locked on Karen and she smiled in her wide-open, unreserved way. It took Karen's breath away to be the object of that intense focus. To be the reason Bianca smiled. She couldn't force her gaze away, even though her feelings must have been painted clearly across her features.

Bianca didn't seem capable of looking away either. She didn't move or break eye contact as Karen closed the distance and stopped in front of her. They stood there, face-to-face, grinning at each other like a pair of lovesick fools while the kids filtered into the classroom. As the last of the students passed, Karen finally found her courage. She was opening her mouth to speak when Benji appeared out of nowhere and stepped between them. Karen had to shuffle back a few steps to make room for him as he looked up at Bianca.

"Good morning, Mrs. Harper."

"Hello, Benji. Did you have a good weekend?"

Bianca's gaze flicked up to her for a moment when she mentioned the weekend. A rush of giddiness flowed through Karen at the memories of Bianca beneath her.

"My mom took me to the library. I was looking for a book about Faith Ringgold."

"That's great." Bianca's tone was engaged, but her gaze was back on Karen. "I'm glad you liked the lesson about her quilts."

"I found two books. I wasn't sure which one would be better. I wrote down the titles. I'm at my limit for books to check out. My mom said I had to pick one. Would you help me pick?" Benji held out a folded slip of paper, the ragged edges where it had been torn from a spiral notebook dangling.

"I'll take a look once we get everyone settled."

Benji wasn't taking the hint to go inside. They weren't going to get the chance to talk. Bianca's resigned expression as Karen said goodbye did a lot to ease the sting of losing out on a private conversation. She really wanted that moment of reconnection. Maybe she could convince Bianca to skip the teachers' lounge and have lunch with her? She'd have to wait until after class to find out.

"I'll see you soon." Bianca smiled back at Karen as she escorted Benji into the class and shut the door.

Karen couldn't focus on anything during her break. Normally, this was her most productive time of the day, when she had free time but wasn't so exhausted by a full school day, but the brief interaction with Bianca only whetted her appetite for more. She started and stopped a half-dozen projects and even forgot to go to the bathroom though that need was hard to ignore. In the end, she gave up on getting anything accomplished and headed back to the art room earlier than usual.

As she passed the library's wall of windows, Sheila looked up and waved. Karen waved back and tried to look casual. It was unusual enough for academic teachers to give up any part of their break, and this was the second time in as many weeks she'd gone to Bianca's classroom early. Considering that she wasn't giving Sheila or Mary the same courtesy on library or music days, tongues would surely start wagging.

Did the district have a fraternization policy for teachers in the same school? Sheila's husband worked at the high school, but that probably wouldn't be against any rules. Karen didn't know any other couples in the school system. Was her relationship with Bianca something they had to report? If they did have to tell the school, how long should they wait? Would Bianca be offended if she announced it to Roger before they even had a proper date? Or would she think Karen wasn't serious about them if she didn't tell him?

Her anxiety spiral took her all the way down the hallway to Bianca's classroom door. Just like the last time she spied on Bianca, she was busy moving from student to student, encouraging and showering praise. Karen could tell by the way each student glowed in her presence, perking up and proudly showing off their work. This time, however, Bianca wasn't giving them her full attention. In fact, she barely spared them more than a few glances. Her gaze was fixed on Karen and so was her smile.

Now Karen knew what her kids felt. Why they were all so eager to go to art class, even the ones who were less than interested in painting and sculpting. She felt the glow they did when showered with Bianca's attention. She wanted to earn some of that praise herself. Bianca's smile made her want to rip a mountain up by its roots and present it to her. Poor Benji. Karen understood now the overwhelming desire to steal just a minute or two of Bianca's undivided attention.

When the bell rang, they both jumped and looked around as though woken from a haze. At least that's how Karen felt. Maybe Bianca didn't have time to feel that way. She zipped around the classroom, collecting supplies and rounding up the students. Karen at least had a moment alone in the hallway to shake her head like a dog with water in its ears.

"Sorry we're late," Bianca said as she opened the door. "I guess I was distracted."

The breeze of students walking past her to line up in the hallway barely registered to Karen. Watching Bianca through the door was distracting enough. Being this close—hearing her voice, smelling her perfume—was enough to make Karen forget her own name.

"No problem," Karen said.

"Excuse me, Mrs. Harper? You didn't look at my book list," Benji said.

"I'm sorry, Benji. Time got away from us today. I promise to look with you next week."

"I was hoping to check out a book this weekend."

A flicker of annoyance flared through Karen's chest. Benji was trying to steal another moment or two with Bianca. Trying to snag her attention. Exactly what Karen was hoping for. Here she was, competing with an eight-year-old kid for Bianca's attention. She really had fallen hard.

"We'll have to chat about it later. You need to go with Ms. Petersen now. Look, all your classmates are waiting for you."

Bianca's formal recitation of her name reminded her of the way Bianca had whispered her name into her ear with soft kisses over the weekend. Her skin flared hot and cold and suddenly she very much wanted this school day to end. Benji stomped off down the hall to join the other students, his head low and his sneakers scraping over the tile. Karen should rush after him and focus on her students, but she couldn't force herself away from this door without stealing one more moment with Bianca.

"Want to have lunch with me today?" Karen asked.

"Of course. I'll stop by your classroom."

Bianca's smile was nothing short of wicked and Karen had never had to work so hard to turn around. The white-hot burn of Bianca's eyes on her all the way down the hall did unspeakable things to her insides. Benji sulked all the way back to class and then all the way to the lunchroom. Karen's guilt over her jealousy weighed her down. She would make it up to him after lunch. It was against her nature to let one of her students out of her sight when they were feeling so low. Still, she let the lunchroom door snap closed between them and then practically sprinted back to her classroom.

Bianca wasn't outside her door this time. She was in the reading corner, curled up in the armchair, looking perfectly at home in Karen's space. That little show of intimacy was nearly too much to bear and Karen pushed the door closed harder than she intended.

"I was tempted to try stealing a kiss, but there's no way I'll get away with it now that you've woken up the whole school," Bianca said.

The teasing was fun and heartwarming, the need for a kiss to reconnect their bond was overwhelming, but that wasn't what had Karen's heart racing. Bianca was thinking about stealing kisses just as much as she was. When was the last time she dated someone who was as head over heels for her as she was for them? Had it ever happened? All signs were pointing to Bianca being the first.

She might be falling too fast again, but she honestly didn't care. She was too happy being in Bianca's orbit to worry about anything going wrong.

CHAPTER SEVENTEEN

K aren was getting better at focusing on her lessons and her students during the school day, but that hadn't extended to the hours after the final bell rang and the last of the school buses pulled away. Both she and Bianca had to work from their respective classrooms, but they always met up after to connect before Karen drove Bianca home. The drives were short and unsatisfying, even with a fair amount of teenager-style making out at the end of them. They never seemed to have time for more.

Wednesday night, however, was light enough that they had time to go on a date. It wasn't much—just dinner at the Main Street Café—but it was their first official date and Karen was giddy with anticipation. If her constant texting was any indication, Bianca was excited, too. Since the last of the kids left, Karen's phone had chirped every few seconds with a new text. She should let the texts wait so she could power through her grading, but she couldn't do it.

Karen had managed to grade two spelling quizzes in a row before her phone rattled with a new notification. She dropped her red pen like it was on fire and snatched up the phone.

Just a warning, one of the second graders spilled paint on my skirt this afternoon. I tried to wash it out, but there is a distinctly green section near my right knee, Bianca wrote.

Karen laughed. She'd been through many similar accidents in her teaching career, so it wasn't hard to picture the spill. *Sorry about your skirt. Want to swing by your house to change before dinner?*

No way. If we go to my bedroom before the date, I won't let you leave again.

Karen's nerve endings tingled. *I'd have to wait in the car. No way I could keep my hands to myself.*

I don't want you to keep your hands to yourself.

I'm pretty sure Alex doesn't want to hear her sister rattling the walls with her screaming.

Good point. I should've brought a backup outfit so I didn't embarrass you on our date, Bianca said.

You could never embarrass me. Besides, I'm pretty clumsy. I'll probably spill something on myself and we'll match.

Karen turned to another quiz, but she kept one eye on her phone. Unsure she'd actually scored it correctly, she went back and double-checked it before moving on.

Oh are you going to pull the old spill soup on your shirt so I offer to wipe it off for you trick? Bianca asked.

Karen's skin flushed hot. Every night she'd driven Bianca home they'd indulged in a few driveway kisses. The longing that had pent up for so many weeks had bloomed into fully formed desire since their afternoon together. If they didn't find some time and privacy again soon, Karen would crumble to ash.

Is that an option? I might have to take advantage, Karen said.

You don't have to ruin your shirt. I'm more than willing to feel you up without pretext.

Karen nearly dropped her phone her palms were so sweaty. What was more of a turn-on, Bianca's confidence or her openness about her desire? Most people danced around early in relationships, hedging or only hinting at wanting more. Bianca never hedged and her words could never be classified as a hint. She was shocking and wonderful and sexy as hell.

That's good to hear. I'm low on laundry detergent. Karen turned back to her quizzes, but the next text dropped right away.

I can't wait any longer. I'll be in your classroom in five minutes.

She wasn't even halfway through grading and she hadn't looked over tomorrow's lesson plan, but she shoved the ungraded papers back into her desk drawer and jumped to her feet. There hadn't seemed to be much to do to close up her room for the night, but every time she turned around, something else needed tidying.

Karen was grabbing her trashcan to set outside the room when her door burst open. She spun, thinking it was Bianca arriving early, but instead Jessica sprinted across the space in front of the desks, holding out two cans of orange soda.

"Thank God you're still here. I have news. I have gossip. You'll never guess what it is," Jessica said.

"Hey, Jess, look I'm a little—"

She didn't get to finish the sentence since Jessica continued without a pause. "You don't need to be jealous after all."

"Jealous?"

Karen straightened up just as Bianca glided in the door Jessica had left open in her rush.

Jessica handed her one of the orange sodas in that same giddy way she did when she had the juiciest gossip. "That's my news. You don't have to be jealous of Tall, Buff, and Butch."

The proximity of Bianca, looking just as alluring as ever even with slightly frazzled hair, kept the words from penetrating. "Tall, Buff, and Butch?"

"Alex. I wasn't sure if you caught her name, but she's not Bianca's wife. She's her sister!"

Bianca's eyebrow arched and her lips curled into an interested smile.

"Oh, Jess, I already—"

Jessica was too excited to be interrupted. "Bianca is divorced but her teaching license is in her married name and she didn't want to change it. Apparently, you and I are the last to know."

Bianca pressed her fingers to her lips, holding in laughter that shook her shoulders. Karen couldn't help but smile herself. She grabbed the offered soda and popped the tab.

"Sheila accused us of being too antisocial to be in the loop. Can you believe that?" Jessica scrunched her face up like an annoyed child.

"That's so rude," Karen said.

"I know. Imagine thinking you and I are antisocial." Jessica's emotions turned on a dime and she grabbed Karen's hands to do a little gleeful hop. "This is so great, though. You don't have to run around with that hangdog look anymore."

"Hey. I don't have a hangdog look," Karen said.

"Yeah, you totally do, but that's okay. You are free to make your move now. But listen, you need to be quick. Everyone adores Bianca, so someone else will snap her up if you don't ask her out soon."

Something of Bianca's teasing nature must have been rubbing off on Karen, because she adopted a faux serious look. "You're absolutely right. There's no time to waste." Leaning sideways to call over Jessica's shoulder, Karen said, "Bianca, would you like to go on a date with me tonight?"

Jessica spinning around at the sound of Bianca's laugh made the whole thing worth it. Her head whipped back and forth between the two of them as Bianca sauntered across the room and wrapped her arms around Karen's shoulders. Her interest in Jessica's reaction lessened as Bianca leaned in and brushed her lips chastely against Karen's.

Bianca snatched the orange soda from her hand and took a sip. "I'd love to, thank you."

Jessica cocked her hip and rested her fist against it. "How long have you known?"

"Not long, I promise. I just found out last weekend and I was going to tell you. I just, um…"

"You've been busy?" Jessica crossed her arms over her chest and raised an eyebrow, but there was the hint of a smile on her lips.

"Very busy," Bianca said.

Jessica laughed, but Karen wanted to melt into the floor again. She was no match for either of these women. "I'm sorry, Jess. I really should have told you earlier. I just got wrapped up. Forgive me?"

"Of course." Jessica turned on her heel, calling over her shoulder, "I'm very happy for you both, but don't stay out too late. It's a school night."

Bianca sighed. "She's right, damn her. I can't keep you out too late or your students will suffer."

"I think I can survive one day tired."

Karen reached to steal a kiss. Then another. Bianca's lips were far too easy to get lost in, her touch an easy distraction. Karen couldn't help herself. She caressed Bianca's hip bone with her thumb. Was the bite mark she'd left on Bianca's thigh still visible or did she need to refresh it?

Bianca pulled back from the kiss, dragging Karen's bottom lip between hers for a delicious moment. "Careful, Ms. Petersen, or you won't get either your dinner or your beauty sleep."

Karen didn't even open her eyes, just leaned back in, pulling Bianca by her ample hips. "Don't want either."

Bianca allowed her one, intense, knee-melting kiss before stepping out of her grasp. "There's nothing sexy about a hangry teacher. Come on, let's go."

Her instinct was to object, but Karen did have a tendency toward grumpiness when she didn't have three square meals a day. Besides, she couldn't wait to sit down across the table from Bianca and hold her undivided attention for an hour or two.

"Hey there, stranger. How you been?" Annabelle said from her stool behind the hostess stand.

"Hi, Annabelle. I've been just fine," Karen said.

As Karen finished her greeting, Bianca stepped through the door behind her. The series of emotions that traveled across Annabelle's face were hilarious. Her eyes flicked from Karen to Bianca and widened to the size of saucers. Was it Bianca's unique style or the fact that she was clearly not Jessica the cause? Her gaze scanned from Bianca's face to her shoes and back up to the spot where she wrapped her hand around Karen's bicep. Karen could almost see her writing the description she'd give to Sallie Bell later.

The shock slid into a conspiratorial grin. "You've been keeping secrets from me, Karen Petersen. Why don't you introduce me to your lady here?"

Pride bloomed in Karen's chest. This town and its residents weren't perfect, but they never once made her feel different or strange because of her sexuality. "Annabelle Green, please meet Bianca Harper. Bianca's the new art teacher at Bucks Mill Elementary."

"Nice to meet you." Bianca released Karen's arm long enough to shake Annabelle's hand, then immediately took it back.

"Charmed, but you're more than just an art teacher I take it?" Annabelle grinned as she indicated their touch.

Bianca winked and pulled Karen closer in response. It was the most wonderful feeling, to be claimed by her like this, right there in front of Annabelle and half the town taking advantage of the café's cheap beer prices.

"Come on, lovebirds. I've got a nice quiet booth in the back for you. Can't have anyone bothering you on a special night."

Every pair of eyes in the café followed them on their winding path through the dining room. Most folks greeted Karen or at least gave her a friendly wave. Bianca's hand slipped down to entwine their fingers. Hopefully, she couldn't tell how sweaty Karen's palm was. She wasn't used to being the local celebrity.

Despite at least a thousand dinners in her eight years in town, Karen had never been seated at Annabelle's special booth. She wasn't sure she'd ever seen it. As they settled into their seats, the noisy dining room disappeared, muffled by distance and the half-wall between them.

"I'm gonna take care of you two myself so no one else disturbs you." Annabelle handed over a pair of menus that lacked the usual coffee stains and sticky spots. "What can I get you to drink?"

"I have it on good authority that Bianca is a beer girl." Karen winked.

Bianca laughed and slid her hand across the table to grip Karen's. "I sure am."

They sent Annabelle off for two beers and two waters, but Karen didn't look at the menu. For some unaccountable reason, she had a stomach full of butterflies. How was it possible for her to have first date jitters with someone she'd already been to bed with?

Bianca didn't seem to be nearly as nervous. She tucked one leg underneath her and leaned into the table, studying the menu with more focus than the local diner's fare seemed to warrant. "What do you recommend? Everything looks amazing."

"Everything is amazing. Tonight is burger night, but their chef specials are all really good."

"I'll wait until the second date before I let you see me with ketchup running down my chin." Bianca's wink did nothing to expel the butterflies.

"You've already got the paint stain to contend with after all," Karen said.

Annabelle delivered their drinks and turned to Bianca. "Made any decisions? I hope you make this one pay for an appetizer and dessert."

"I was thinking two desserts, actually."

"A woman after my own heart." Annabelle threw a thumb over her should at Karen. "But I think I have to get in line behind her."

Karen's cheeks ached from smiling. She sat back and watched the two of them trade quips and debate the merits of chicken and dumplings versus pot roast. Bianca slotted in so easily here, both into the fabric of Bucks Mill and into her life. It couldn't really be that easy, could it? The longer Bianca held her hand, the more she thought it might just be.

As soon as Annabelle hustled off with their orders, Bianca turned all that charm squarely on Karen. "She's sweet. Thank you for bringing me here."

"Thanks for coming. I know our schedules are hectic, but I missed you this week."

Bianca gave Karen's hand a squeeze. "Sorry about that. I wanted to see you. I just had to deal with some things."

Karen nodded and forced a smile, though she wasn't sure she liked the tone shift. "I understand."

"Do you?" Bianca's gaze was like a pair of lasers, stripping her skin off down to bone. "I guess I should get right to it. Honestly, one of the reasons I wanted this date was so we could talk."

"That sounds ominous."

"I hope not. Although I would understand if this isn't okay with you."

Karen was now certain she didn't like the tone shift. "Even more ominous."

Bianca laughed quietly, but it ended quickly. "I need to be honest with you. I want this relationship, I really do, but I have a lot of baggage from my divorce."

"Of course. Anyone would."

Annabelle arrived with their dinner and made a business of straightening plates and making sure they had everything they needed. Karen tried hard to act like normal, happy even, but she wouldn't be touching her chicken pot pie anytime soon.

Once they were alone again, Bianca said, "I just need to go slow."

Some of the tension broke as Karen let out a strangled laugh. "Not to make light of the situation, but I think that ship sailed last Saturday."

Bianca's wickedly flirtatious smile was back. "Not in that way. Honestly, I couldn't go slow that way with you if I wanted to. You're incredibly sexy, you know."

Karen pulled her plate closer to her to give her an excuse to break eye contact. The heat on her cheeks and in her chest was intense despite her nerves.

"I just need a little time and patience on the emotional side. It's really hard to be vulnerable again. I invested everything in my husband and he gave nothing back," Bianca said.

Karen took a chance and slid her hand on top of Bianca's. She hadn't had the same experience, so she couldn't imagine what Bianca was feeling. But she needed a physical connection now, as much for herself as for Bianca and. Fortunately, she didn't pull away.

"I'm trying really hard not to make you suffer because of that asshole, but it's going to take time. I'm really sorry, but this is all I can offer right now. Can you accept that?" Bianca asked.

The doubt in Bianca's voice broke Karen' heart, so she didn't hesitate. "Yes, of course. I'm fine with taking it slow."

Even as she said the words, a burning knot of fear twisted in her gut. What exactly did that mean? Bianca was all in physically but not necessarily emotionally? She wanted them to date, but she didn't want to be vulnerable. It was so strange and unexplained, but Karen didn't want to push. Hadn't she just promised she wouldn't? Starting that by asking for a list of do's and don'ts would make Bianca doubt her. She didn't want that. She was all in emotionally and she could be for the both of them.

Bianca's happiness was palpable as she finally started on her dinner. Karen forced herself to take a bite and used the time she chewed to give herself a pep talk. She could do this. She could do and be whatever Bianca wanted. She was over the moon about Bianca and she could be patient. She could be anything if she could be Bianca's girlfriend.

CHAPTER EIGHTEEN

The third time Karen shivered, Bianca laughed and scooted closer. Bianca's coat was purple velvet with a furry trim all around, and Karen was afraid it would pick up a smear of road dust from the slide across the trunk of her old Civic. Then Bianca's warmth enveloped her and who cared about dirt anymore?

"I know it's dark, but it's still a great view," Bianca said.

Karen let Bianca plan their second date in as many days. She wanted to treat Karen to her favorite dinner meal of all time. It shouldn't have surprised Karen that Bianca's favorite dinner was ice cream.

Karen transferred her dripping waffle cone to her other hand so she could rest the left one on Bianca's knee. She had taken to wearing a stylistically broad array of leggings, but today she had done away with them. Still, while Karen was shivering under her coat, Bianca's skin was warm, almost hot to the touch. It made her want to wander underneath the hem of Bianca's coat.

"It is a great view, but don't you think it's a little too cold for this?"

"Maybe you should get a thicker coat?"

"Maybe I should be drinking hot apple cider instead of eating ice cream," Karen teased her.

"Cider's great, but it doesn't compare to ice cream."

"Normally I would agree, but ice cream is a summer thing."

"You take that back. Ice cream is an any time of year thing, and I won't hear anything else."

Karen watched jealousy as Bianca ran her tongue along the line between ice cream and cone. Ever since their explosive afternoon the previous Saturday, Karen had ached for more. Now she was jealous of ice cream, for goodness' sake. A smear of green escaped the corner of Bianca's mouth. Her gaze locked with Karen as she flicked the tip of her tongue out to collect it, then licked across her full top lip. Karen followed its path hungrily until it slipped back inside. She wasn't cold anymore. In fact, her blood was positively boiling with anticipation.

"I wouldn't dream of contradicting you." Karen tried to match Bianca tease for tease. "Even if I am freezing to death."

"We can't have that, can we?"

"Maybe you could find a way to warm me up?"

Bianca purred as she leaned close, rubbing their cold cheeks together until her lips were inches from Karen's ear. "Let's see what I can do."

Bianca left a trail of sparks behind as she kissed agonizingly slowly along Karen's neck and then her jaw. Karen's eyes fluttered shut, all her attention on the sensations Bianca's touch elicited. The way the tiny hairs on her own face brushed against Bianca's. Her smooth, slightly sticky lips like velvet as they moved across her cheek. The gentle scrape of teeth every now and then, sending a completely different type of shiver through her.

Because her eyes were closed, Bianca's kiss surprised her. She gasped, sucking in the warmth of Bianca's breath. The kiss tasted like mint chocolate chip and cookie dough. Bianca had always moved like a dancer, but her tongue was even more agile. It swept across Karen's bottom lip, begging for entrance that she eagerly gave. They moved together, sweet and sticky, with a shared rhythm that Karen rarely found with a lover.

Bianca broke the kiss sooner than Karen would've liked, leaving her reeling. As her eyes fluttered open, she caught the teasing glint in Bianca's gaze and the faintest hint of a smile swept across her lips. She tried to cool herself down with ice cream, but her waffle cone was no match for Bianca.

"So what's your weird thing?" Bianca asked.

"My weird thing?"

"Yeah. Everyone has a weird thing. I like ice cream outside, even in winter. Alex can't sleep unless she has a cup of fully caffeinated coffee after dinner. What about you? What's the one quirky trait inside that perfect body and sexy mind?"

Karen was stuck on the sexy mind and perfect body part of the sentence and couldn't think of anything at all, certainly not something playfully quirky about herself. She dove back into her ice cream to buy time.

"Come on, no more stalling." Bianca playfully poked her in the ribs.

"I can't think of anything. I'm boring. Like vanilla ice cream." Karen brandished her dwindling treat.

"There are chunks of cookie dough in that ice cream."

The response was so sweet it made Karen's heart thrum. No matter how hard she tried to distract from herself or see the mundane in her quiet life, Bianca wouldn't let her. Given that encouragement, her brain kicked into gear. The answer popped into Karen's brain, her face heated up just thinking about it. She sighed. It was okay. She could trust Bianca. Besides, better to get all the unsexy things about herself out into the open early. "I sleep in socks."

"Oh, come on, that's not weird. I put on bedtime socks if it's really cold. Based on how chilly the bottom floor of my house is already, I think I'll be a sleeping-sock girl for the next few months at least."

Karen winced but forged ahead. "Not just when it's cold. Year-round. My feet get really cold in bed for some reason and I can't sleep without socks on. Sometimes, um, just socks."

That got a lift from one of Bianca's expressive eyebrows. "Oh really? Now that's something to add to my overactive imagination." Bianca smiled and snuggled in close. "That's really cute. I love it. Thanks for telling me."

Karen nearly said "I'd be happy to show you," but Bianca leaned in for a kiss before she could say a word. Sitting side by side on the trunk of her car, the angle was all wrong for Karen to deepen the kiss. A bubble of frustration grew as she tried to slide closer, to make their lips fit better together, but couldn't quite manage it. Bianca slid her free hand over Karen's shoulder and gripped hard at the back of her neck, holding her close.

The bubble of frustration in Karen burst. She tossed her ice cream cone to the ground and slid off the car, careful not to break the kiss. Bianca held on and laughed as she moved, but the laughing trailed off into a groan when Karen pushed Bianca's knees apart and settled between them. Bianca's cone landed with a splat next to her feet and she cradled Karen's face.

Karen stepped further into the shelter between Bianca's legs, grabbing her hips to pull their bodies flush. This angle was infinitely more comfortable and infinitely more intimate, and Karen took advantage by deepening the kiss. She pressed so hard into Bianca that she bent back, but still Karen pressed harder. Bianca had felt so good in her arms, and she was desperate for that feeling again. Her warmth and her smell and her very essence wrapped around Karen, threatening to drown her in shared desire.

When Bianca wrapped her legs around her waist all new possibilities opened. She was dizzy with them. Dizzy with need. Dizzy with Bianca. She slipped a hand under the loose hem of Bianca's shirt and slid it up the intoxicatingly soft skin of her side. The slight dip of Bianca's ribs under her fingertips was the softest of all. She was getting carried away. After all, they were both elementary school teachers and in public. If a parent or, God forbid, a student happened upon them they would have a lot to answer for. She caressed the soft swell of Bianca's breast and very much wanted to get carried away.

Bianca felt so right in her arms. Saturday was a lifetime ago and Karen had been dripping with need almost since the moment she'd left Bianca's house. All week she'd been waiting for a moment the two of them could slip away and relish each other's bodies again. But now that they'd finally found time to be together, they were in this public place. Sure, the hilltop was sparsely populated even in warmer months, but they were in full view of the whole parking lot and the entrance road. They simply couldn't indulge in the sort of activities Karen craved. Not when the possibility of being seen was so present.

Finally getting her libido under control, Karen slid her hand out of the danger zone and took a step backward, putting a little space between them. Bianca, apparently, didn't approve of her plan. She grabbed Karen's belt buckle and pulled her in more forcefully than she'd expected. Tripping on her feet, she fell forward. Her momentum pushed them both back on the trunk, Karen only barely managed to catch herself with a hand on either side of Bianca.

They slid and pressed against each other in ways that were definitely not appropriate for public, but Bianca wouldn't let her go. Not that Karen tried hard to get free. Or tried at all. In fact, the movement had finally forced them to break their kiss and Karen's mouth was inches from Bianca's cleavage. She wanted to lavish it with the same attention she'd given to her recently discarded ice cream cone. Bianca's shirt was thin and gauzy, doing little to hide the stiff peaks of her nipples.

With monumental effort, Karen stood up straight. Her core throbbed in protest. Unfortunately, Bianca laid out in front of her, legs still wrapped around her hips, did nothing to quench the fire raging inside Karen.

Bianca's voice was raw with need when she said, "Please don't go."

Karen watched like a spectator at a show as Bianca pushed herself back up and slid her thumb over Karen's lips. She swallowed hard, hypnotized by the naked hunger in Bianca's eyes as she stared at her mouth. She risked a glance down and it was nearly her undoing. Bianca's skirt had slid up—or possibly Karen had hiked it up, she couldn't quite remember—and her bare thigh pressed against Karen's khakis. Karen followed the perfectly shaped skin, pale as winter moonlight, until it was interrupted by the folds of her skirt. But the bunched brown and gold had slid back just enough to show a thin band of scarlet wrapped around the apex of her thigh and the ghost of a bruise in the shape of several teeth. Karen looked away quickly before she fixated on the sight.

Bianca caught her chin and dragged her back, rubbing her thumb over Karen's lip. "I want you. I can't stop thinking about your mouth on me. Please."

Despite herself, Karen slid her hands up Bianca's thighs, pushing her skirt up and out of the way. The red lace wasn't just a border. Bianca's panties were a swirling pattern of lace, thin enough to show the outline of the tight line of curls beneath.

Karen managed to whisper, "We can't. Not here."

"I can't wait." Bianca punctuated the words by pressing her hips forward, the darkening patch at the center of her panties pressing hard against Karen's khakis. It took everything she had not to grind back into her.

"Anyone could come up here. If someone sees us…"

"It's getting dark. No one will see. Please, Karen. Touch me."

Karen's resolve, thin as it was, snapped at the pleading note in Bianca's voice. She swiped her thumb across Bianca's clit. The thin barrier of underwear couldn't hide how swollen and ready Bianca was. Ready for her. Desperate for her. Bianca rocked into the touch, trying to prolong it. A flush crept up her neck and spread across her chest, the color mesmerizing. Karen's heart raced at the obvious desire, urging her to swipe her thumb again. She nearly gave in. But she just couldn't shake the thought of someone watching them.

Karen pulled her shaking hands away and Bianca whimpered. The sound was heartbreaking. Maybe there was somewhere they could go? Some clump of trees or wall of stone they could duck behind. Bianca was right, their need was too great to survive a drive to either of their houses. Karen was intimately familiar with the landscape out here, though. There was nothing that could give them the privacy they needed. Her own whimper echoed Bianca's and her core gave a stab of need, but what could she do? She was helpless out here, so close and yet so far from relief.

She was so distracted, she hadn't noticed Bianca's hands creep to her belt buckle. Not until she had teased the tail loose and turned her attention to the button on Karen's khakis.

"Baby, we can't. Not here." Karen's voice was like a whine.

Bianca's hand plunged past her waistband to cup her. Karen was so swollen and wet with need. "You're sure you don't want to?" Bianca asked.

There was no use denying it. "Of course I want to, but someone could see."

Bianca teased her with light, agonizing touches. "What about your car?"

Even as her hips lurched forward into Bianca's touch, Karen blanched. Screwing in the back seat of her Honda Civic wasn't exactly what she had in mind when she fantasized about them together. It was hard not to feel like this was less the start of a beautiful relationship and more a tawdry fling. Was that what Bianca really wanted? Was that how she felt about Karen? Karen's heart dropped into the soles of her shoes. She knew that wasn't the case, but the previous night's discussion of going slow was tying her in knots. They shouldn't have started their sexual relationship so early. Wasn't this exactly why people waited?

Bianca's hand stilled. The desire leaked away from Bianca's eyes, replaced with confusion and then the regret. Just like that, Bianca broke all contact and the loss of her heat was like physical pain.

"I'm sorry. I got carried away and I hurt you," Bianca said.

There was a thickness to her voice that sounded like the edge of tears and Karen felt even worse. If that was possible. "No, you didn't. I'm sorry. I'm not the adventurous type."

Bianca backed further away and the steel was cold through the fabric of Karen's pants. The cold wasn't just on her skin, though. It had settled deep into her guts. What if this was how they ended? This thing between them was so new and so fragile.

"It's not about the adventure. I hope you know that," Bianca said.

"No, I know." Karen said the words but didn't really believe them.

"I want you, Karen." Bianca's voice stroked the syllables of her name with an almost carnal indecency. "I want you so bad it's driving me wild, but I don't want to screw things up."

A flicker of hope rekindled in Karen's chest and, if she was honest, a little bit lower as well. Finally brave enough to meet Bianca's eyes, she was glad she did. There was nothing but truth in her features. She stroked her palm across Karen's cheek and it was like a balm to her soul.

"Can you possibly forgive me?" Bianca asked. "Please give me another chance. I promise I'll control myself. Just give me another chance?"

"You don't have to control yourself." Karen could barely hear herself over the relief that flooded through her like a wave. "I want you, too. Just not here."

"No. Not here. I'm sorry."

"It is okay. I promise."

Bianca's breath came out like a burst of laughter. "Thank God. Thank you."

Bianca wrapped her arms around Karen and buried her face against her chest. Karen pulled her in tight and held her in a full body hug. Tears prickled her eyes and she forced herself not to let them fall. Every time she started to doubt, Bianca said or did something that showed how important Karen really was to her. How important a relationship was.

They held each other as the sun went down and Karen's smile made her cheeks ache.

CHAPTER NINETEEN

The rest of the night had been a wash of confusion for Karen. The tightness in her lower belly had seeped away during a quieter than usual ride to Bianca's house. When they arrived in her driveway, the orange glow of her porchlight throwing weird shadows across Alex's truck and the thinning azaleas, Bianca had turned to her with a radiant smile and a gentle kiss as though nothing at all had happened on Jouett Hill. She had hopped from the car and bounced up the stairs, turning to blow a kiss Karen's way before disappearing inside.

Had she imagined the awkwardness of their intimacy that evening? The lingering taste of waffle cone soured on her tongue, and she went straight to the bathroom to brush her teeth and end this day. She'd lain awake for ages, though, mulling over her conflicted feelings. She was certain Bianca cared for her, but Karen was ready to dive in with both feet and Bianca wasn't. Karen's head knew that had nothing to do with her, but her heart wasn't getting the memo.

She'd eventually fallen asleep, but the feeling didn't fade overnight. In fact, the next morning she was even more miserable. She went through the motions of washing blueberries for her yogurt, spreading hummus on bread, and filling her travel coffee mug, but there was none of the pep she usually had in her step. Sighing in resignation that today would be a struggle, she headed out early for school. It wasn't until she had climbed into her car that her phone buzzed with an incoming text.

Thanks for an amazing first week of dating. Can't wait for the next one. Bianca said.

That was all it took to turn Karen's day around. That tiny moment of encouragement—the acknowledgment that she wanted more with Karen—was balm to her battered ego. After replying with enthusiastic agreement, she smiled all the way to school.

Morning lessons flew past in a blur of enthusiasm and the squeak of marker on whiteboard. Having settled into the new school year, Karen's class threw themselves into all their lessons and several of them had already told her she was their favorite teacher ever. That would change as they grew up and formed bonds with other teachers, but it felt good nonetheless to have them enjoy her class. She had made her students her sole focus for so long. If she couldn't find fulfillment in her personal life, then she would find it here. In the shaping of young minds. In fostering a love of learning. She led her class to the lunchroom. Maybe a world existed where she could have both?

The moment they passed through the doors to the cafetorium, her students scattered to the winds, hurrying to get in line to buy the usual Friday pizza or carrying their lunchboxes to the tables where their friends sat.

"No running, Ava." No sooner had she called out the admonishment, Karen's gaze fell on Bianca, strolling down the aisle toward her. She tried to hide her grin, but she was failing miserably. "Nice to see you, Mrs. Harper."

Bianca twirled to stand next to her, a burst of floral perfume wrapping around Karen. She leaned in close and whispered, "I really need to get my license changed. I can't believe you have to call me that here."

"I can't imagine the questions I'd get from the students if I called you Bianca."

"All the more reason to see more of each other outside of school."

"I like the sound of that," Karen said.

"Me too." A pair of first graders ran past them and Bianca sighed. "That's my cue."

"You're a cafeteria monitor today?"

"Unfortunately, yes. Before I go, though—I'm taking Alex to lunch tomorrow for burgers and beers. She's having a rough time. Business is not booming. Maybe you and I could hang out after?"

Karen's heart gave a little skip at the thought. "I'd love to."

"I'll text you when we have firm plans?"

"Sounds great."

Bianca hurried off after the wayward students and Karen marched happily back to her classroom. Her heart was lighter than it had been in ages. She could really get used to this.

"Hey there, stranger."

Jessica's voice snapped Karen back into the present and she found that her feet had carried her back to her classroom door. Jessica was leaning against the frame, a mischievous smile on her lips and her violently purple lunch cooler in her hand. Karen's heart soared at the sight of her.

"Hey, Jess. You crashing my party for one?"

"It depends. Can I grill you for girlfriend details while we eat or are you going to make me help with grading?"

"I gave a spelling quiz this morning, so I do have a lot of grading to do."

Karen held back her smile, but she didn't have to wait long. Jessica pulled a plastic bag from her lunch and waved it around. "This batch of white chocolate toffee cookies says the grading can wait."

"Are you trying to bribe me for romantic secrets?"

"Is it working?"

Karen laughed and snatched the bag from her hand. "Absolutely. Come in."

They settled into their usual spots on either side of Karen's desk and spread their bounty out on the surface.

A smile spread slowly across Jessica's lips. "Should we skip the lunches and go straight for the cookies?"

Karen couldn't stop her own smile. Jessica always did this. She wanted to get to the sinful treats, so vegetables and protein be damned. "When we do that you always complain about getting sleepy in the afternoon."

"A sugar crash is Afternoon Jessica's problem."

"Yeah, well Afternoon Jessica is cranky and Afternoon Karen doesn't want to deal with that. Eat your sandwich at least."

"You're such a mom." Jessica pouted, but unwrapped her sandwich anyway.

"And you're such a kid."

Karen laughed and tucked into her hummus and cucumber sandwich, knowing they'd both thank her later.

Jessica crossed her legs under her on the hard wooden seat. "Okay, spill. How long have you been dating?"

"I told you, I just found out she was single last weekend."

"Yeah, but the chemistry between you two is off the charts. You can tell me if you shared an illicit kiss before you found out the truth."

Karen furrowed her brow. "You know I would never do that. Cheating is completely off limits for me."

"Is just a kiss cheating?"

"Of course it is. Would you be okay with Brandon kissing someone else?" Karen asked.

"No way. I'd kill him. And her."

"Thank you for making my point."

Jessica swallowed a mouth full of sandwich, eyeing the cookies like a leopard eyeing its prey. "Okay, but she isn't married anymore. So you've kissed, right?"

Karen dropped her gaze to the desktop, but it wasn't the lure of cookies that drove her. She wasn't embarrassed that she and Bianca had started the sexual component of their relationship early, but she had a feeling Jessica wouldn't be so open-minded.

"Karen?"

"Yeah. Of course we've kissed."

Karen shoved far too much sandwich into her mouth, making it more difficult than usual to chew. Or maybe it was the fact that her throat felt like it was closing up under Jessica's penetrating stare. Apparently, Jessica could still read her like a book, because after only a few seconds, her eyes flew open wide and her jaw dropped.

"Karen Suzanne Petersen, you did not!"

"What?"

"You slept with her already? It's only been a week!"

Karen shushed her but it was too late, her cheeks blazed with heat. "Would you keep your voice down? Jesus, Jess."

Jessica dropped her sandwich on the desk. She leaned forward and hissed, "How the hell did that happen? When did it happen? Why did you let it happen?"

Karen's hackles raised at the implications. Jessica was the one who had encouraged her from the start and she was excited at the idea of them kissing before Karen knew Bianca was single, but this was a bridge too far?

"I know it's been a while since you've had sex with a woman, but I don't think I need to tell you how it works."

To her surprise, Jessica didn't laugh or smile or anything. Instead, she furrowed her brow seriously and crossed her arms. "Answer my question."

Karen sighed and crossed her own arms, matching Jessica's defensiveness. "We had sex the first time last Saturday, after I found out she was single and we decided to date. Not that it's any of your business."

"You found out she was single and immediately fucked her?"

"Would you not use that word? You make it sound like it didn't mean anything," Karen said.

"How could it mean anything when you literally started dating five minutes before."

"It's not like we're strangers. We've been spending all sorts of time together as friends. Bianca had been flirting with me the whole time and you know how much I like her."

"Like her. Not love her. That's the problem." Jessica was still scowling like a disappointed father.

"Oh, and you waited to sleep with Brandon until after you knew you loved him? You and I both know that's not true. Why are you being such a jerk about this?"

Jessica's face softened, but not by much. "I'm not trying to be a jerk. I'm trying to keep you from making a huge mistake."

"I'm a big girl, Jess. I can take care of myself."

"Are you though? You fall for people too fast and they always break your heart. I don't want to see you hurt."

Karen's anger was still bubbling, but Jessica really did care. Besides, that little voice in the back of her head that had been so loud all morning had said a lot of the same things. But Bianca had been lovely and sweet afterward and the night before. Bianca cared about her, too, she was sure of it.

"I'm not going to get hurt. This is real, and I want you to be happy for me."

That was enough to thaw Jessica completely. She dropped her arms to her lap and her face took on that loving expression she reserved for just Karen and her husband. "I am happy for you. I'm sorry. I shouldn't have freaked out. You know what you're doing."

Relief flooded through Karen. If Jessica really had believed Bianca wasn't the right woman for her, she would have kept fighting. That gave her the confidence to shut up that little voice in the back of her head again. She grabbed the bag of cookies, then handed one to Jessica.

She snatched the cookie from Karen's hands. "You're forgiven." Karen laughed.

They groaned in unison at the first bite. Jessica's cookies were a work of art only matched by Sallie Bell's creations. They were thick and chewy and packed to the gills with toffee and real chunks of white chocolate, not those vanilla flavored baking chips. After devouring her first cookie, Jessica snatched another and turned a conspiratorial grin on Karen.

"So how was it?"

"There is absolutely no way I'm answering that question."

"That good, huh?"

Karen smirked. "Better."

Jessica giggled and fell back against her chair. "Oh my God, that's amazing. I'm so happy for you, friend."

The nagging doubts hadn't fully disappeared. In fact, oddly enough, they had come back a little louder now that Jessica was all in on their relationship. Still, having Jessica's approval felt good. "Thanks. I'm happy, too."

"You deserve it." Jessica handed over the last cookie to Karen.

Some weeks it felt like Saturday might never come. After getting Jessica on her side, Karen's day seemed to drag on interminably. One of her students had gotten into some sort of trouble with an older student on the bus home and was now surly and uninterested in class. A pair of boys were getting unruly nearly every day and she would have to separate them soon. And then there was Benji whose grades and attention were slipping when it came to everything but art class and library time. All in all, she had been thrilled when that final bell rang on Friday afternoon.

Her typical Saturday would entail laundry and binge watching whatever new documentary series Netflix had to offer, but things had changed drastically for her recently. She was up early to get her chores done so she could shower and change, ready to jump at a moment's notice when Bianca's text came in. A little cluster of butterflies erupted in her stomach. Whatever their plans, hopefully, they would end right back here, in her apartment. Mostly in her bed. What were the chances she could convince Bianca to spend the night?

Just as her mind threatened to spiral into a half-thrilling, half-terrifying whirlwind, Karen's cell phone rang. The butterflies in her stomach dropped dead. Experience told her this would probably be Bianca canceling. She knew it was too good to be true. No one ever really wanted to spend this much time with her. When she checked her phone, however, she was shocked to see her mother's picture.

Since her mom rarely called, Karen answered by saying, "Hey, Mom, is everything okay?"

"You always think I can't take care of myself," her mom said through laughter. "Can't I just call to look in on my daughter?"

Karen's heart swelled and she felt a little guilty. She should really stop thinking the worst of people. "Sorry, Mom. Of course you can call to check in. I love it when you do."

Karen took the phone back to her armchair and sat while her mom asked about her week at school.

"It was fine. A couple students are giving me trouble, but nothing I can't handle."

"Of course you can handle it. You're a wonderful teacher. What are they doing?"

Had Karen heard that right? Her mother had never once, in her eight years of teaching, told Karen she was a wonderful teacher. Or had she? Maybe Karen was so disposed to think the worst of her that she didn't take it in.

"Thanks, Mom." Karen fought back a lump in her throat.

"You really ought to start believing in yourself, you know."

Karen just laughed. It probably came out a little bitter. What sort of alternate universe had she dropped into?

"So tell me all about it."

Before Karen could start the story, her phone beeped in her ear. Of course, Bianca's text for date details would come through right now.

"Hang on one second. I just got a text."

"I'm not interrupting your day am I?" her mom asked.

"Just meeting someone later and she texted details."

"Oh, is it Jessica? Tell her your father and I said hello."

"It's not Jessica. One second."

Alex says misery loves company and wants you to join us for lunch at Main Street Café. Are you free? Bianca wrote.

Karen's heart fluttered with anticipation and she quickly fired off a response.

I'd love to. On the phone with my mom, but I'll be there soon.

A heartbeat later, she replied, *Perfect. Also, Alex promises to make herself scarce after lunch so we can have some alone time.*

She couldn't think of a more perfect Saturday. Alex seemed really cool and she was excited to be friends with her girlfriend's sister. Add in a date after and she was on cloud nine.

When she finished the conversation with Bianca, she fully expected her mother to ask who she was meeting if not her best friend. After all, she'd been so interested in a possible girlfriend back in the summer, and Karen was excited to tell her it had actually happened.

Her mother, predictably, didn't ask and Karen ended up chatting about her students for a few minutes with a few "hmms" and "oh nos" from her mother. Eventually, Karen wrapped up her story.

"Have you heard your brother's big news?" her mother asked the moment she finished.

"No, I haven't spoken to Derek in a few weeks."

"Well, he's had another amazing breakthrough at the firm."

Karen stopped listening while her mother gushed about the huge stacks of money her brother was making. Why was she surprised? This was their relationship, after all. Her mother didn't call to check on her students. She didn't care that Karen had a girlfriend. Their connection revolved around her brother. Everything had always been about the golden boy.

A ping announced a message from Bianca and Karen happily took the phone from her ear to read it.

Take all the time you need talking to your mom. I'm so excited for today that it won't feel like a wait at all. Thanks for letting Alex tag along—she's been so lonely recently and I really think you'll be good friends.

She didn't have to let that distance with her family break her anymore. She had someone in her life who was genuinely interested in her. Someone who was thoughtful and kind and wanted to know all her weird quirks without judgment. Not to mention, she had the prospect of another friend, one who was masc, too, and could understand her in ways Jessica couldn't.

Karen had everything she ever wanted waiting for her at Main Street Café and she wanted to focus on that. She didn't need to suffer through one of her mother's monologues about her perfect brother. She could focus on the things in her life that made her happy and let her indifferent family take a back seat.

She raised the phone back to her ear and cut her mother off mid-sentence. "Sorry, Mom, I have to run. I'm very happy for Derek, but I've got folks waiting on me."

"Oh. Well, okay, dear. Have fun with your friends."

Her mother sounded surprised, but unfazed. As though it didn't really matter whether she talked to Karen or not. That stung a little, but not nearly as much as it would have without Bianca and Alex waiting for her. She hung up her phone and set out to meet her girlfriend and new friend at the café for the start of something new.

Chapter Twenty

Night had fallen and darkness enveloped the street between the sparse streetlights when Karen, Bianca, and Alex spilled out onto Main Street. They were all laughing, Alex and Bianca clutching their stomachs as they doubled over. Karen's pride swelled that her simple joke about the seats in their booth having permanent grooves from their butts had caused the reaction. Of course, it might have been the lingering effects of the several beers they'd each had.

They were supposed to have just had lunch and a drink, but Karen had been having too much fun and Alex had looked so sad when she said she should go home. As much as Karen wanted alone time with Bianca, she wanted her new friend to be happy too.

"Why don't you stick around?" Karen had said.

Her reward had been a shocked but grateful look from both the sisters. Bianca had wrapped her hands around Karen's bicep and asked if she was sure. Her reassurance had come out in a stammering, lovesick sort of way and Alex had teased her about it while she ordered them another round.

"We'll get our date tomorrow. Unless you have other plans?" Karen had asked.

"I was worried I'd have to kidnap you to keep you tomorrow, too," Bianca said.

So lunch and a drink had turned into several drinks, and then dinner and a couple more drinks, and now here Saturday was basically over and Karen had accomplished nothing productive. She had never been happier in her life, either. It had been a perfect day. Bianca was hanging onto her arm, leaning her head on her shoulder. Karen loved how tactile she was. She always seemed to want to be in contact with Karen and the warmth of her was intoxicating when Karen had spent so much of her life alone. That warmth fed her soul.

They were strolling down Main Street toward Alex's truck, Karen dragging her feet to prolong the night, when there was an unexpected burst of light. She pulled them all to a stop and hung back, awkwardly trying to keep out of the pool of orange light from the nearest streetlamp.

"What's going on?" Bianca asked, her voice low and concerned.

"Can we just wait a minute until they're gone?" Karen's voice was clipped compared to Bianca's lilting tones.

When the sisters met her with blank stares, she sighed and pointed across the street. The side door to Bamford Insurance was still open and Mr. Bamford didn't seem to be in a big hurry to close it. He was laughing in his slimy, overly familiar way. The woman at his side, a tall, painfully thin woman with white-blond hair and thick enough makeup to hide the first appearance of lines around her eyes and mouth, echoed his laugh and put her hand on his arm. The gesture was sickeningly similar to the way Bianca still held Karen.

"Okay, I'll bite," Alex said, her voice low. "Who are they?"

"That's Mr. Bamford and his secretary. I think this one's name is Annette, but he changes them so often I can't always keep track. That's his insurance company."

Bianca's eyebrows crinkled. It was clear she could see how annoyed and embarrassed Karen was, but she was still working out why. "Is there something wrong with them being here? If you're late paying your car insurance, I'm sure it's not worth hiding in the shadows."

Mr. Bamford finally let the door swing shut and started off down the street, but Karen kept them where they were. "No, it's not that."

"So then what's going on?" Alex asked.

"The problem is that married Mr. Bamford isn't leaving his office. That's the side door, and it leads up to the two apartments over the business."

Alex cottoned on and shook her head. "And he's leaving one of those apartments with his secretary."

"Yeah." The sick feeling in her gut hadn't quite passed and her voice had a bite when she said, "He's a real piece of garbage."

"Sounds like it, but why does it bother you so much that one guy in this town is a jerk?" Alex asked.

"I live in the other apartment up there and I hate that my landlord is a cheater. His granddaughter is one of my favorite students ever and it makes things so awkward when I see her."

Bianca let out a little gasp. "Bamford. As in Tinley Bamford?"

"Yeah."

"Oh no, not poor Tinley. She's so sweet."

"Yeah, she is. I see her around here sometimes when I'm in and out of my apartment. I don't think she knows or anything, but I know."

"That really stinks," Alex said.

They all shuffled around awkwardly for a moment, each trying in their own way to snatch back the joy that had suffused the night before Mr. Bamford ruined the mood. Karen shouldn't have worried, though. Nothing could bring the mood down long around these two.

Alex was the first to break back into a goofy grin. "So, you live right over there, huh? I didn't know that."

"Me either." Bianca's voice held a lingering note of smoke and suggestion.

Karen's eyes went to her and were trapped. She was radiant standing there in the moonlight, a thin glow of orange from the streetlamp kissing her cheek. A tingle of anticipation spread across Karen's skin. Why hadn't it occurred to her how close they were to her apartment?

Her tongue was heavy in her mouth when she said, "You want to come up for a tour?"

One of Bianca's eyebrows gave the briefest flick up and back down. She clearly remembered what happened the last time one of them had offered the other a tour of her home. Images of that afternoon slammed into Karen like a physical blow and suddenly she could think of nothing else. Bianca's skin against hers. Her fingers sliding through her hair when Karen settled between her thighs. It had only been a week ago, but her body ached as though a century had passed.

Alex cleared her throat pointedly and Karen finally broke eye contact. Her skin was hot against the cool night air, and not just her obviously blushing cheeks, but every inch of her. She couldn't make eye contact with either of them right now. In fact, she couldn't settle on anything with her heart pounding so hard in her chest.

"That's my cue to drive myself home," Alex said with a laugh.

Karen's cheeks blazed even hotter, but Bianca didn't seem the slightest bit embarrassed. She slapped her sister hard on the butt. "Drive safe and don't wait up," she said.

Karen was mortified, but apparently, she was the only one. Alex laughed and tossed her keys in the air, catching them before she waved over her shoulder and marched off down the street. Karen watched her go for a whole block before she turned to Bianca.

For all her confidence and joking, now that they were alone, Bianca looked almost as nervous as Karen felt. "I didn't mean to sound presumptuous. It's just...well, I've been wanting time alone with you all day. All week really. But I don't want you to think—"

Karen cut her off with a fierce kiss. Who cared that they were standing on the street in the middle of downtown? Who cared that Alex knew exactly what they were going to do? All she cared about was getting her hands on this incredible woman and she didn't want to wait one more instant.

Karen was uniquely aware of her body as she climbed the stairs to her apartment, Bianca two steps behind her. The chill of the air on her lips and how it warmed instantly as it traveled through her body to her lungs. The weight of her feet on the soles of her boots, pressing down on the creaky old stairs. The jingle of Bianca's necklaces clinking against each other filling her ears.

Being around Bianca was starting to have this effect on her. It was like a superpower, being in her presence. Warmed by her aura. Karen knew it was dangerous. One day it would either catapult her into the heavens or pitch her over a cliff into a deeper hell than she'd ever experienced. Somehow the murkiness of their future was just as compelling as it was frightening. She was a moth desperate to be closer to the flame that was Bianca.

As she fitted her key in the lock, a pulse of emotion coursed through her. There was anticipation, of course. All her nerve endings were attuned to the reality that she would have Bianca in her arms again soon. But there was also a new apprehension. The first time they had been intimate, lust had driven them and everything had been fantastic and new. What if Karen found herself unable to repeat the performance? What if they fumbled through the motions and found they didn't fit so neatly together after all? Would she survive that?

Her hand shook as she pushed the door open. She was so nervous it felt like she had never had a woman back to her home before. Should she step over the threshold or let Bianca precede her? Maybe Bianca sensed her apprehension. Maybe she was just the kind of woman who took charge in every situation. Either way, she stepped forward, sliding delicate fingertips down Karen's arm until their fingers locked together, then she led them through the door together.

"It's so cute." Bianca released Karen's hand and marched into the center of the kitchen.

"It's nothing special. Not nearly as big and fancy as your place."

Fortunately, autopilot took over as she closed the door and dropped her keys into their little wooden bowl on the mail rack. She flipped on a few lamps as she followed Bianca around her space.

"Sorry, it's, um, cramped and you know there's no overhead lighting so that makes it feel even smaller." She grabbed a couple pillows off the sofa and tossed them into the basket under the window. "I really should have less clutter in this tiny apartment."

"Don't be silly. It's wonderful."

Her body language showed that she meant it. She moved through the apartment the way she moved through everything in life. Without clear purpose, just flowing from place to place. She ran her hand across the crocheted blanket draped over the back of the couch as she scanned the view of Main Street from the tall windows. She stopped at the end table wedged between couch and chair to pick up first the half-read library book and then the framed photo of Karen and Jessica at their first sunflower festival. Bianca glanced up from the photo version of Karen's face to meet her gaze and a slow smile spread across her lips.

"It's cozy, and I don't mean small," Bianca said before Karen could object.

"It is small, though. And the view is great but there are like five parades a year down Main Street and it's so loud I can't hear myself think."

Bianca set down the photo and picked her way across the room. She peeked into the bathroom before twirling around and giving her another sweet smile. "You are never going to convince me that it isn't perfect. I'm sticking with cozy. Cozy like curling up under a blanket. Cozy like walking into one of your hugs."

Bianca winked and then disappeared down the hallway to the bedroom. She vanished just in time. Karen needed a moment to close her eyes and take a deep breath. In truth, she loved her little apartment. It was small, but she didn't really care. It was perfectly sized for her, and she loved the big city feel of being able to walk to everything she needed, matched with the small-town ability to lean out her window and wave at friends and acquaintances walking by. She spent so much of her life feeling overlooked and insignificant, but here she was able to create a cocoon of familiarity that made her feel special. And Bianca had seen that the moment she stepped through the door. Karen didn't need much in life. Just comfort and security and now, suddenly but definitively, she needed Bianca.

She gave herself just enough time to wipe the silly grin off her face and check that her clothes were straight and unwrinkled before following Bianca down the hall. The sight that greeted her in her bedroom took her breath away. The tiny, shaded lamp on the bedside table lit just enough of the room to capture Bianca's form. She stood on the edge of the pool of light the way she had stood on the edge of the light from the streetlamp, like she was just arriving to bring her warmth into Karen's life. The glow kissed her cheek and the curve of her breasts and the long tangle of necklaces piled on her chest. She turned to look over her shoulder and her features were cast into shadow. She looked thoughtfully at Karen, then back at the room around her.

"It's the exact opposite of my room," Bianca said.

Karen looked at her bedroom. She had never examined it through someone else's eyes before. What did the room say about her? Bianca wasn't far off. Instead of hardwood floors covered in every stick of furniture imaginable, Karen's bedroom floor was wide open gray carpet, lush and newly installed after a prolonged fight with the notoriously tight-fisted Mr. Bamford. A single dresser spanned one wall, a closed closet door and full-length mirror opposite. The queen-size bed was neatly made with a heavy duvet and cable-knit blanket runner across the foot and two lonely pillows at the head. Beside it, a single bedside table with a single lamp and a scented candle she couldn't remember ever lighting. It looked like the bedroom of an uptight, single lesbian.

She laughed nervously and rubbed the back of her neck. "Yeah, I, um, should probably get more pillows."

The moment the words left her mouth, she wanted to drag them back. More pillows? That was all her brilliance could come up with when a creative, free-spirited, goddess stood next to her bed. Bianca threw her head back and laughed. It wasn't a cruel laugh or even a teasing one. Embarrassed as she was, Karen couldn't help laugh along, though in her much more subdued way.

"You're so fucking cute, you know that?"

Karen's throat went dry and her heart pounded. Bianca's praise made her feel somewhere between a simpering acolyte and a ten-foot-tall hero.

"I thought about rummaging through your drawers." Bianca sauntered across the room as she spoke, her hips swaying in a distinctly distracting way. She stopped in front of Karen and slid her hands over her shoulders and around behind her neck. "But I thought I'd let you keep your secrets for one more night."

"I don't have any secrets. What were you hoping to find?"

Bianca purred and leaned in, placing a slow kiss on Karen's neck. "A huge drawer full of sex toys maybe."

Karen closed her eyes, focusing on the feel of Bianca's mouth on her skin. She rubbed her thumbs in circles over the points of Bianca's hips. "I hate to disappoint, but I'm pretty vanilla."

"You said that before, but there are pieces of cookie dough in your vanilla, remember?"

Karen tingled at the thought. "Maybe."

"A strap-on?"

Bianca caught her earlobe between her teeth and Karen hissed as a pulse of desire like a thousand fingertips stroking her skin tore through her. "Yeah. I have one. Do you want me to use it?"

"Do you want to use it?"

Karen pushed up underneath Bianca's shirt, pressing into the soft flesh and pulling her close. "I want you. I'll do anything you want."

"We moved so fast last time. We never had a chance to talk about what we liked." Bianca slipped the top button of Karen's shirt open, then traced down to flick the second open. "What do you like, Karen?"

As she whispered the words, Bianca took advantage of the opening in Karen's shirt to slip inside and cup her breast. Karen's nipple hardened in an instant and Bianca pinched it just hard enough to make her groan but not hard enough to hurt.

"Oh God, I like that."

Bianca kissed at her neck and massaged her breast, making it hard to think, but still she pressed. "More. Tell me how you like to come. Do you want me inside?"

Karen's mind whirled with possibilities. No one had ever asked her that before. What's more, she'd never asked the women she'd slept with—and there had been a respectable number, though not many recently—what they wanted. Why hadn't she done that? How much better could the sex have been if she'd actually talked to her past lovers?

"Please tell me," Bianca whispered. "I want to make you feel good."

Karen stroked her hands up Bianca's sides, arriving simultaneously at her large, tantalizing breasts. Her nipples were already hard and she gasped when Karen teased them between thumb and forefinger.

"Inside is fine, but I prefer...um..." She trailed off, hoping Bianca would let her get away with it, but that wasn't Bianca's style.

She nuzzled closer to Karen's ear and whispered, "Tell me."

Karen pressed her eyes shut as hard as she could. Could she really say it? Bianca wasn't pushing. She would probably let Karen chicken out and still do all the things Karen wanted her to, but is that what she wanted? Could she be brave?

"My clit." Karen's voice was so soft it was barely audible, but a burst of mingled desire and pride flooded her that she said the words.

Bianca immediately rewarded her by cupping Karen, pressing the heel of her hand hard against her clit. Her soaked underwear and the zipper of her jeans ground into her, sending an arcing flash of pleasure through her. She bucked hard into the pressure and Bianca laughed low and throaty.

"Like that?" Bianca asked.

Karen's breath came out more like a gasp. "Yes."

"What else?" Bianca's hands were back at her shirt buttons, more frantic than before. "Oral?"

Karen's eagerness took over, too. She walked Bianca back toward the edge of the bed, pulling her shirt off over her head in one, whipping motion. The necklaces flew around and then settled against the pale skin between her breasts. She was mesmerizing and Karen discovered a new turn-on she hadn't known existed.

"I prefer to give than to receive."

"Receive what?"

Karen's cheeks were on fire and she focused on Bianca's breasts so she didn't have to look into those luminous eyes. "You know what I mean."

Bianca's finger stroked her jaw, gently forcing their eyes to meet. "No, I don't know. Tell me."

The glimmer in those fathomless mahogany depths teased but also begged. She didn't want innuendo or guessing. She wanted to make sure their lovemaking satisfied Karen. How breathtaking to have a lover so intent on Karen's pleasure. It was intoxicating.

"I want to taste you. It'll make me come faster if I lick you," Karen said.

Bianca pulled herself up onto the mattress, dragging Karen to her by her belt. "Seriously? Could you be any more perfect? I love your tongue on me."

"You want that now?" Karen was warming to the discussion. Each new insight sent a fresh flood of desire between her legs. "Can I taste you?"

"Maybe later. I want to see you. I want you naked."

Karen took a step back and stepped out of her boots while unzipping her pants. Any thought of a slow, sexy disrobing abandoned thanks to the building desire low in her belly. Bianca slipped her skirt off without taking her eyes off Karen. She lounged back on the fully-made bed, spreading her legs wide. Karen was caught in that awkward moment of bending over to peel off socks and jeans together, but Bianca, swollen and dripping for her stopped her dead.

The curls between her thighs were the same dark brown of her eyebrows. They were wild and unkempt and somehow all the sexier for it. Karen's rigid shaving routine seemed silly and unnecessary when she saw how alluring a natural look could be. Hastening to complete her task, Karen was less graceful than she'd like, but at least she was naked quickly. No sooner had she stood to her full height than Bianca crooked a finger at her, beckoning her between the welcoming cage of her legs.

"Christ, you're sexy," Bianca whispered as Karen stood in front of her.

Bianca slid her hands delicately over the plane of her stomach to the tops of her thighs. Karen sighed as Bianca's hands and eyes devoured her. Soon she added her mouth to the mix, kissing and licking across the inside of her elbow and the row of ribs on her left side over the light scar from a bicycle accident in her teens. Bianca's attentions remained on all the non-intimate areas of her body, but it was far more erotic than anything she'd experienced before. By the time Bianca took one of her nipples into her mouth, Karen cried out in need.

Bianca purred as she released her nipple with a final light flick of her tongue. "Mmmm. So expressive. I like that."

"You're driving me wild."

"Maybe I want you that way."

Bianca scratched lightly down her abdomen, through the tight line of blond curls. Two fingers caged her clit, stroking hard and fast for a glorious moment. Karen would not last long through teasing. She pressed her hand on top of Bianca's to stop her movement but keep the pressure.

"Wait, not yet. You first."

Bianca chuckled and flopped back on the bed, her breasts and long necklaces swaying. Karen's mouth watered.

"Don't tell me you're a controlling top."

Karen let her hands wander up the thighs wrapped around her. Bianca's position, laid out on the bed with their pelvises locked together, was so hot Karen had to force herself not to grab those delicious hips and grind into her.

"Not controlling. I just like to make you come." Karen shook off the image of last time so she could lower the heat for a little while. "Besides, you haven't told me what you like."

Bianca slid her hands behind her head, the picture of relaxation. If Karen couldn't feel the evidence of her desire against her own skin, she might think they were discussing art or their latest reads.

"I like it all. Oral and penetration are my favorite. But I should warn you, I'm no pillow princess. I like to be on top."

"Why doesn't that surprise me about you?"

"Does it bother you?"

"I don't think it will. I've never tried it before."

"Why don't you get out that strap-on and we can find out?"

It had been a very long time since Karen had used her harness, but it wasn't buried too deep in her bedside table. She brought it out along with her dildo and a bottle of lube.

Bianca pulled back the sheets and nodded toward the lube. "We won't need that tonight. In fact, you might want to grab a towel unless you want to sleep in the wet spot."

Her wink and wide smile had Karen hustling to the linen closet for a beach towel. She'd never had a girlfriend who ejaculated before, but the way Bianca had soaked her own quilt was burned into her brain. She couldn't help but take it as a compliment and she loved that Bianca was confident it would happen again.

When she returned to the bedroom, Bianca had propped up both pillows against the fabric headboard and was kneeling in the center of the bed. She licked her lips as she watched Karen step into the harness and fit the dildo in place. Just having it there, firm pressure against her clit, was nearly enough to send her over the edge. She breathed through waves of pleasure, willing herself to wait.

"Sit here and lean back against the pillows," Bianca said in a determined tone that was almost identical to her teacher's voice.

Okay, new kink number two for Karen today.

No sooner had she settled into place than Bianca straddled her knees.

"Is this okay? Are you comfortable?" Bianca asked.

"Yes." Karen's voice was a tight, throaty croak.

Bianca reached down to coat her fingers between her lips, then stroked the dildo. The toy wasn't realistic, but a swirling blue and purple shaft. Bianca seemed to appreciate it, since she wasted no time moving forward, bracing one hand on Karen's shoulder, and using the other to guide the toy inside herself.

Karen was determined not to thrust, but she needn't have censored herself. Bianca slid down the toy in one, fluid movement, taking Karen to the hilt and only stopping when their bodies met. They groaned in unison, Bianca an octave higher and Karen's eyes rolling back in her head.

"Oh God, you feel so good inside me," Bianca said.

She immediately picked up a slow but constant rhythm, lifting off Karen and thrusting into her again. Both her hands were on Karen's shoulders now and Karen gripped hard at her hips to keep grounded. She easily matched Bianca's rhythm, mesmerized by Bianca on top of her. Bianca's hips snapped eagerly, determined to take her own pleasure. Karen burned, each thrust pressing the toy's base against her clit and taking her closer to ecstasy. Too close.

"Bianca, I…"

"Yes. Do it. Come with me."

Bianca leaned back. She gripped Karen's legs below her knees and her thrusts became more and more erratic. Her palms were like matching flames, her touch hot on Karen's slick skin. Karen reached down to circle her exposed clit and Bianca cried out. Her orgasm pounded closer and closer with each thrust, but Karen fought through the haze to make sure Bianca came with her. Her breath came in the same quick, shallow bursts. A bead of sweat trickled down her forehead and tickled her nose. They both went silent for a heartbeat, the sounds of their bodies slapping against each other the only noise in the room, and then they both screamed.

Karen ground her thumb hard into Bianca's clit, slipping and skipping off target as she crested. Bianca's hips jerked hard and then she let loose, a flood bursting from her and coating Karen's abdomen and legs. She was entranced, her heart hammering twice as hard as her orgasm, and was nearly eclipsed by the joy of seeing Bianca's.

They came down slowly. Karen recovered first, giving her the gift of watching Bianca's final pulses and aftershocks. Eventually, Bianca fell forward again. Karen pulled her, flushed and sweaty, into the closest of hugs. Both their hearts raced as they rested against each other.

Bianca purred and snuggled closer into her. Her voice was muffled in flesh and pillow when she said, "Like I said, you give the coziest hugs."

Karen's chuckle shook their bodies. Or maybe it was a shared laugh, she couldn't tell. She pulled Bianca close and held on as tight as she could.

CHAPTER TWENTY-ONE

Sometime in the middle of the night, Karen woke with a start, her limbs heavy with sleep. What had brought her out of her dreams? She recognized her surroundings, but something was different. Rather than the softness of her sheets, something scratchy and coarse bunched beneath her. Rather than the chill of empty sheets beside her, an intense heat filled her bed.

A glimmer of awareness fought through the fog of sleep. The towel they'd put beneath them before they'd had sex hadn't been enough to protect the sheets and mattress. Karen had fetched a fresh towel to lay down before they succumbed to their exhaustion. Bianca had thanked her properly for her chivalry. Twice.

Bianca. That was the heat beside her. The sheet had fallen off her shoulder as she slept and her body rose and fell gently as she breathed. She made a sweet, gentle noise that wasn't quite a snore but was more than a simple breath.

And she was warm. More than that. She radiated heat like her own sun. That's what had woken Karen. She was so hot her whole body was sweating and she desperately kicked off the sheets. She wasn't wearing socks. She always wore socks to bed. Her feet were always cold. She couldn't sleep without them. And yet here she was, waking up in the middle of the night because she was too hot, not too cold.

With the sheets off her, she was starting to get cold, though. She turned and snuggled up against Bianca and her eyelids immediately grew heavy. Her last thoughts before tumbling back into a deep sleep was how warm and soft Bianca was. Warm, soft, and perfect to cuddle with.

When she next woke, the bright light of morning slashed across the carpet from under the edge of her heavy curtains. It must be really late for the light to be so bright like that. Being on the third floor, it took ages for the autumn sun to light her apartment. Her bedroom had just one window, with blackout curtains she kept tightly closed most days. That gave it a wonderful, cave-like atmosphere perfect for sleeping in. It was her active mind and body that usually woke Karen, but neither of those were ready to be up that Sunday.

Beside her, Bianca stirred and groaned as she slowly awoke. Karen watched her move, transfixed by her presence. She wanted to memorize the look and feel of this, the first morning she woke up next to Bianca.

She'd been so worried about them starting their sexual relationship early, especially since her conversation with Jessica at lunch. The fear that Bianca would lose interest like everyone else had loomed so large for the last week. But there was nothing better to settle that fear than waking up next to her. People didn't sleep over with casual sex partners, right? They slept over with their girlfriend, though.

"Good morning." Bianca's voice was croaky with sleep as she turned a smile on Karen.

"Good morning to you."

Bianca's eyes opened slowly and were even more slow to fix on Karen's. When they did, they were filled with the sort of gentle affection Karen craved. She leaned in and brushed her lips against Bianca's. She pulled back, but Bianca followed her, begging for more. Discarding worries about morning breath or bed head, Karen melted into the kiss. It was slow and sensuous and brought her body alive far more effectively than coffee. Obviously, Bianca felt the same, because she pressed hard against Karen.

Deepening the kiss, Bianca slid a leg between Karen's. She opened her legs gratefully, her body on autopilot as she responded to Bianca's. To her great frustration, Bianca's thigh barely grazed her core before it slid down her leg. Karen thought she was preparing to climb on top, but Bianca's movements abruptly halted as her foot tangled with Karen's.

"Oh shit, babe." Bianca pulled back, staring at Karen with a look of horror. "I forgot to get you socks."

With her clit throbbing, Karen had difficulty making sense of the words. "What?"

"Socks for you to sleep in. I was going to search your dresser for some, but I fell asleep. Did you sleep a wink? I'm so sorry."

A warmth that had nothing to do with arousal flooded through Karen. She'd remembered that Karen always slept in socks and she had planned to get them for her. It was a little thing, but it was also another clear sign this relationship meant as much to Bianca as it did to Karen. She shouldn't be surprised anymore, but it was hard to feel worthy.

"I didn't need them, actually," Karen said.

"Really?"

"Yeah. Not sure if you know, but you sleep really hot. In fact, the only time I woke up was because I was too hot."

"I probably should have warned you about that," Bianca said with an embarrassed smile.

"It's great, actually. You were like my personal furnace."

Bianca slid close with a wicked smile. "Well, that is a service I'd like to provide for a long time to come."

Time swam in a sea of bliss as they reacquainted themselves with each other's bodies. Before anything could get too out of control, Bianca broke things off for a much-delayed trip to the bathroom. After they'd both brushed their teeth and emptied their bladders, they snuggled back into bed. Hours floated by as they chatted about everything and nothing, sharing their lives as freely as they had shared their bodies. Neither of them seemed inclined to get up or dressed, even when their stomachs rumbled.

"I can't remember the last time I've stayed in bed this late on a Sunday," Karen said.

Bianca had snuggled up against her side, her head resting on Karen's shoulder and her fingers drawing patterns around her bellybutton under the sheet.

"Get used to it, because I have no plans to let you go away any time soon."

"Is that a kidnapping threat?"

"Are you complaining?" Bianca's fingers swirled lower as she spoke, tracing the edges of the neat line of Karen's curls.

"Depends."

Bianca's touch wandered lower. "On?"

"How hard you plan on working to convince me."

Bianca rolled on top of her, kissing her way toward Karen's hardening nipples. "I can be very persuasive."

Her lips wrapped around Karen's nipple and she bucked up into Bianca. "Won't Alex be worried if you don't come home soon?"

Bianca kissed her way across to Karen's other nipple and slid a hand between their bodies. "I frankly don't care about Alex right now, and I'm going to make damn sure you don't think about her any time soon either."

Her mouth latched on to Karen's nipple and her fingers found her clit. Karen closed her eyes and dissolved into the moment that felt so much like a dream come true.

On Monday evening, Karen made her way through the empty halls of her school. Only a handful of the classrooms she passed were still lit and all the windows were dark. Autumn and winter drove many of her colleagues home early, as they preferred to fine-tune lesson plans under blankets on their couches rather than in their chilly, concrete-block-walled classrooms. She couldn't blame them. She didn't want to be here any longer either, but that was only because she had spent a tortuous twenty hours away from Bianca.

True to her promise, Bianca had kidnapped Karen from the wider world all of Sunday. In fact, they'd spent very little time out of her bed. They'd skipped breakfast and snacked on crackers for lunch, the crumbs tumbling under the sheets with them when they turned their attention back to each other. Dinner had been ordered from a pizza place outside town, but left on the doorstep. When Alex had texted to say she was downstairs, ready to pick Bianca up and take her home, they'd both pouted like teenagers. It had been the most magical weekend of Karen's life.

Dragging her pleasantly sore body out of bed the next morning had been a chore, but she cheered herself up by changing the sheets. After all, she expected them to get much the same treatment that night as they had all weekend. But the school day had dragged by at a glacial pace and she couldn't ignore her backlog of paperwork. Now she had powered through all of it and was skipping toward Bianca.

When she arrived at the art room, however, she found the front table littered with construction paper in browns, yellows, reds, and oranges. A noise from the far corner of the room drew her attention and she caught sight of Bianca, marching out of her supply closet with even more stacks of paper.

"I guess we aren't going to be grading papers in bed this evening after all," Karen said with a laugh. "What's all this?"

Bianca's face lit up like a candle in a winter window at the sight of her, making Karen's heart skip a beat. Rather than answering the question, Bianca dropped the stack of construction paper on the table and grabbed a fistful of Karen's shirt. She yanked her across the room, into the corner of the classroom almost entirely occupied by a pottery kiln and a rickety old bookshelf. They'd discovered the previous week that this was one of the few spots in the classroom where they couldn't be seen from the hall.

"I missed you." Bianca growled as she pushed Karen against the wall.

Karen barely had time to suck in a shocked breath before Bianca's lips were on hers, hot and insistent. She slammed her eyelids together and fell into the kiss, the need that had enveloped her all weekend washing back over her on Bianca's lavender-scented air. Bianca kissed her thoroughly, her thigh slipping between Karen's to stoke her need. She kissed back with all the frustration that had built in her in the last day.

When they broke the kiss, they were both panting and, if the hazy gleam in Bianca's eyes was any judge, both aching with desire. Bianca didn't move far away, instead settling her head on Karen's shoulder while her hands kept a firm grip of her hips.

"It's pretty clear we aren't heading home any time soon." Karen indicated the stacks of paper. "So, this isn't as effective an apology as you think."

Bianca gave her a flirty wink, then hurried over to the table. "Come here. I need your hands."

"That's exactly what you're missing out on by not taking me home."

Bianca laughed and slapped her shoulder teasingly. It was so domestic and charming, Karen's heart swelled more than she thought possible. This was definitely a girlfriend task, and Karen was really good at girlfriend tasks.

"It just came to me when the final bell rang. I figured out how to make Thanksgiving a smash hit at Bucks Hill Elementary this year."

"With construction paper?"

Bianca ignored her, shuffling the different color papers into piles. "With the Halloween festival coming up at the pumpkin patch and your big winter talent show plans, I've decided to go old school and simple for Thanksgiving."

"I like old school and simple."

Bianca turned that wide smile on her again. "I know. Me too. And it's perfect because that's the whole vibe of Bucks Mill. Classic small town."

Karen couldn't keep her hands to herself. She slid up behind Bianca, wrapping her arms around her waist and using her extra height to look down over her shoulder. "Am I part of that happy vibe Bucks Mill gives you?"

Bianca turned to look at her, their lips centimeters apart. "You're the biggest part. That's why you are the first to participate."

Bianca caught her hand that had been wandering up underneath her thick, cable knit sweater, and placed it palm down on the table. For a moment, Karen thought she had something kinky in mind, until she felt the pencil tracing along her pinky finger.

"Umm, what are you doing?" Karen asked.

"I told you. I need your hands."

Bianca spread Karen's hand wider on the paper, then completed the outline. A memory from her youth tickled at Karen's mind, but she couldn't quite sort it out.

"I had hoped you wanted it for something else."

Bianca smiled devastatingly at her, then bumped her out of the way with her hip. "Later."

Shrugging, she took the safety scissors Bianca handed her and dutifully cut out the outline of her hand from the brown construction paper. It wasn't until Bianca started cutting out feathers from the yellow, red, and orange paper that she finally realized what was going on.

"Oh, we're making paper hand turkeys," Karen said.

Bianca shot a quick glance at the door to make sure the hallway was empty before leaning over and pecking her on the lips. "That's right. We'll draw eyes on the thumb, then add feathers over the fingers. Everyone will get one folded-over brown feather—the turkey's wing. They'll write a secret message of what they're thankful for on that one."

"That's fun." Karen grabbed a roll of double-sided tape and the first colorful feather from Bianca's stack.

"We'll hang them around the school and on the last day before break, we'll pass them back out to the students. They take them home and read what they're thankful for to their families during Thanksgiving dinner."

With Bianca cutting out feathers using a cardboard template and Karen wielding the tape dispenser, they made quick work of their turkeys. Karen wasn't nearly as artistic, of course, but she had slightly bigger hands, so that made her turkey a bit more impressive. Bianca compensated by drawing long, blue marker eyelashes on her creation.

Shoving a larger, partially folded brown feather at her, Bianca said, "Now write down what you're thankful for so we can hang these up and I can take you home to do unspeakable things with you."

Heat crept into Karen's cheeks, but it wasn't from the not-so-subtle innuendo. She knew exactly what she wanted to write on her feather, but she also knew she was playing with fire. It was too soon, she knew that, but she had already fallen for Bianca. If she was honest with herself, she never stood a chance.

Picking up the thin marker, Karen smiled. The best part of this plan was that she got to write her feelings down now, but didn't have to share them for another month. That would give her enough time to be able to say it without making it too soon. Turning her shoulder to block Bianca's view, she wrote: *I'm thankful for you, Bianca. I love you.*

If Bianca noticed that she snatched the tape a little more quickly and sealed her feather with a bit more secrecy than was strictly necessary, she didn't mention it. Karen tried not to read too much into the fact that Bianca didn't share her message either. She led them down to the main hallway leading to the office, where she'd set up a ladder next to one long wall.

She gave Karen a smoky, promising look. "Think you could hold the ladder for me?"

Karen stepped close until their bodies nearly brushed. "Of course. Although I can't promise I won't look up your skirt."

"Exactly what I was hoping you'd do."

Bianca dodged her attempted kiss and hurried up the ladder. It squeaked and wobbled, so Karen really did have to hold on tight. Heaven knew where Bianca got the ladder, and how long it had been in the school's possession. She was so busy worrying about it falling apart with Bianca on top of it, she missed out on the opportunity to ogle her.

"There we go. The first two turkeys of the year are up." Bianca climbed down, grabbing Karen's arms when she arrived at the bottom so she could wrap them around herself. "Maybe you could help me hang them all up as they come in?"

"I'd love to."

Karen's throat closed up with nerves and she barely finished the sentence. Why had she said the L word? She hadn't said it about her feelings for Bianca, but the syllables still felt raw and terrifying after having written them down. She tried her best to act normal as they packed up the ladder and tucked it into a storage closet. Bianca chatted in her usual carefree style as they walked back to her classroom and tidied the paper into a turkey making station, but Karen couldn't focus on anything. If she had this much anxiety about a casual use of the word, how would she manage a not-so-casual use of it?

Even after just a few weeks, this thing with Bianca was special. The first time she told her she loved her needed to be equally special. Something big and showy and brave like Bianca herself. Without really intending to, she'd already set the stage for it. She would make a big production of it at Thanksgiving dinner. Bianca loved Thanksgiving. She loved family and tradition and putting a big mark on an often-overlooked holiday. That was one of the first things Karen had learned about her and it had been the moment she knew this woman was special. What better way to honor her first big project at a new school than to use it to show her how amazing she was?

Before she lost her nerve, Karen took the plunge. "So hey. I know you normally do a big thing with your family for Thanksgiving, but would you have any interest in coming with me to my parents' place this year? It's nothing special, just the traditional meal and my dad and brother watching football on the couch, but it would be so great to have you there."

Even as the words were leaving her mouth, Karen feared the answer. Why in the world would Bianca say yes? It's not like she was offering some amazing event, and besides, she had just moved away from all her family. Surely, she'd want to go see them. There was no way Bianca would accept and then she would feel stupid and sad.

"I'd love to come."

Karen blinked a couple times as the words soaked in. "Really? Are you sure?"

Bianca laughed her tinkling, angelic laugh and wrapped her arms around Karen's neck. "I've never been more sure of anything in my life. I want to have Thanksgiving with you and your family."

CHAPTER TWENTY-TWO

Karen stood in her usual place in the hallway between the library and her classroom as students dribbled in for the start of school. It was the last week of October and the temperature had plummeted over the weekend. Of course, she had barely noticed. She'd spent the entire weekend ensconced in Bianca's bedroom except for the brief breaks to shower or sneak upstairs to raid the kitchen. Alex had been away visiting their oldest sister, so there had been no reason to keep quiet or clothed.

She shook those tantalizing memories from her hormone-riddled brain as a surge of students entered the hall. Most of the group were rowdy fifth graders. She'd gotten used to quieting down this particular group. She couldn't imagine the relief their bus driver felt when it came time to unload them every morning and make them Karen's problem. Fortunately, several of them had been her students two years previous and still held a grudging respect for her. She even made Benji's brother, Cliff, laugh with one of her comebacks.

The next group to arrive included Tinley Bamford and Lily Hanson, two of her all-time favorites. Lily spotted her first and ran over, Tinley hot on her heels.

"Hi, Ms. Petersen. Are you coming to the Halloween festival this year? It's at Carter Farms again and my aunt Carter says it's going to be the best ever," Tinley said.

Strange how this mention of Carter and her approaching marriage to Lily's aunt didn't bring its usual pang of sadness and jealousy. Of course, that might've been because she was distracted by a glimpse of

Bianca crossing the hall in front of the library, a crying kindergartener in tow. Bianca didn't look up at her, she kept her attention on her forlorn charge, but that didn't stop Karen from looking her fill.

"I, um, think I might miss it this year. Sorry, Lily."

"What? You can't skip it," Tinley said, her voice an octave lower than Lily's but dripping in the same sadness.

"It's just a really busy time and I—"

"The festival wouldn't be the same without you, though." Lily whined.

Just before Bianca passed out of view, she looked up and caught Karen's eye. She gave the tiniest of winks and Karen felt it in her whole body. Like a cool breeze on a hot day at the beach.

"I—I'll try my best to make it. Okay?" Karen said, forcing her focus back to Lily and Tinley.

They squealed happily and in unison before hurrying off, arm-in-arm, toward their classroom.

"Don't think I didn't catch that," Jessica whispered.

Karen tried and failed to hide her smile. "Catch what?"

"That wink. You two are ridiculous."

"Oh, like you and Brandon didn't act the same way."

"Of course we didn't. He's a man. He's genetically incapable of being sweet," Jessica said.

"I call BS. You would never settle for a guy who wasn't as romantic as you are."

Jessica shrugged, but she couldn't hide her smile any more than Karen could. She leaned against the wall and Karen leaned beside her, trying to play it cool. She counted silently in her head, and made it to five, as she expected, before Jessica asked, "So how've you been?"

"Fine."

"Now I call BS. I've never seen you so happy. You didn't even give me a hard time for canceling our lunch date last weekend."

"I did too give you a hard time."

"Did not."

"I said there's no such thing as a pumpkin emergency, even the weekend before Halloween," Karen said.

"Yeah, but you said it like you meant it and you didn't even sound sad."

"You want me to be sad?"

"Not all the time. Only when I'm a jerk and cancel on you last minute," Jessica said.

Karen stifled her laughter and forced a straight face as a group of fourth graders walked past them on the way to their classrooms. Honestly, she had completely forgotten about their lunch date on Saturday. She'd been picking up pastries to take over to Bianca's when Jessica had called, so she was right when she said the ribbing had been less than full-throated. Still, it wouldn't do to let Jessica know that, especially since there had been loads of times recently when she had, in fact, made Karen very sad by canceling.

"Okay, I was a little sad, but I understand that your family comes first."

To her surprise, Jessica put a hand on her arm and turned to her with a worried look. "That's not what happened. You're really important to me, Karen."

A little of the old bitterness sprung up in Karen's chest as she looked at Jessica. Of course, Karen understood she was attached to her husband, but the cancelations were constant. It would have been infinitely better for her to just not make plans with Karen in the first place. Especially since she tried to involve Brandon in their time together. How could she deny how often she had let Karen down? How could she not see how frightened Karen was of losing her best friend?

The feeling passed as quickly as it had come, though. It was easy to forgive Jessica when she had someone who put her first now. She had someone who wanted to be with her all the time. Bianca had even gone so far as to cancel with her own family to spend Thanksgiving with Karen. Other people putting her second hurt a little bit less now.

"I'm just teasing. Did you get the perfect pumpkin?"

The loving smile returned to Jessica's face in an instant and she gave a hilarious account of traipsing through the pumpkin patch in search of a white pumpkin. By the time she finished the story and rushed off to help one of her students, Karen was sure she had fully smoothed things over with Jessica. She checked her watch to see that the bell was about to ring.

As she turned to retreat to her own classroom, she saw Benji dragging his feet as he turned the corner. Normally he hustled down the hallway from the back entrance to the library, but this morning he was coming from the far side of the school.

"Hey, Benji. You better hurry, you're about to be late," Karen said.

"Oh, hi, Ms. Petersen."

"Is everything okay? Did something happen on the bus? Is that why you're running late?"

"No. I'm fine. I just went to Mrs. Harper's classroom, but she wasn't there," Benji said.

"I think she was taking a student to the nurse. What did you want to talk to her about?"

To her surprise, Benji's eyes went wide and he blushed furiously. "Nothing. I was just—I didn't want—I mean, um, I should get to class."

He hurried past her, his face growing redder by the moment. The bell rang the moment his overlarge backpack disappeared through the doorway, so she followed, but a suspicion took root in her mind as she closed the door.

After hanging the first few turkeys from the students next to their own, Karen dragged Bianca to the teachers' lounge to help make copies of the math quiz she was giving the next day. They only got through five copies before the machine jammed.

"Does this thing ever work?" Bianca asked.

Karen rolled up the sleeves of her button up and yanked open the side cover. "Not really, but I've gotten really good at fixing it."

Bianca leaned on the heel of her hand and gave her a devastating look. "I love a handy butch. I bet you never call your landlord to fix things, do you?"

Karen rolled her eyes as she slapped the side cover closed and knelt down to open the front cover. "Mr. Bamford pay to fix anything? You must be joking. When I first moved in I told him that the kitchen drain was leaking and we needed a plumber. His son—Tinley's father—showed up four hours later with a Philips head screwdriver and nothing else."

There was a beat of silence before Bianca said, "I'm guessing that's bad?"

Karen shook her head as she moved rollers to get to the jammed papers. "Alex would have laughed her head off at that."

"My sister is the reason I have no idea what you mean. She's been the handywoman at every apartment and house I've ever lived in."

The paper gave way but sent a shower of dry toner all over Karen's hands and arms. She displayed her dirty palms to Bianca. "I'm happy to show you a few tricks if you want."

"I'll pass, thanks."

"Ah so it isn't just lack of experience then?"

Bianca leaned in close, but kept her clothes well out of reach of the mess. "Maybe I just like watching you get your hands dirty."

Karen's lower belly gave a pleasant little twist at the innuendo. "I do like it when you watch."

Bianca chuckled low in her throat. "Go wash your hands and finish up so I can take you home to…watch."

She didn't have to be told twice and hustled to the sink. When she got back, her hands smelling of fake mango scented soap but clean, she found Bianca scanning the quiz. Her eyebrows furrowed in an adorable little pout.

Karen closed the copier and set it to work again. "What's the matter? Not a fan of math?"

"I would totally fail this quiz."

"It's only long division," Karen said with a laugh.

"Of fractions. That's dark magic if ever there was any."

"You really are the most remarkable woman. Didn't you just teach my class how to mix different amounts of paints to make different tones of primary colors? That's just ratios, you know."

"Mixing paint is like cooking with garlic, you measure with your heart. No numbers involved."

Karen laughed and gathered together the finished quizzes, heading for the stapler. "That's the only time I've heard you sound truly Italian."

"Just wait for Thanksgiving, when I make my famous Thanksgiving stuffing focaccia."

"You make stuffing back into bread? How?"

"You'll find out in a few weeks, won't you?"

"My family makes oyster stuffing. It'll be fun to compare the two."

"Oyster stuffing? What's that?" Bianca asked.

"You'll find out in a few weeks, won't you?"

Bianca leaped over at her, attacking her with tickles. Karen laughed as she defended herself, wrapping her arms around Bianca and pulling her close. The sparkle in her eye as she stood on her tip toes to smile at Karen was too much. How could she possibly hold off telling Bianca she loved her until Thanksgiving dinner?

Bianca twisted gently out of her arms and turned her attention to the counter strewn with paperwork. "Okay, you, focus on these so we can get out of here."

As they worked, Bianca straightening the three pages together and handing them to Karen to staple, she remembered her encounter with Benji that morning.

"Someone in this school has a crush on you," Karen said.

"I don't mean to be critical, but you aren't exactly hiding your crush very well."

Karen's heart skipped a beat and she nearly dropped the stapler. "Okay, there are two people in this school who have a crush on you."

Bianca gave her a faux grumpy scowl. "The quizzes are supposed to be for the kids, not me. Spit it out."

"Okay. Okay. I believe that Benji has developed his first teacher crush."

To her credit, Bianca didn't deny it. She sighed and shook her head, but didn't make fun of him. "I was worried about that."

"He went by your classroom this morning, but you weren't there."

"That would make three mornings in a row. I think I might've gone a little overboard in encouraging him."

Karen stapled the last quiz and turned to her, sliding along the countertop until they stood hip to hip. "It's not your fault. You're extremely easy to form a crush on."

Bianca's furrowed brow smoothed and the tilted her face up tantalizingly close to Karen's. "Is that so?"

It wasn't exactly that Karen forgot where they were, it was more that she couldn't care less. It had been far too long since she'd tasted those lips. She closed the distance between them and captured Bianca's mouth with hers. Her kiss was tender and slow but left no doubt her intentions. Bianca met her with the same obvious need, sliding a hand up to cup her cheek and hold her close.

Just when things were getting interesting, a loud throat clearing from the doorway made them jump apart like a pair of teenagers caught in the act. Karen frantically straightened her clothes, trying to figure out how to explain she was a little mussed not from making out, but from fixing the copier.

Bianca was the first to speak. "Roger. I'm so sorry. That was all my fault—"

"No, it was mine. I shouldn't have—" Karen said.

Roger saved them the trouble of stammering through coherent apologies. "Look I don't care about what everyone does in their free time, but when you are on school property, you're on my time."

"Yes, of course," Bianca said.

Karen chanced a glance in her direction in time to see the color receding from her cheeks. It almost looked like she was fighting back a smile. Looking over at Roger, she saw he was smiling, too. It was his Condescending Father Look, but since he wasn't firing them, Karen forgave him. She never had looked into the school's fraternization policy.

"You know how much I hate mediating complaints, Karen. Just keep it professional here."

"Yes, sir. Sorry."

His lecture over, Roger's face relaxed. "On a personal note, I'm very happy that you two are happy. Just maybe be happy at home, okay?"

With that, he beat a hasty retreat back to his office. It took a long moment for Karen to get up the nerve to look at Bianca, but she had recovered much more quickly.

Bianca burst out laughing. "You look terrified."

"I am."

"He's happy for us, though."

Karen's shoulders relaxed and she managed a smile. "Yeah. That's pretty cool."

Bianca slid close to her again. Not close enough to be scandalous, but close enough to whisper. "He had a very good idea, though. Shall we go be happy at your place or mine?"

Now that they had settled into the routine of a relationship, Karen had been able to get back to her professional routine as well. After the final student had left for the day, they would go to their respective classrooms and work for around an hour. Then they would meet in Karen's classroom and some days she would drop Bianca off at home, but most days they would stay at Karen's overnight. They were too busy and tired for traditional dates during the week, but they had decided they would go out more on the weekends. It was all very domestic. Exactly what Karen had been searching for.

On the Wednesday after Halloween, however, Karen worked her obligatory hour, then packed away her computer. She puttered around her classroom, straightening desks and tidying shelves while she waited for Bianca. After ten minutes, she ran out of mundane tasks and headed for Bianca's classroom.

Bianca was there, stuffing her things fiercely into her bag. It only took one look at her face to know something was terribly wrong. She looked like she wanted to tear the bricks out of the wall, but rage sat uncomfortably on her warm features.

"Are you okay?" Karen's heart lurched with concern.

Bianca went back to her furious packing without so much as a smile for Karen. "I was going to text you. I can't hang out tonight."

Karen jerked away from the words, they'd been spit at her with so much venom. The way Bianca characterized their time together didn't feel great either. If Karen wanted to define their time together, she would use more intimate words than hang out.

"Okay. If that's what you need. But can you tell me what's wrong?" Karen said.

"Frank fucking Harper."

"Who?"

Bianca came to a halt, one hand fisted on her hip, the other pinching the bridge of her nose. "My fucking ex-husband. I'm sorry, I know we had plans, but I need to go home and talk to my sister."

"Is everything okay? What did he do? Are you in danger? Is Alex?"

"No. No, it's fine." Bianca grabbed her bag and marched toward the door. "He's just being an asshole. It's what he does."

Karen caught up with her, and, while she wanted to grab Bianca's arm to stop her, she thought better of it. "Does what? Please talk to me. I'm worried."

Bianca's exasperated sigh cut ever so slightly. As though Karen was being a nuisance by worrying. "I got an email from him. Or rather from his lawyer since he's the only person I'm allowed to talk to apparently. He does this once or twice a year just to piss me off and obviously he succeeded."

"That's awful. I'm so sorry. Let me drive you home."

"No, it's okay. Alex is waiting out front."

So Bianca had known about this for a while. Long enough to get Alex to come all the way out to the school. Alex had known well before Karen. "Oh. Okay. Well, do you want to talk about it while you walk?"

Bianca gave her a distracted smile but was starting to look a little more like herself. "You're sweet, but I really need some sister time for this one. I'll call you tomorrow, okay?"

With that, she swept through the door and down the hall. Karen was left alone and reeling, staring at bare painted concrete walls and paint-splattered floor for a long time. Eventually, she wandered back to her classroom.

Bianca had blown her off. That was the only way to describe it. It stung a little that she had turned to Alex in her time of need. It was probably just too early for Bianca to talk to her about everything. There was a lot of back story when it came to Bianca's previous marriage. It sounded like this was something Alex would be used to and could manage without a long, painful explanation. This was what Bianca had warned her about. This was the going slow she had needed.

That explanation worked enough to get Karen through closing down her classroom. Once she stepped out into the chilly night, the few stars poking through the clouds and the partially obscured moon doing little to combat the gloom, her mood soured. A little voice in the back of her head kept telling her Bianca hadn't confided in her because she wasn't worth the big, personal stuff. She was just a friend to have sex with. She didn't come first for Bianca like she thought she did. She sat in her car, closed her eyes, and focused on her slow breathing. She was overreacting, but she needed to acknowledge the feelings before she could let them go.

The long march up the stairs to her apartment felt twice as long carrying all the weight of her disappointment. She had just settled onto her couch for a long night of sulking when her phone chirped with a new text message. She nearly knocked over her newly opened beer in her haste to grab her phone to see what Bianca said.

What's that beer from Richmond your father loves so much this time of year? Her mother asked.

Karen dropped her head back on the cushion with a disappointed sigh. *Hardywood's Gingerbread Stout.*

That's it! Can you bring some for Thanksgiving? They don't sell it out here and you know how much he loves it.

Thanksgiving. Karen's mind flashed back to the joy on Bianca's face when she agreed to come with her to her family's Thanksgiving. That meant something, right? In that moment Bianca had picked Karen over everything else, even her family. Even Alex. She had picked Karen and you didn't do that with someone you just wanted to have casual sex with. It meant something. All the disappointment swimming through her right now wasn't about Bianca. It was about her own feelings of inadequacy. Her body tingled with anticipation of her big plans for Thanksgiving. Tonight was a blip, this thing with Bianca was real.

Just like that, all the sadness and doubt fled from Karen. So what if Bianca needed Alex for this one thing? Bianca cared for her and she was being selfish.

Karen typed back to her mother excitedly. *Sure, I can do that. By the way, I'm bringing someone with me to Thanksgiving this year if that's okay.*

She sent the message before her nerves got the better of her. Her mother would call the moment she read the message and that made her unbearably nervous. It was silly to be nervous, but she was. She knew exactly how this call would go. Her mother would bring up how long it had been since she'd brought anyone home with her. Then she would shout the news to her dad and he was sure to jump on the phone to ask about her friend. They would be disappointed that Bianca was another teacher and unlikely to make the kind of money her sister-in-law made. Eventually, they would lose interest and that would probably be the worst part. It shouldn't bother her, but it did and she knew better than to try fighting it.

As predicted, her phone rang and her mother's face popped up on the display. She took a deep breath. Even if they did all the things she expected them to do, she couldn't change their reactions. She had to accept them for the way they were, and, though they didn't show it the way she wished they would, they loved her in their own way.

"Hi, Mom."

"Who are you bringing?" Her mother's voice positively dripped with excitement.

"Her name is Bianca." Deep breath. "She's my girlfriend."

Her mother squealed and she could practically hear her jumping up and down. Karen couldn't help smiling. It did feel good to hear her mother so happy for her.

"Oh, darling that's so wonderful. It's been so long since you've brought a girlfriend home to meet us."

Karen sighed and made a little check mark in the air in front of her. One down. "It hasn't been that long. Please don't say that when you meet her, okay?"

Her mother didn't answer right away and she could hear her father's voice shouting in the background. "No, Arthur, it's Karen. She's bringing someone home for Thanksgiving."

There was a scramble and scuffle of fabric and the muted sounds of her parents arguing about how to turn on speaker phone before her father spoke. "Karen? Tell me about your friend."

"She's not a friend, Dad. We're dating. Her name is Bianca and she teaches art at my school."

"An art teacher? Well, that's okay. There's not much money in art though," her dad said.

"Or in teaching," her mother said.

"Guys, please don't start with that. We both teach because we love teaching. I don't care how much money she has."

"Exactly right. The important thing is that she makes you happy. Does she make you happy, sweetie?" There was a hopeful note in her dad's voice.

"She makes me very happy," Karen said. She had to push aside memories of how sad she'd been a half hour ago, but that was normal in relationships. Nothing was perfect all the time.

"Well, we can't wait to meet her," her mother said.

Karen smiled and for the first time in a long time when talking to her parents, she really meant it.

CHAPTER TWENTY-THREE

The door she was leaning against burst open so unexpectedly, Karen nearly fell flat on her back. The only thing that kept her upright was Bianca's hand flying from the door handle to her hip. The door banged hard against the wall and Karen was pretty sure she heard the crunch of Sheetrock denting under the impact of the doorknob. Bianca kicked it shut, making the wall rattle with the force of the impact. Karen stumbled down the hall backward, feeling her way through the house without the benefit of lights.

During the entirety of the adventure, neither of them broke their intense kiss. Karen was careful not to jar their mouths too badly as she bumped off walls, furniture, and doors, but she was entirely focused on Bianca. Her need was practically bursting through her skin.

They usually didn't spend Thursday nights together because of the weekly staff meetings after school. Those days were long and frustrating and they usually took them to decompress alone. This week was different, though. Bianca had had her hands full for over a week dealing with the fallout from the email exchange with her ex. Then planning meetings for the winter talent show had kicked off and overeager parents had monopolized Karen's evenings.

Karen had hoped they'd at least get a chance to talk. They'd had much more than that. Bianca had been so sweetly apologetic and had been effusive about how much she'd missed Karen. They started making out before they'd even left school and it had been a chore to focus on driving the short distance to Bianca's house.

"Oh, I forgot to tell you." Bianca ripped her sweater off over her head. "Your class made their turkeys this week."

"Yeah, they told me." Karen tried stepping out of her shoe and ended up tripping ungracefully. "They said it's been their favorite project this year."

Bianca was naked from the waist up and Karen suddenly had no interest in talking turkey. She took one long stride across the room and captured her in a searing kiss. Bianca pulled her in tight, wrapping a leg around her waist.

"God, I missed the feel of your skin against mine," Bianca mumbled into the kiss.

Karen lifted her with a forearm under her ass and carried her across the room. "I missed you, too, baby. I'm sorry the show is taking so much of my time."

Her knees banged against the mattress, but Karen wasn't quite ready to set her down. Holding Bianca up, her thighs wrapped around her waist, was like being a hero in an action movie. It didn't hurt that Bianca looked at her like a hero, too. Like she reveled in being the prize Karen had won.

"How are the parental volunteers? Sheila said some of the moms at this school are a handful."

Karen finally placed Bianca on top of the bed. Bianca didn't release her legs, but lay back seductively, arching her back to present her breasts at a truly delicious angle. If she wasn't so eager to get Bianca's skirt and panties off, she'd take her time in memorizing the tableau.

"I pawned the worst off to Jessica for the Halloween festival," Karen said. "And that's the last I'll say about school for the rest of the night."

Bianca chuckled low in her throat. When Karen reached for the zipper on her skirt, Bianca pushed her hands away. She raised an eyebrow and stroked the fabric covering her hips. "Eager, are you?"

"Very."

Bianca started unzipping her skirt, one tooth at a time. "Well, then I should probably not tease any longer?"

Karen whimpered but wasn't willing to give up her dignity so easily. She could play this game, too. She slid her palm beneath the waistband of her khakis, tugging lightly at her shirttail. "Yeah, I probably shouldn't tease you either, huh?"

Bianca had a fetish-level interest in Karen's abs. She didn't have a six-pack, but there was a fair amount of definition to the muscles and Bianca spent hours tracing them with her tongue. Watching the slow exposure of her abs and the band of her boy shorts, Bianca's tongue traced the line of her own upper lip in sympathy.

The standoff only lasted a moment or two, and Bianca broke first, attacking the zipper with unnecessary force. Then she stripped the skirt and her damp panties off in one quick movement. It was Karen's turn to laugh, but the sight of her naked girlfriend splayed before her was too much to ignore for long.

Karen dropped to her knees, took firm hold of Bianca's thighs, and dove between her legs with a feral intensity that surprised even her. They groaned together as Karen's tongue found home. Her first taste set her wild, and she set up a punishing rhythm. Bianca's fingers curled into her hair, holding her in place as she licked and sucked with reckless abandon.

She was addicted to the taste of this woman. Addicted to the smell of her and the sound of her and the feel of her. She couldn't contain herself when they were together. All she could think of was making Bianca feel as good as being around her made Karen feel. She forgot to breathe and forgot to think.

If she was in her right mind, she would have taken her time to prolong their shared pleasure. But she wasn't in her right mind. She never was when Bianca was in her arms. Within moments of her first touch, Bianca was screaming her release and the desperate animal in Karen's chest was purring its happiness.

Karen watched Bianca as she screamed and moaned and then screamed again. As she came down from her orgasm, however, Bianca burst into a flood of tears. Fear clenched Karen's heart. Had she done something wrong? Had she hurt Bianca in some way?

Bianca fell backward on her bed, her hands covering her face and muffling her sobs. Before she could even think, Karen was off her knees and crawling across the mattress. As she landed at her side, Bianca turned her face into Karen's shoulder and sobbed even harder. Karen wrapped her arms around her and Bianca grabbed her back, clutching Karen to her with such pressure little bursts of pain radiated out from the spot where each finger gripped.

"I'm sorry," Bianca said between gasping sobs. "I'm so sorry."

"Shh. It's okay. I've got you."

The reassurance only made Bianca cry harder and another bolt of worry coursed through Karen. All thought of her own desire had fled as she held Bianca.

As the crying slacked, Bianca was able to speak more. "I don't know why I'm so emotional. I'm okay. I promise. I'm better than okay."

Karen stroked a light touch across her back, completely lost as to what to say.

Bianca looked up at her, tears sparkling in her eyelashes in the dim light from a single bedside lamp. "I just missed you and I'm really, really happy."

Emotion too intense to name coursed through Karen. That was love, right? Crying during sex because you're so happy was love, wasn't it? Would she say it? Was it possible that Bianca would be the one to take the first emotional leap?

"Me too," Karen said.

Her words set Bianca off again and she buried her head back into Karen's shoulder. She cried the way she laughed and made love. Without boundary or shame. She cried loud and long and she was crying because of what she felt for Karen. Tears formed and fell from her own eyes in her own way. Quiet and hesitant but undeniably real.

Karen had spent so much time waiting for her person. Though she hadn't admitted it, even to herself, she had lost faith that her person was out there. That she would ever have someone who felt for her as strongly as she felt for them. Now here she was, holding Bianca as she cried about how much she loved Karen. Sure, she hadn't said it in those words and it seemed unlikely she would tonight. Still, when Karen said it at Thanksgiving dinner next week, she knew in her bones that Bianca would say it back.

Bianca quieted, but kept her face buried in Karen's shoulder. "I've spent so long giving my time to people who think I'm too much or not enough. No one who's ever accepted me for who I am."

"I'm actually a really big fan of exactly who you are," Karen said quietly.

"I know you are. Thank you."

Bianca looked up at her and Karen gently wiped the tears from her cheeks. "You don't have to thank me. I'm the lucky one here. You're incredible, you know that?"

Bianca shook her head, but she smiled. Did she believe Karen's words? If there was anyone in the world who deserved to know how amazing she was, it was Bianca.

In that charming way she had of switching from one thought to another, Bianca's mood changed with a snap. The only warning Karen had was a quick peck on the hinge of her jaw, then Bianca pushed her on her back and straddled her hips.

"Enough of that." Bianca ripped Karen's shirt tail out of her waistband and raked her nails down her stomach. "Now I want to make you scream my name so loud that Alex bangs on the floor to tell us to shut up."

Karen was too happy to be embarrassed at the thought.

The Tuesday before Thanksgiving, Karen arrived at school earlier than usual to help Bianca take down all the paper hand turkeys to distribute to students and staff. It was amazing how the school had embraced the project. From those first two offerings Karen and Bianca had placed, the number of turkeys had grown and grown. Now they covered the top third of every hallway from the music room all the way to the fifth-grade classrooms. The office and custodial staff had theirs in the main lobby, dotting the thin band of wall above the huge windows showing off Dana's desk. Roger had drawn a crude Hawaiian shirt on his turkey with a silver paint pen.

Bianca was waiting with her ladder in front of the office, chatting happily with Doug. Karen couldn't help but laugh at the admiring look fixed on his face, so reminiscent of the way Benji looked at her. Just how many people had fallen in love with her anyway? When Bianca had arrived, looking like the stereotypical hippie art teacher, most of the staff had been wary. Or giggled about her behind her back. Now, just a few months into the school year, she had everyone wrapped around her little finger. As she looked over at Karen with a wide, devastating smile, Karen embraced the fact that she was the one wrapped tightest around that finger.

"Good morning. Thanks for being my assistant," Bianca said.

A hint of a whine entered Doug's voice as he said, "You should've asked. I could've helped you with this."

Karen decided to give Bianca an out. "I insisted. We've had fun hanging them up so I wanted to help hand them back out. Besides, you're here to keep us safe, not do all the manual labor."

Doug didn't seem to like the answer, but he ambled off without protest. Once the office door closed behind him, Karen dropped her bag on the floor and hurried out of her coat. Bianca's eyes scanned her body as she moved, sending a little shiver of joy through her.

It took less time than they'd thought to pull down the turkeys. Karen had suggested folders for each classroom to make passing them out to the students easier, but Bianca had gone one step further, separating a box into different grades and breaking those down by teachers. The attention to detail and careful organization was much more in line with Karen's personality than Bianca's, and she didn't hesitate to tease her about it.

"What can I say, you're rubbing off on me." Bianca added a wink and a sly smile that underlined the suggestiveness of the statement.

Karen's blush lasted through three more trips up and down the ladder.

"I spent too much time on this box, though, so I'll need to go home after school to pack," Bianca said.

Since they were leaving early for Kilmarnock, they'd decided Bianca would spend the night at Karen's house. She hadn't had much time there recently, spending more nights at Bianca's than her place, so she had a fair amount of tidying up to do before her apartment would be in a fit state for Bianca. "That's fine. Want me to pick you up when you're done or will Alex drop you off?"

"We'll play it by ear. She left for her job site early this morning, so I didn't get a chance to guilt her into it."

They'd worked their way through most of the school now, with only the main hallway left. As they turned the corner, Karen spotted her own turkey, the edges a little curled from hanging on the wall so long. Just the sight of it made her nervous about the trip. How would she make it through another two days without freaking out? As she climbed the ladder, she took a deep breath and gave the speech she'd been avoiding.

"So, listen, I wanted to warn you about my family," Karen said.

"That sounds ominous. Are they vampires? Or werewolves? Is Thanksgiving on a full moon?"

"No vampires or werewolves. It's just…they aren't like you and Alex. They're…kind of cold." Bianca didn't tease or joke. She gave Karen a thoughtful look that was hard to read. "Just don't expect too much."

"Okay."

Bianca's smile held all the warmth the thought of her family lacked, and it somehow made her feel guilty. Maybe she was being too hard on her family.

"The food will be good, though. Especially the oyster stuffing. It's only the company that will leave a lot to be desired."

Bianca's smile dropped a fraction. "I'm still not sure about this oyster stuffing."

"I'm still not sure about the stuffing focaccia, so I guess we're even."

Karen handed over the last of the paper hand turkeys for Bianca to sort, only a minute or two passed before the loud rumble of the first bus arriving signaled the start of their day.

"See you tonight." Bianca dropped a quick, chaste kiss on Karen's lips.

The sound of racing footsteps caught her attention, dragging her focus away from Bianca. Jessica raced up to them and stopped with her hands outstretched.

"What do you think? Cute right?" Jessica said.

Cute was one word for it. She was wearing a knitted sweater with a massive, stitched turkey on the front. Around her neck was a big plastic turkey hanging from what looked like bright red Mardi Gras beads, and matching earrings dangled almost down to her shoulders.

Before Karen could tease her, Bianca gave a little squeal of delight and clapped. "I love it! Where on Earth did you find all that?"

"Etsy can be a magical place."

"Magical is one word for it," Karen said with a laugh.

"Don't mind her," Jessica said, throwing her arm around Bianca's shoulders. "She doesn't appreciate this wonderful holiday like we do."

"Since when do you love Thanksgiving?" Karen asked.

"Since the two of you decorated the school and put us all in the mood for a super fun turkey day."

"I think you look amazing. Your students will love it," Bianca said.

"Thanks. I hope so." Tiny voices filtered through the doors as the students arrived, so Jessica hurried on. "I just wanted to come collect my turkey before the crush."

Bianca sorted through and found Jessica's turkey in the staff folder. It wasn't nearly as gaudy as Roger's, but Jessica had taken a moment to add red construction paper earrings and a yellow construction paper necklace to it. The way she clutched it to her chest after showing it off, it was clear she was as excited by her artwork as the kids were likely to be.

"Want to see what I wrote under my wing?"

Jessica had nearly peeled the folded over paper up when Bianca grabbed her wrist. "Don't do that. You have to wait until the Thanksgiving Day meal."

"Oh, we aren't doing anything special. Brandon's parents are on a cruise and mine are going to see my sister in California. We got turkey frozen dinners and cheap beer to eat in front of the TV during the dog show."

"It doesn't matter. This is tradition. You still have to read it at dinner," Bianca said.

Jessica laughed. "Okay. If you insist."

"Speaking of." Bianca rummaged through the box and pulled out two turkeys, holding them out to Karen. "Here are ours. Can you pack them?"

Karen's hand only shook a little as she took the papers from her. If she only knew what was written inside one of those turkeys. "Sure. I can do that."

CHAPTER TWENTY-FOUR

With that, Bianca turned left toward her classroom, leaving Karen and Jessica to turn right for theirs. The first few students ran past them, backpacks banging and laughter in their wake. Since it was the last day before holiday break, neither Karen nor Jessica stopped them. There was no chance of getting any focus or calm on days like these, so it was better to let them have their fun. Besides, Karen was too nervously excited to care too much about how the students behaved.

"How do you think Thanksgiving with your parents will go?" Jessica asked.

"It'll be a disaster, I'm sure, but as long as Bianca's there, I'll survive."

Clearly, her nerves were showing, because Jessica pulled her to a stop and gave her a searching look. "Why are you freaking out? What's wrong?"

"Nothing's wrong. I'm not sure why I'm so nervous. I'll be fine."

Jessica's stare softened and she put her arm through Karen's. "You always do this, you know."

"Do what?"

"You always build things up to be bad where your family is concerned."

"That's because it always is," Karen said.

"They always come through in the end."

"Name one time."

Jessica squeezed her arm as they walked. "That's no fair, you only tell me the bad stuff. They were super nice when they met me."

"That's because they know your parents are rich and they thought if they were nice enough we'd get back together."

Jessica laughed and said, "Even if that's true, it still means they love you."

"They have a funny way of showing it."

"When they see the two of you together, they'll see what the rest of us see and they'll love Bianca. And if all else fails, lie to them and tell them her parents are rich."

Karen couldn't join in on her laughter. It might be a joke to Jessica, but they weren't her parents. She didn't have to live with the knowledge that the only way she could ensure her family was nice to her girlfriend and respect their relationship was to lie to them. In the end, the whole conversation made her feel ten times worse. She turned to walk away, but Jessica called her name to get her attention.

"Don't expect the worst, okay? Give them a chance to surprise you."

Karen gave her a wave of acknowledgement, but her stomach fell even further. How many chances had she already given them? How many times had they let her down? Jessica's attempts to pretty it up only made it worse. It was tantamount to telling Karen she was overreacting, and she hated to think Jessica wasn't on her side with this.

Her mood did not improve that day. Instead, everything was so much worse. Even though she promised to be there, Jessica did not come to lunch in the teachers' lounge, leaving Karen to eat alone at a table while everyone else was chatting and laughing with friends. Instead of a fun time with her best friend, she got a visit from Roger, dragging Ethan along like a frightened puppy.

"Glad we caught you, Karen." Roger threw an arm around Ethan's shoulders, nearly knocking him to the ground. "Ethan here has volunteered to co-chair the winter talent show with you this year."

Karen had to work to stop grinding her teeth enough to speak, but she managed it. "The show is in less than a month."

"It isn't a lot of time to get him up to speed, but it should take some pressure off you. Plus he's eager to help. Aren't you, Ethan?"

Karen didn't bother listening to Ethan's mumbled assent. What was he playing at? She had done so much work. She had endured the meddling of overeager PTO parents who wanted their child to be the star. She had missed evenings with Bianca. Now Ethan wanted to come in at the last moment so he could get a few kudos from Roger and take a bow onstage like he'd done anything?

"It'll be very helpful next year, but I've got everything set for this year already. Thanks anyway," Karen said.

Ethan blushed and scuttled away, but Roger turned a hard look on her. "Ethan is having a hard time fitting in here, Karen. I thought you would be a lifeline for him."

A wave of guilt crashed over her. Of course, Roger was right. She should be doing more to help Ethan fit in, but not this. Not giving him her thing. Especially after she'd already done so much work. Before she could defend herself, Roger marched out of the room. It felt like every eye was on her as she packed up the remains of her lunch and slunk back to her classroom, the anger and guilt still warring inside her.

Her mood was rock bottom even when Bianca came by after lunch to hand out her class's paper turkeys. The fawning look Benji gave her when he accepted his turkey wasn't cute or pitiable today. It made her want to scream with frustration. The wink Bianca gave her as she left the room did little to crack the shell of annoyance around her, but the crack healed quickly.

As she packed up her classroom for the break, her phone pinged with a series of notifications. Rather than flirting from Bianca, however, it was a grocery list from her mother.

Just a few ingredients I need you to grab while you pick up Dad's beer.

Was there a sly insinuation in there that she had forgotten she was supposed to bring the special beer for her father? She hadn't forgotten. In fact, it was waiting in her fridge at home and she'd had no intention of going to the store on this, one of the worst evenings to pick up groceries. Then there was the fact that her mother hadn't asked, but told her to go to the store. What was she? The pack mule for the family?

Of course she went to the store without complaint. What other choice did she have? The parking lot was packed when she arrived, telling her this would not be a quick trip. That prediction proved out as she elbowed her way through the crowds to grab fried onions and piece together the last of the golden potatoes in the produce bin. Then she hit every red light on her drive home, which was impressive since Bucks Mill only had two stoplights.

Her patience was worn so thin by the time she arrived home that she slammed her front door like a sulking teenager. The framed photograph of sunrise on her special beach spot in Kilmarnock fell off its nail from the impact. The sound of wood cracking as it hit the tile was the last straw.

Karen stood in her entryway and closed her eyes. She took a deep, steadying breath and said out loud to the empty room, "It's fine. Everything will be fine. Just go pack and before you know it, Bianca will be here."

The pep talk actually worked, and she was able to shake her grumpiness while she cleaned her bathroom and packed her clothes. She was so calm, in fact, that it didn't occur to her until her stomach started growling how late it was. She had planned on having dinner with Bianca, now she was starving and there was no sign of her. Karen fired off a quick text before checking her fridge for something to make them for dinner. This time she recognized quickly that there was no response. Where was Bianca and why wasn't she answering Karen's text? The grumpiness she had worked so hard to shed earlier was back with a vengeance.

Karen's annoyance was starting to turn into concern when her doorbell finally rang. When she flung the door open, she was so relieved to see Bianca that she didn't pick up on the details. After the relief dissipated, however, she noticed two things. First, that Bianca was still wearing the clothes she'd worn to school, and second, she didn't have a suitcase with her.

"Sorry I didn't call," Bianca said as she swept into the apartment. Karen tried not to be hurt that she didn't greet her with a kiss or even a hug. "I've been at the ER with Alex."

"Oh no, is she okay? What happened?"

"Yeah, she's fine. She fell off a ladder and cracked a bone in her foot. They put her in a walking cast and told her to stay off it as much as possible for the next few weeks."

"She must be in a lot of pain. Does she need anything?"

Bianca kept her back to Karen and her eyes on the countertop. Her body language was so strange. Was Karen getting the whole story? "No, they gave her some pills and she says she's fine. It isn't a bad break. She's had worse."

"That's good news."

Bianca was quiet for a long time, so Karen guessed what was coming even before she spoke. "She's not up to a nine-hour drive to Boston, and I can't leave her alone on Thanksgiving. I can't go to your family's."

Karen swallowed hard, forcing herself not to break down even though everything inside her wanted to. "I'm sorry about Alex. But she's up to a two-hour drive, right? She can come with us. She'll have the whole back seat to stretch out."

"No. It's too late to call and ask and Alex hasn't been invited."

The explanation had come too quickly and there was an odd formality to it that was so unlike Bianca. "My parents are cold, but they aren't Victorian. They won't refuse her because they didn't offer an official invite. I'm sure they won't be upset to have Alex along. There's always plenty of food and they have plenty of space."

Bianca turned an angry glare on her. "She's already upset about missing our family's dinner. She doesn't want to be a third wheel. Plus, she's tired and we'd have to leave early tomorrow morning."

"Okay, well what if we—"

"Why are you pushing so hard on this? I'm sorry, but I have to stay home with my sister. That's just how it is."

Karen took an involuntary step back in the face of so much unexpected hostility. She could understand Bianca being worried about her sister, but why was she being so angry and unkind about it. All of her frustration and annoyance from the day boiled over, now laced with a heavy helping of embarrassment. Not only had she made this grand plan to declare her love during dinner, with Bianca bailing at the last minute her family would obviously think either she made up a girlfriend or that the relationship wasn't that big a deal if she would cancel. It was all too much. Suddenly she was matching Bianca's anger with her own.

"Why am I pushing? Maybe because I thought this was as important to you as it was to me. Maybe because this is just the latest of so many examples of how you've put Alex before me."

Bianca's voice was deadly calm when she said, "That's not fair. She's my sister."

"And I'm your girlfriend, but you don't treat me like that."

"How can you say that?"

"Because it's so obvious. Any time you're upset and want a shoulder to lean on, you go to her. You never come to me."

"If this is about the day I got the email from Frank, I explained that. I couldn't handle going through the whole sordid history of my divorce. It was too much."

"It's not just that one time. That was just the most recent." Karen was warming into her anger now. She paced back and forth in front of the door as she growled out her grievances. "What about the time the fifth grader shouted at you or when those parents complained about your curriculum? It's any time you need to vent, you do it to her, not me."

"I can't be everything for you all the time. My love for my sister is not a threat to our relationship."

"Sometimes I wonder how much of a relationship it is. You give her all your emotion and you give me nothing. Do you really want a girlfriend at all?"

Silence rang in the apartment for a long time. She hadn't meant to say that. Everything just built and built until she couldn't hold it in anymore. That fear that had been tickling the back of her brain from their first afternoon together burst out of her. She was half ashamed of her outburst, half relieved she'd finally spoken it out loud. The longer the silence stretched, however, the less she was sure it was the right thing to do.

Bianca's eyes hadn't left her since they'd started arguing, and now they hardened with resolve. She took a step forward and held her fists at her sides, jutting her chin out like a child delivering a speech. "I told you from the start that I needed time. You said you were okay with that, but I see now that you weren't. I have done everything in my power to make you feel special, but you insist on holding me accountable for everything other people have done to hurt you in your life. I'm not perfect, I know that, but this is what I can offer you right now. That's either enough for you, or it isn't."

Karen wanted to respond, but she couldn't drag enough oxygen into her lungs to form words. Or thoughts for that matter. Bianca dropped her chin and relaxed her fists, then she marched past Karen without another word or touch and left the apartment. Karen heard the sound of the door click shut and Bianca's footfalls on the creaky wooden stairs. She heard the door to the parking lot swing open and crack lightly against the wall. Whether the wind had caught it as usual or Bianca had slammed it, she wasn't prepared to say.

Karen continued standing, staring at the spot where Bianca had been, for a long time. She should follow after Bianca. Chase her down so she didn't leave. But what would either of them say? They'd both already said quite enough. Too much. She was hurt and worried and she didn't want to say anything else she might regret.

Instead, she moved numbly around the apartment, turning off lights. She moved her suitcase from the bedroom to the entryway next to the front door. She had intended to go to bed but could not imagine a time when she had been less likely to fall asleep. Eventually, she walked over to her couch and sat down in the dark.

CHAPTER TWENTY-FIVE

Since she'd become an adult, Karen had joined the tradition of Petersen women getting up early on Thanksgiving morning to make homemade cinnamon rolls and get a head start on pies for dinner. The men also woke up early, but they went fishing. The best time of day to catch catfish was sunrise, though Karen suspected her father and brother at least fell asleep the moment they cast out. Their absence, however, gave the women plenty of space to roll out dough and measure out spices. Coffee always flowed freely, as did gossip.

This year, however, the process was nearly silent. Karen performed her usual task of rolling up the prepared rolls and cutting them for their final proofing before baking, but her mother and sister-in-law were definitely avoiding eye contact. They'd acted the same way the previous evening when Karen was making the dough. She'd been alone in the kitchen then, and she had the distinct impression everyone had been talking about her behind her back. A kindly voice in the back of her head argued that they were worrying about her. It was probably a little of both.

She'd arrived later than planned on Wednesday and the whole family had come out to greet her. She'd never gotten that treatment before, and that made the explanation that Bianca wouldn't be joining them both awkward and chilly. There had been a long, humiliating moment of quiet before her mother had bustled them all inside out of the cold wind. Her mother made a halfhearted attempt to get an explanation from Karen, but everyone could see she was upset and they let it go. It was probably evident that she hadn't slept and had spent the entire drive crying. The crying was why she'd been late. She'd stopped at a gas station to clean her face and give herself a stern talking to, but the desire to turn her crappy car back toward her crappy apartment and her crappy everyday life had been tough to overcome. It would have been even more embarrassing to not show up herself, so she'd continued on.

As usual, the smell of cinnamon and sugar baking into bread drew the men back inside just as the rolls were coming out of the oven. There was a relieved sort of bustling around as they removed coats and boots and accepted new mugs of coffee. Karen ignored it all, focusing unnecessary attention on the process of spreading icing over the rolls.

"The fish weren't biting this morning?" Angela said.

"What? Oh. Umm…no. They were sluggish this Thanksgiving," her father said.

There was something in his halting tone that made Karen look up. This time she actually caught her father shoot her mother a meaningful look and a nod in her direction. When he saw that Karen had caught him, he blushed bright red and took a gulp of his coffee. Since it was fresh from the pot and piping hot, he yelped and spit it back into the cup. Normally that would earn a teasing poke in the ribs from her brother and laughter all around, but no one laughed. No one teased. No one looked at her.

Karen was caught in a swirl of emotion, trying to decide if she wanted to burst into tears or scream bloody murder. She was equally furious that they were treating her like she might break at any moment and that they couldn't find the right words to make her feel better. They never knew the right words, though. She had always felt like a stranger in this group. Apparently, she always would.

"I'm going to my cottage to unpack," Karen said. "I'll be back in a while to start the stuffing."

"Don't you want a cinnamon roll, dear? They smell incredible," her mother said.

"I'm not hungry."

Before anyone else could speak, Karen made her escape through the kitchen door and down the path to the guest cottages. A cold front had brought a snap of winter to the air earlier in the week and had hit its stride. The wind whipped off the bay with the force of a slap. Karen let it push her around. She let it cut through her thin sweater and jeans. She reveled in the cold because that discomfort was nothing to the staring, pitying looks of her family.

Why had she come here? Why had she thought this would be better than a pitiful, lonely meal in her apartment? It's not like these people meant anything to her. Not enough to try making her feel welcome and loved when she was so low. All she was to them was the person who fixed the leaky roof and kneaded bread dough. She was a worker, not a confidant. Just like she was to Bianca.

Thinking of Bianca was a mistake. Not that she had been far from Karen's thoughts since she'd slammed the apartment door shut Tuesday night, but at least she had been quiet for a moment. But thinking of her brought her right up to the surface and all the pain with it. She had so been looking forward to having Bianca here to make her feel special. Be a buffer between the callous disregard of her family and the softer parts of Karen's heart.

Karen pushed through the door of her cottage just as the hot wave of shame washed over her. Was her embarrassment about her reaction to Bianca's canceling plans or the way her family looked at her when she pulled up to the house alone? There had been a moment while she explained Bianca's absence, she was almost certain of it, when her brother had smirked in a way that seemed to say he had never expected Bianca to show up. That smirk had devastated her, but it was nothing compared to the way Bianca had looked at her when she'd said Bianca was using her for sex. She had felt it at the time. Hell, she'd felt it for weeks, but now she wondered if that was just her lack of self-confidence getting in her way. Had she ruined the chance of something amazing with Bianca for nothing? The thought had kept her up all night for two days and she was now physically ill with worry.

One thing Karen knew, she would drive herself up the wall if she didn't talk about this. She couldn't talk to her family—they'd never been people she could confide in—so she reached for her phone. Jessica answered on the first ring.

"Don't tell me you're already mad at your mom," Jessica said with laughter in her voice.

Karen wasn't sure what made her cry. The rush of relief at her best friend's voice or the undercurrent of teasing that always made her feel loved. Maybe it was the muffled sound of the television in the background reminding her that other people were enjoying a normal Thanksgiving because their worlds hadn't crumbled. Whatever it was, the muffled sob was the only answer she could give.

Jessica's voice was calm, but sharp with worry when she spoke again. "Karen? What's wrong? What happened?"

Guilt that she had worried Jessica held the true tears at bay, and she started with an extended apology. It faded quickly into a long, detailed description of the fight with Bianca and the strain with her family. When she had it all out, she honestly felt a sliver better, but exhaustion filled that space inside her. She leaned back against the headboard and let out a deep breath.

"That's a lot. Honey, I'm so sorry," Jessica said.

"I just can't believe this is happening," Karen said. "Everyone else has their person and I don't. I thought I did, but I don't know. I can't help feeling like I'll never have anyone."

"Sweetie, you always have me."

Karen was just feeling terrible enough to pour salt in her own wound. "Come on. You have Brandon."

"I can care about more than one person, you know?" There was teasing in Jessica's words, but they still felt like a lie.

"But for how long?"

Now Jessica sounded frightened herself. "What does that mean?"

"Nothing. Never mind. Forget I said it."

"Oh no, we're not doing that. Talk to me."

Karen closed her eyes and let the pain in her chest radiate out. "I know how these things go. Best friends drift apart when one gets married. They want to spend less time with their friend and more time with their person. It's happening now. That's why I keep inviting Brandon to stuff. I thought if he was a part of our hanging out then I wouldn't lose you."

Silence filled the line for a long time. Had she done it again? Had she lost the other most important person in her life? Her track record this week was just about perfect.

Finally, Jessica spoke and, to Karen's surprise, she didn't sound angry. "You've felt this way for a while, haven't you?"

"Yeah."

"I knew you were upset about the sunflowers and the pumpkin thing."

"And you never met me for lunch in the lounge on Tuesday," Karen said.

"Shit. I forgot."

"Yeah."

"Look, sweetie, that isn't about you. I...have this thing going on."

"What thing?" Jessica didn't immediately respond. She was probably pushing too hard. "I'm sorry. You don't have to tell me."

"I want to tell you, I just don't know how." Jessica sighed and then said in a rush, "I'm worried I'm losing myself. I love Brandon with all my heart, but I don't want to turn into his twin or his arm candy and sometimes I worry that I'm letting myself get swallowed up in his personality."

"He does have a big personality."

Fortunately, Jessica laughed along with her. "Right? So much."

"But you love that about him."

"I do. I really do. But when I'm with you, I just get to be me before I was with him. It's like a reset that keeps me Jessica. I want that and I need that, but I also really like hanging out with my husband."

That was how she felt with Bianca. She could easily fall into the same pattern. "I get that."

"That's why I don't want him to come along with you and me, but I also sometimes can't drag myself away."

"That makes sense," Karen said.

"I promise to be better, though. I haven't been fair to you and I'm sorry."

"I haven't been fair either. I probably should have said something before."

"Yeah, you should have. You can trust me, you know? You can tell me when I'm a jerk," Jessica said.

"I'll try."

"This is supposed to be about you and Bianca though. How are you feeling now?"

"Awful."

"That's to be expected. You had your first fight."

"What if it's our last fight?" Karen had held back that fear, but she had to say it now.

"It won't be."

"How can you be so sure?"

"Duh. Because I've seen you two together. You two are going to make it. I know it."

Karen said, "I'm glad you're so confident."

"I'm also right."

"Always."

After hanging up, she didn't exactly feel better, but she felt able to face the world. Deciding she might as well be true to her excuse, Karen unpacked the suitcase that her Wednesday afternoon malaise made her avoid. It didn't take long and her clothes took up a depressingly small fraction of the closet and dresser. She dropped her computer bag on the small desk, intending to plug in her laptop, but her hand landed instead on the pair of paper hand turkeys. The sight of them sucked the last of the energy from her and she dropped onto the edge of her bed. A pit of emptiness like she'd never known opened inside her chest.

The longer the project had gone, the more elaborate the turkey decorations had gotten. Most of the fifth graders had added tennis shoes to theirs. The youngest students had tried to decorate but had less skill, and many had turned out like abstract works of art. Glitter pens had been deployed to excess among a group of the younger teachers. Karen's turkey, being the first, had been less elaborate. Still, she was neither the jewelry nor the glitter type, so she would probably have made the turkey just like this one even with the pressure of other artists. She was a simple woman with simple tastes and she liked her turkey. Vanilla with the bits of cookie dough well-hidden.

She could still feel the swooping lift of her stomach when she'd written the message inside. She'd felt brave and scared and certain all at once. Sitting there, alone on the neatly made bed with her distant parents whispering about her in the main house, she wished she didn't still feel the same way she had when she'd confessed her love on a scrap of brown construction paper. She wished she'd been mad at Bianca or hurt enough to make her break up with her. She wasn't, though. Far from it. The emptiness she felt whenever she and Bianca were apart only reinforced the knowledge that she was in love. Truly, madly, deeply, and oh so painfully in love.

But what about Bianca? Was she feeling like this? Probably not. She was with Alex, the person she shared everything with. Her pain and joy and disappointment. Alex was the shoulder Bianca leaned on. The arm that supported her when couldn't stand on her own. She was everything for Bianca that Karen wanted to be. They were probably having an amazing time. Making a dinner for two and preparing to watch the parade on TV.

No, Bianca probably wasn't feeling empty like Karen and that was the whole problem. That was always Karen's problem. Just like Bianca said, everyone in her life had let her down. She'd thought that trend had ended, but apparently not.

Karen arranged the two turkeys side by side on the night table by her bed. They had curled slightly from being taped to the wall, right between a heating vent and a bank of fluorescent lights. They wouldn't stand up against the lamp, no matter how she tried to arrange them. Bianca's turkey kept slipping down and sometimes falling off the table. It felt like a metaphor for their relationship. Karen's turkey perched upright, waiting for Bianca's to stay beside her.

Eventually, she gave up and put them both down flat on the surface of the table. Sometime during the arrangement of the decorations, she started crying. Not crying. Sobbing. Bianca's words during their fight kept coming back to her. The way Bianca had stood in her kitchen and said "this is what I can offer right now." There'd been a look in her eye that Karen had read as a challenge. Now she realized it was more in the manner of a plea. A desperate request for Karen to tell her what she had to offer was enough. But Karen hadn't said that and Bianca had left.

"Oh God, what have I done?"

Karen wasn't entirely sure she said the words out loud. If she had, they'd been swallowed into one of the endless sobs she couldn't hold back.

She'd done to Bianca exactly what her ex-husband had done. She'd made Bianca believe she wasn't worth fighting for. Wasn't enough. She'd been hurt and she'd lashed out at Bianca in return. She'd be frightened and insecure and she'd done the one thing she never wanted to do. She loved Bianca and Bianca loved her back. Because the bottom line—the thing she knew more than anything else—was that Bianca was her person. They were each other's person and she might have ruined that because she was selfish.

She curled up on the bed and let herself cry like she'd never cried before. She lost track of time as she swam in tears and indecision. She may even have cried herself to sleep, because she jumped when she felt a soft hand on her back. For a wild moment, she thought it might be Bianca, but when she looked up it was her mother's face looking down at her. There was a softness there that Karen could never remember seeing. A softness she'd craved to see there her whole life. Her mother pulled her up off the mattress into her arms and Karen fell apart all over again.

Even when she ran out of tears, her mother didn't let her go. She held her quietly, one hand stroking her back and her cheek resting on Karen's head. Eventually, her mother spoke quietly, not letting her go. "Will you tell me now what's going on?"

As she told the story, Karen felt herself falling into old habits. She started to smooth over the ways she was sensitive about being ignored by her loved ones, but it quickly became clear that she couldn't tell the whole story without admitting the ways her parents had opened the wound to start with. Especially since she had to be vague in the extreme about the way she and Bianca hurried into their sexual relationship.

"Oh, honey, it's just one dinner. Why did you put so much pressure on this weekend?" her mother asked.

The patronizing tone made Karen want to scream. "It isn't just a dinner, Mom. Don't you see why I'm so hurt? Don't you understand why I want one—just one person in my life—to put me first?"

"Sweetheart—"

Karen wouldn't let her speak. Couldn't let her make excuses. Maybe if she hadn't let this fester for so long, she wouldn't have taken it all out on Bianca. "You don't get it. It's everyone. Jessica cancels on me every time we make plans."

"She's got her husband and—"

"It's not just her. What's your excuse? You and Dad?"

Her mother flinched away as though she'd been slapped. "What do you mean?"

"You know what I mean. Derek is the only one you've ever cared about. He gets all your attention and all your love. I'm just here to do your chores so you can take the boys out on the boat and brag about how much money Angela makes. You've never once said you're proud of me. You've never once asked about my life. I show up without my girlfriend and you just shrug and move on."

"We didn't want to upset you by bringing it up. You've been so obviously heartbroken about it."

Karen jumped to her feet, throwing up her arms in frustration. "I was heartbroken about it. I am heartbroken about it. Didn't it occur to you that I would want to talk to my mom?"

She expected her mother to argue. To make excuses. She hadn't expected her to stare at the toes of her shoes and speak in a voice watery with emotion. "I should have. I know that. I just…didn't know how."

All the anger and frustration leaked out of Karen, returning her to her new normal feeling of emptiness. She dropped back onto the mattress and stared at the toes of her own shoes. What a picture they must have made. Two grown women not knowing how to look at or talk to each other.

Her mother spoke first, a gentleness Karen had never heard from her coloring her voice. "I know your father and I haven't been the most attentive. The truth is your brother couldn't fight his way out of a wet paper bag. We've always had to take care of him. But you're so capable and strong. We knew we didn't have to worry about you."

Karen's laughter sounded bitter, even to her own ears. "Well, not worrying about me felt a whole lot like you not caring about me."

Her mother made a quiet sound that sounded somewhere between a sob and a cry of pain. Karen looked over and saw tears running like a river down her mother's face. It was heartbreaking and wonderful in a tragic way.

Without warning, her mother reached out and grabbed both her hands. She squeezed them hard and ran her thumbs over Karen's knuckles. "I'm so sorry, sweetheart. I never meant to make you feel that way. Your father never meant to either. Oh, darling, you're so wonderful and special. I'm so sorry."

The way she was breaking down and apologizing, Karen felt awful that she made her mother feel that way. Part of her—the old part who wanted to please everyone else and never mention her own feelings—wanted to take back the words. She forced herself not to. No matter how uncomfortable it was, she had to be true to her feelings now or she never would be.

All Karen could manage was a nod and a watery smile, but apparently that was enough. Her mother pulled her into a tight hug and started crying all over again. Karen joined in and, while all this crying was starting to give her the devil of a headache, it felt good to get all this out. Like cleaning out an old wound.

Sitting up straight and wiping the tears from her cheeks, her mother put her stern face back on despite the puffy eyes. "Now I know it's a bit late for me to be butting in, but I'm your mother and it's my job to talk some sense into you. You need to fix this thing with Bianca."

"Mom…"

"No. No, young lady. I will not have you lose the best thing that ever happened to you because you have a couple of substandard parents and a flighty best friend."

She probably should have argued that they weren't exactly substandard parents, but there was a look in her mother's eye that said she wasn't going to put up with arguments. Instead, she dropped her eyes back to the toes of her shoes and admitted, "I don't know how."

"Well, for starters, you can get yourself back to Bucks Mill and start groveling."

"I wouldn't know what to say."

"Don't be silly," her mother said in that tone that refused to accept argument. "You're not as brainless as your brother. You know exactly what to say, and if you don't now, you will the moment you see her. That's how love works."

The tears came again, no matter how much Karen wanted them to stop. She could barely speak her fear out loud, but she knew she had to. "What if she doesn't want me anymore?"

Her mother rubbed a strong hand across her shoulders and the pressure and compassion of it was almost too much to bear. "If she didn't love you as much as you love her, she wouldn't be so hurt right now, would she? Go on, dear. Go get your girl."

The thought wasn't exactly happy, but it lit a flickering flame of hope in her chest. She grabbed her keys off her bedside table and ran to the door before she lost her nerve.

She stopped with her hand on the knob and said, "Mom?"

"Yes, dear?"

"I'm thankful for you, too, you know."

"I've never doubted it for a moment. One day I'll be better at showing that."

CHAPTER TWENTY-SIX

Karen was driving far too fast for the old engine in her beat-up car. It was Thanksgiving Day and she'd left her parents' house before most people were up for breakfast, so there was very little traffic even on the interstates. She made incredible time, but the closer she got to Bucks Mill, the more terrified she became.

As soon as the blue-purple forms of the mountains appeared in front of her, the fear set in. She kept telling herself Bianca was too good and kind to refuse her a second chance, even if she didn't deserve one, but she couldn't quite make herself believe it. It helped when she set her teeth and determined she would find a way to earn that chance. She would happily spend the rest of her life earning it. She probably shouldn't analyze too closely the spark of joy that lit when she thought about spending the rest of her life with Bianca, even if she did spend it groveling.

She pulled her car to a stop, parking in front of Bianca and Alex's house far before she was ready. She sat there, hands still on the steering wheel, staring at the front door for a creepily long time. She took a deep breath, then hopped out of the car and practically ran to the front door. That kept her from chickening out, and she rang the doorbell before she had really decided what to say.

It felt like an eternity, standing there, waiting for Bianca to appear in front of her. She took another deep breath, then another. Her nerves started to get the better of her as she analyzed why it was taking her so long to come to the door. The rattle of the chain and lock really started to freak her out.

"You can do this. You can do this. You really can do this," she whispered to herself.

When the door opened, however, it wasn't Bianca standing in front of her. Alex was wearing a worn green flannel shirt and sweatpants, with one leg pulled up to show the boot on her foot. She leaned back, resting on her crutches and staring stone-faced at Karen.

"Alex...I, um, look I'm really sorry. I'm sure Bianca told you about our fight and I hope you know I wasn't trying to be dismissive of your injury or anything. I'm sure it came across that way and I'm really, really sorry for that."

Stumbling through that first apology relieved some of her fears, but they all returned in spades when Alex didn't say a word, just continued to stare at her.

"Um, I...Well, your friendship is super important to me. Not just because you're Bianca's sister, but because I don't have a lot of queer friends. Especially masc lesbian friends. So I really hope you can forgive me, because our friendship is almost as important to me as my relationship with Bianca."

"So your relationship with my sister is important to you," Alex said.

"Yes, absolutely." She was so relieved that Alex spoke to her, she could have cried. In fact, as she spoke, she felt the tears close to the surface again. "It's the most important relationship in my life. That's why I was so upset when she canceled. I want so desperately to share her with my family. So they can see how special she is, too."

Alex's eyebrows came together and her scowl was so similar to Bianca's it made Karen's heart hurt. "She is special and she deserves to be treated that way."

"She absolutely does and I failed at that. I want to apologize and try to make it up to her."

The tears came then. Not the sobs wracking her body like when her mother held her, but to her horror, they made her bottom lip tremble. She was so embarrassed to cry like that in front of Alex that she almost turned away. To her surprise, Alex reached out with one arm and pulled her into a hug.

"Everything's going to be okay," Alex said.

Karen wrapped her arm around Alex to return the hug, careful not to pull her off balance or make her drop a crutch. If Alex could forgive her—comfort her even—maybe Bianca could forgive her too?

Alex pulled out from the hug and hopped back onto her crutches. "Truth is, Bianca and I have always had this twin-like closeness. It's screwed up things for both of us once or twice, but that's Bianca's story to tell, I think."

"Do you think I could come inside to grovel to her face-to-face?"

Alex slapped her on the shoulder in that bro sort of way and gave her a pitying look. "Sorry, pal. Bianca realized she'd been an idiot around the same time you did, I think."

Karen tried to make sense of the words, but couldn't really keep up. The headache from crying all day was really starting to blossom and she hadn't eaten much in a couple of days now. "What do you mean?"

"I mean she left a couple hours ago to drive to your family's place so she could do this same begging for forgiveness on the doorstep dance."

Karen just stared at her. Bianca wasn't here. She couldn't apologize because Bianca was gone. Dimly, it registered that Bianca was coming to her to apologize, and that seemed to indicate her own apology would be well-received. If she was ever able to give it, of course.

Karen groaned and leaned against the doorframe, and almost immediately, her cell phone rang in her back pocket. While Alex laughed good-naturedly, Karen looked at the screen. Her mother's face stared back at her.

"Hello?" Karen said, her voice hollow with exhaustion.

"Hi, sweetheart." Her mother sounded trapped between nervous and confused. "Are you still driving?"

"No, I made it back to Bucks Mill."

"Oh good. Traffic wasn't too bad then." After an awkward beat, her mother said in an extra cheery tone, "Bianca's just arrived looking for you."

Karen closed her eyes and lightly tapped her forehead against the doorframe. "I know. I just got to her place and found out she isn't here."

"What would you like us to do?" her mother asked.

Karen took a moment to think. The kindness in her mother's voice and the conspiratorial firmness made her realize she'd been stupid. All her fears about what Bianca would think of her family and how they would treat her were ridiculous. She wanted Bianca in her life. In all of her life. The messy parts, the parts that were still growing, and the parts that had begun healing. Bianca would fit into all those parts because the two of them fit together.

"Just be nice to her. I'm on my way," Karen said.

"Well, we had planned on poking her with spears and locking her in the basement, but I suppose we could welcome her into our home and show her baby pictures of you instead," her mother deadpanned.

The unexpected humor made her burst out laughing. "Thanks, Mom. See you soon." She looked up to see Alex smiling and shaking her head. "Oh, and, Mom? There'll be one more for dinner, okay?"

Alex gave her a wary look as she hung up the phone. "What did that mean?"

"Pack an overnight bag. You get to try oyster stuffing for the first time."

❖

Like most houses on the bay, the Petersens used crushed oyster shells for their driveway and parking area. They made a completely uniquely quiet crunching noise under Karen's tires. She'd never been happier to hear it in her life. If she'd thought the drive to Bucks Mill that morning had been full of fear and anxiety, it was nothing compared to the drive back. With Alex stretched out in the passenger seat, she couldn't be outwardly nervous. That meant her internal angst had been doubled at least. Now, with the main house in sight, she broke out into a cold sweat.

Parked in her normal spot close to the house stood Alex's massive, fire-engine red pickup truck. It was jarring to see it there and realize Bianca had driven that monster all that way. Karen hadn't even realized she could drive. She figured Alex picked her up out of necessity even if the rides she got from Karen were intended to prolong their time together.

Beside her, Alex let out a long breath. "My baby's in one piece."

"She doesn't drive much, huh?"

"Never." Alex turned to her with a conspiratorial grin. "It can't really be a surprise to you that my sister is a passenger princess."

Karen couldn't quite meet her eye and she felt the heat on her cheeks that made Alex laugh. She smiled, but couldn't quite bring herself to laugh. It was weird to be joking about that with her girlfriend's sister, but more than that, she was scared of what was to come.

She stared at the truck but made no move to open the car door or go inside. Alex reached out and squeezed her shoulder.

"It's going to be okay," Alex said. "Bianca's nuts about you. The two of you can figure this out."

"You know I'm nuts about her, too, right?"

Alex nodded and Karen expected some sort of reference to all the loud sex they'd had in her house, but she didn't say it. She just kept that friendly hand on Karen's shoulder. Was this what having a sibling was supposed to be like? What she wouldn't give to have this relationship with her own brother. Maybe if everything worked out like Alex expected it would, she'd get to find out what it was like to have a sister.

"What if I can't do this?" Karen asked. "What if I'm too old or set in my ways to make a relationship work? I want this more than anything else and I've already screwed it up. What if I'm too damaged?"

Alex kneaded her shoulder, reminding Karen again of how affectionate a family they were. Another thing missing from her life. Another thing she craved and loved so much in Bianca. When they were together, Bianca was always touching her, and not just in a seductive way. She always had a hand on Karen's knee or arm. It was so comforting and intimate in a way she had never known.

"Everyone's damaged. Damage doesn't make you unlovable. In fact, you're by far the least damaged person in this car. Bianca doesn't mind my damage, so I know it's not a dealbreaker with you."

Karen watched Alex's face grow cold and distant. She had the burning desire to hear Alex's story, but now wasn't the time. She needed to get inside the house and talk to Bianca. And possibly save her from the awkwardness of her parents.

The kitchen door opened and Karen's dad stuck his head out, most likely worried about Karen sitting in the car for so long without coming in. She gave her a thumbs up and opened her car door.

"Thanks, Alex. It means a lot that you support me in this."

"I'm supporting my sister. Sometimes she can be really stubborn. Besides, I like you a lot better than that douchebag she married."

With a laugh, Karen said, "At least I got that going for me. Come on inside."

Navigating the oyster shells on crutches was tricky, so their trip to the house was slow going. Just before they got there, Alex stopped and looked at Karen skeptically. "That oyster stuffing thing was a joke, right?"

Karen slapped her shoulder in that bro way Alex always did to her. "Not even a little bit. Trust me, you'll love it."

"You must be Alex. Nice to meet you, I'm Karen's dad, Arthur."

Alex balanced on one crutch to shake his outstretched hand. "Thanks for having me."

"The more the merrier. You like football, Alex?"

"How could you tell?"

He waved her inside. "Bianca's told us a few stories. Come on in, second half just started."

Karen hesitated on the stoop, taking a deep breath before taking the plunge. The first thing she heard when she entered the kitchen was a long burst of laughter from her mother. She kept up the giggling as she poked her fingers into a deep pan. Bianca was beside her, wearing a silly apron covered in drawings of fish and crabs, directing her mother's work. She idly noted that her mother was poking at some bread dough covered in a load of olive oil.

Karen didn't give the dish much attention, though. She couldn't keep her eyes off Bianca. She was the woman Karen was so desperately in love with, but she was different somehow. The light in her eyes when she teased Karen wasn't quite there. Her face was drawn, like she hadn't been sleeping any better than Karen had. Still, that special spark that was so unique to Bianca could never be dimmed.

As though she could feel eyes on her, Bianca looked up, her gaze zeroing in on Karen. All the air went out of the room and Karen struggled to breathe. She always did when Bianca looked at her like that. Like she was the only person in the room.

It wasn't until her mother cleared her throat that Karen realized the room had gone quiet. She blinked and looked around to find everyone staring at her.

"Welcome back, honey. Bianca was just teaching me how to make her Thanksgiving stuffing focaccia," her mother said.

Karen wasn't interested in looking away from Bianca to give her attention to the bread. "It looks great."

Bianca's smile grew slowly on her lips. "Just wait until we bake it."

The smile alone gave Karen the strength to have the conversation she knew was coming. No matter what, she couldn't live without at least trying to get that smile back. To have Bianca love her.

"Mom, is there time before dinner for me to take Bianca for a walk on the beach?" Karen asked.

"Of course. The turkey needs another hour at least. Besides, we have to get Alex settled, don't we?"

Alex, who was standing behind the couch, said, "Thanks so much for having me, Mrs. Petersen."

"Certainly, dear. Would you rather have wine and gossip or beer and football?"

"Definitely football."

Bianca laughed at her sister as she untied her apron, then she took Karen's hand and led them out the kitchen door.

Wind cut in off the water and tugged at Karen's top knot. A few strands came loose to swirl in front of her eyes. Bianca had pulled her hair together and tied it up with a scarf from around her neck. It was actually the first time Karen had seen her with her hair up, and it leant her a completely new look. She liked being able to see the graceful curve of Bianca's neck, and the scarf whipped around in a blur of color.

They hadn't spoken since leaving the house, even when they stopped at the border between grass and sand to remove their shoes and, in Karen's case, socks. Bianca carried her sandals dangling from her fingertips. Karen had tied the laces of her tennis shoes together and slung them across her shoulder. She'd rolled up her jeans into loose cuffs just above her ankles. The wind blasted stinging sand against her skin. The back of Bianca's skirt trailed across the ground, picking up a fine layer of sand as they walked.

Karen noted all the details with a manic need to focus on something, anything other than the silence between them. She should start the conversation. She was the one who needed to apologize, so it was up to her to start the groveling. Since she had no idea where to start, she just focused on the details. Like how Bianca watched the waves and didn't look at her. Or how they weren't holding hands, but were walking close enough that their fingers occasionally brushed. Bianca wasn't pulling her hand away or shifting her path to put more space between them, but she wasn't reaching out either. What did that mean? On that note, what did it mean that Bianca had driven all the way out here?

There was only one way to get the answers to the questions buzzing around inside her brain, and she was about to ask when Bianca finally spoke. "It's beautiful out here. And peaceful. Why does it look so familiar?"

That threw Karen off-kilter. She hadn't expected to talk about anything other than the fight. When Bianca finally looked over at her, she managed to kick her brain back into gear and answer. "I have a picture of sunrise here in my apartment."

Bianca turned back toward the water, then she closed one eye and swept her fingertips in an arc, drawing the coastline. "Right there. With the sun coming up over the water just there. This is a special spot for you, isn't it?"

Karen swallowed hard. Bianca was right, of course. She'd never shown this spot to anyone before. Even her parents and brother, who had seen that photograph and must have seen this spot of sand and water, hadn't recognized the importance. Bianca had, though. Bianca always did.

She turned back to Karen and said, "Thank you for bringing me here."

And just like that, they were on the same team again, and it felt really good. "Thank you for coming. I like having you at all the places that make me happy."

Bianca came to an abrupt stop. "Are you happy?"

"I am. In fact, I'm happier now than I've ever been." The desperation was back. This was it. They were talking about it now. It was time to be brave. She took Bianca's hand in both of hers and dropped to her knees to beg. "I was an idiot and I'm so sorry for how I acted. I was selfish and unkind and insecure. I hope you can forgive me for how I acted."

"Stop being an idiot and get up."

It was a bit of an overreaction and Karen felt a little silly, but when she did get back to her feet, she noticed Bianca was blushing. It was such a rare sight, she was left speechless.

"You weren't being selfish or unkind. I was the one who freaked out and took out my insecurity on you," Bianca said.

"What do you mean?"

Bianca stared at their clasped hands. "Last week when we were in bed after being apart so long and I cried, you remember?"

"Of course. It was beautiful."

"It was vulnerable and I don't do vulnerable. I'd gotten that fucking email from my fucking ex and then we were busy and didn't get to see each other. I sort of—I don't know…"

She trailed off and looked back out at the waves crashing against the shore. Karen got the distinct impression she wouldn't finish the thought unless she made her. She reached out and cupped Bianca's cheek, drawing her attention back to them. "It's okay. You can tell me. You're safe with me."

Bianca closed her eyes and a tear fell down her cheek. "I know. That's why I lost it that night with you. I'd just been reminded of a relationship I'd wasted years on. A partner who never once made me feel the way you make me feel every day. It was just so wonderful and I couldn't hold it in."

"It is wonderful. You don't have to hold anything in with me. I want you to share it with me."

"I know you do, but I'm scared. It didn't work out for me last time."

"I understand," Karen said.

"You were right, you know? I haven't been sharing everything with you. I lean on Alex. I always have. Frank was so jealous of how close we are. He said he never could get any attention because I was always attached to Alex's hip."

Karen tried not to see the parallels of how she'd felt Tuesday night, but they were hard to miss.

"When he stopped trying to get my attention, I blamed him. Especially when he left. He said it was my fault and I said it was his, but deep down I knew I shared some of the blame," Bianca said.

"It doesn't give him the right to be an asshole."

"Doesn't it? He wanted the same thing you want now."

Karen stepped closer and held her hands tighter. "I have my own baggage and it wasn't fair of me to put that on you. It's not fair to expect you to be everything to me all the time."

"But you don't understand. It was an excuse. I used Alex as an excuse."

"You didn't push her off the ladder, did you?"

Bianca's smile matched the teasing one Karen wore, but it melted away quickly. "No, but I probably would have. I just took advantage of her being a klutz to do my normal thing."

"What thing?"

"I was holding you at arm's length just like I did to him. Meeting the parents is a big step and I didn't realize how scared I was until it was about to happen. People don't always like me. I'm loud and obnoxious and—"

Karen cut into her speech that descending into rambling. "You're bold and passionate and that's just one of the reasons I love you so much."

Other than the howling wind, everything went quiet. Bianca stared at her with eyes wide and then Karen realized exactly what she'd said. Her heart lurched at having blurted it out that way, but she wasn't afraid of it. Not anymore.

Stepping closer so their noses nearly touched, Karen looked straight into Bianca's eyes. "I love you, Bianca. I love you more than I've ever loved anyone in my whole life. And it isn't just you. I love Alex, too."

Bianca's eyebrows shot up. "Um, is that really what you want to tell me right now?

"You know what I mean. Not like that. I love that in you I found a girlfriend, a new friend, and a family all in one. I can't imagine anything better than a life with you. You're allowed to be close to your sister. You're enough for me just the way you are."

"There's a difference between me being enough and what I can offer being enough."

Karen took a deep breath and steeled herself for the admission she'd been planning during her drive. "I've been having some really important conversations today. Some people I care very deeply about have been honest with me because I was honest with them. That's the part I'm not good at. Being honest with people about what I need."

"What do you need?"

"You. That's all I need." Karen pushed back her fear and plowed on. If she didn't put all her cards on the table now, she would never shake old habits. "When we talked on our first date, you were very honest about your needs. I wasn't honest about mine."

There was concern written deep in Bianca's expression, but she proved her bravery by asking, "Okay. What if we try that conversation again now."

"What do you mean?"

"Would you have still wanted to date me?"

"Yes. Absolutely," Karen said without hesitation.

"What would you have asked for then? What could I have offered to help us avoid this?"

Karen took a moment to think. She didn't want to frighten Bianca, but she had a feeling Bianca was as invested in this as she was. She could be honest, just like she was with Jessica and her mom. She might even get what she needed if she learned to ask for it.

"Those times when you need to pull away. When you can't be vulnerable with me, but need to go to Alex or be alone. Can you just, um, reassure me?"

"What would that look like?"

Karen's palms were wet and her heart was racing. She felt now like she'd felt before when Bianca had pulled away. What would calm her down now? What would calm her down then?

"If you told me something like 'I have to do my own thing right now, but I'm coming back.' I think if I heard something like that—if I knew you were coming back—I'd be okay. I think it would help," Karen said.

The moment she said the words, Karen wanted to take them back. Panic filled her. She had asked for too much. Bianca was bound to say no. She wanted a girlfriend, not someone whose ego she had to babysit. Karen should have just shut up and accepted whatever Bianca had to offer.

Bianca's smile was half sad, half flirty. She reached out and ran a thumb over Karen's forehead. It wasn't until the touch that Karen realized she had scrunched her face up and lines of worry were showing. Bianca's touch smoothed them out.

"You know that's not a lot to ask, right? It's completely reasonable and something I can definitely do."

Karen swallowed hard, not ready to let the hope fill her quite yet. "Really?"

Bianca took both Karen's hands in hers and used them to pull her close. She pressed their joined hands against her chest. "You are allowed to ask for what you need. I did in that conversation and you didn't hate me for it, right?"

"Of course not."

"Then why would I be upset with you for doing the same thing? You're worth fighting for, Karen. You should really start fighting for yourself."

Karen's whole body felt weak, even as her heart felt so light. "I can try. It might take a little time, though."

Bianca pulled her even closer and Karen found herself falling into those coffee-dark eyes. "I guess I'll have to remind you often."

"Does that mean…" Karen had to let the question trail off. Could she ask outright?

Bianca said, "I'm all in. Are you?"

"Absolutely. Yes. Completely." She stopped rambling when the sound of Bianca's light laughter cut in. "I love you, Bianca."

"I love you, too. I love you so much it scares the crap out of me."

"Same here."

"You've got nothing to be scared of. I'm the lucky one. No one has ever been unreservedly on my side before. No one has ever accepted my attachment to my sister and all my assorted weirdness."

"I like your weirdness. Besides, no one has ever really done that for me either. And I don't even have a sibling to lean on since my family are the worst offenders."

"That's just another reason to love you. They haven't always treated you the best, but you love them anyway."

Karen would have argued the point, but then remembered the conversation she'd had earlier with her mother. It felt like a lifetime ago, but it was so new and different to have her mother on her side. Maybe this Thanksgiving would start a brand new life for her in so many ways.

"They're better from a distance," Karen said.

Bianca laughed and then pulled her into a sweet, deep kiss. She forgot about the wind and the cold and everything else the world had to offer. When she pulled back, Bianca cupped Karen's cheek and gave her a moment to let her toes uncurl.

"I won't argue the point," Bianca said. "As long as you give me the chance to find out for myself."

"Sounds like a great plan to me."

CHAPTER TWENTY-SEVEN

After Thanksgiving dinner, the whole family lounged in the living room, sleeping off the turkey and emptying the wine bottles. Since there were limited seating options, Karen sat on the floor, her head in Bianca's lap. Alex was on the loveseat beside her, her booted foot resting on an ottoman. Her parents curled up on the sofa, her nephews between them, both kids more interested in their iPads than the rest of the family. Her sister-in-law was dozing in an armchair after being surprisingly lively at dinner thanks to far more wine than she usually drank. For the first time, Karen could understand why her brother stared at her with heart-eyes from his armchair. She could be charming if she wanted to be.

Karen had taken her hair down to pull it into a neater knot, but Bianca had asked her to keep it down. Once she'd settled on the floor, Bianca finger-combed her hair while they all chatted. The tingling warmth of that repetitive touch was hypnotic. She might have even dozed off herself, because she jumped at a loud bark of laughter from her dad.

Alex sat forward, talking excitedly with her hands as usual. "It's true. The ability to pressure when you're shorthanded is way more critical than a good power play. A shorthanded goal is the best way to break the opponent's spirit."

"In my day, the best way to break a team's spirit was with a right hook, but they don't like fighting in the NHL these days," her dad said.

"A good fight will never go out of style. God, I love the sight of mitts flying and two brutes squaring up against each other. The Bruins haven't had a good fighter in ages."

Karen's dad scooted forward on his seat, earning a grumble from Mason when the movement jostled the iPad out of his hand. When was the last time she'd seen him so engaged? It must've been rare, based on the complacent smile her mother directed at him.

"What are they talking about?" Karen asked Bianca quietly.

"Ice hockey."

"How'd they get on that?"

"They ran out of football talk, so they switched. Alex can talk for hours about any and every sport."

Mason joined the conversation, clearly charmed by Alex. "Is that how you hurt your foot? Playing ice hockey?"

Bianca laughed. "God, no. She can't skate to save her life."

Alex stuck out her tongue at her. "No, not playing ice hockey. I fell off a ladder at work."

"Did you fall from really high up?"

"Not too far. I was coming down the ladder after working on someone's roof."

"You should have Karen do the roof stuff. She replaced the roof on her cottage last summer. She loves doing that stuff," Karen's mom said.

It was sweet how much her mom was trying to impress Bianca on her behalf, but it was making her feel self-conscious, so she demurred. "I don't love it, exactly. I'm just good at it and Derek's afraid of heights."

"Am not," Derek said defensively.

Angela was apparently awake enough to hear, because she laughed. "Are too. I can't even get you to put the star on the Christmas tree."

The boys joined in the laughter and Derek blushed, but he was smiling so he couldn't have been too embarrassed.

"Alex is a professional contractor. She doesn't need any help from an amateur like me," Karen said.

"I don't know. I could use an extra hand around the house come summertime," Alex said.

Her mother sat forward, for all the world as excited as her dad talking about football. "That's a great idea! Then Karen can move out of that tiny apartment and have some room to breathe."

Bianca's hand paused in its course across her scalp and Karen's jaw dropped open. Clearly, her mother didn't realize the pressure she'd just put on them to move in together and Karen didn't want Bianca running for the hills when they'd just patched everything up. "I love my apartment, Mom. Besides, you've never even seen it."

"Wait, what?" Alex's eyebrows scrunched together in confusion. "You haven't seen Karen's place? I thought you've been there a while?"

"Five years," Karen said.

Her dad cleared his throat. "We keep meaning to get up to Bucks Mill."

Her mom broke in. "It's just that we're ocean people, not mountain people."

As the banter continued back and forth, Bianca leaned forward to whisper in Karen's ear, "Are you okay?"

"I'm great. Why?"

"Well, normally you get upset when we talk about how your parents don't give you enough attention."

She was right, of course, but she wasn't this time. What was different this time? Looking around, especially at Alex extolling the virtues of little Bucks Mill, she was pretty sure she knew. She had always felt outnumbered in her family. No one ever noticed her. No one ever coddled her. Now she had a girlfriend who noticed everything and a friend who was taking her side.

Without the bitterness in the way, she realized her parents weren't that bad. Sure, they nagged and maybe even criticized, but it wasn't because they didn't love her. They were just set in their ways and they trusted her to take care of herself. Now she recognized that was their way of showing love and she could accept what they had to offer.

Reaching up, she pulled Bianca into a quick kiss. "Nothing could upset me when you're here, looking at me like that."

Bianca's smile was like the sun, warming her and everything around her. Karen couldn't tear her eyes away. Just that morning she was wondering how they could ever make it work between them. How could it not work when they loved each other so very much?

Alex cleared her throat, dragging them out of their reverie. Looking around, Karen realized everyone was smiling at them. Well, not the boys, they were still killing aliens or whatever on their devices, but the rest of her family were looking at her like they couldn't be happier. Karen was embarrassed, of course, but she was also secretly thrilled. How could she have ever thought they weren't on her side?

Karen's mom slapped her knees and stood up. "Well, Alex dear, do you think you could manage some rickety old beach house stairs on those crutches? I think it's time for bed."

"Um, Mom, there aren't any stairs in my cottage," Karen said.

Alex laughed and everyone else rolled their eyes. Apparently, no one had expected Alex would want to share a tiny cottage with the two of them after that display of affection. If she was honest, Karen was fine with her taking the guest room in the main house. She wanted Bianca all to herself tonight.

"Okay, well, if you're willing to submit to the tender mercies of my parents, that's fine by me," Karen said.

"It's extra fine by me," Bianca said.

Karen felt the heat on her cheeks and she thought even Bianca blushed at the not-so-subtle implications. Derek gave her a little bit of a hard time about it, but he also gave her a wink as he said good night. Before she knew it, Bianca had taken her hand and pulled her out into the night, the glow from her cottage window leading them home.

Karen and Bianca didn't speak as they strolled to their cottage. Bianca held her hand and rested her cheek on Karen's shoulder, and the wind forgot to howl and the ocean forgot to crash as they walked. They moved together without urgency, but it was clear they both felt a certain anticipation for where the night would lead.

For the first time, there was no thin thread of doubt coursing through Karen's desire. They had a long way to go and there would be other fights and other misunderstandings, but now her belief in their future was solid. She knew that she would not wake up in the night wondering if Bianca was using her for sex. For the first time in several nights, she would have her personal furnace in bed with her, so there would literally be no room for cold feet.

Bianca lifted her head so Karen could push open the cottage door. Unsurprisingly, there was an extra suitcase inside now. Her parents must have brought Bianca here when she arrived.

"It's really cute. You stay here every summer?" Bianca asked as she looked around. Just like her first trip to Karen's apartment, she moved around the little building, inspecting the furnishings and decor.

"For a few weeks, yeah, but I never stay the whole summer."

"Let me guess. You come back to Bucks Mill the moment Roger tells you that your classroom is ready?"

Karen shrugged. "You know me."

Bianca turned from the ceramic lighthouse on the end table to look at her. The fire in her eyes made Karen's throat go dry. "Yeah. I do."

With that she turned and sauntered off toward the bedroom. There was no other word for the way she swayed her hips and floated across the floor. Everything Bianca did was a turn-on, but there was nothing more erotic than the seductive way she walked when she wanted Karen to follow. And follow she did.

Karen stayed a few steps behind her to watch her move. Bianca clearly knew she was being watched. She reveled in being watched. As she passed through the door to the bedroom, she stepped out of her sandals, throwing a half-glance over her shoulder. It seemed to state very plainly that she expected Karen to strip as she followed.

They left a trail of discarded clothing behind them as they traveled toward the bed. As usual, Bianca's discards were fewer than Karen's. She rarely wore much in the way of underwear and she never seemed to feel the cold. Within a few steps she was down to nothing but the scarf tying back her hair and the necklaces hanging between her breasts. Karen struggled to peel out of undershirt, bra, and boxers while also watching her bare hips sway.

Bianca stopped at the foot of the bed, waiting with her gaze on the far wall. Karen slid up behind her, circling her waist with both arms to pull their bodies flush.

"I've missed you," Bianca whispered.

"I've missed you, too."

Bianca turned in her arms, settling her palm over Karen's racing heart. "I love you so much. I don't want to go through that ever again."

"Me either, baby."

Bianca led them around the bed to lie down without separating their bodies. She moved like she didn't want a breath of air between them ever again and Karen was happy to do the same. They lay down and twisted into each other, limbs and lips locked into an intricate knot.

They only separated far enough to allow Karen to slip a single hand between their bodies. They moved together, whispering promises and hopes and dreams while they touched. Bianca was unusually quiet that night, her pleasure clearly as intense as always, but wanting to keep the sounds of her pleasure inside the tight bubble they shared. Karen made no noise at all, the stiffening of her muscles and catching of her breath the only indication of her release. It was as though their bodies had decided that this time—the first time they made love rather than had sex—was too sacred for more. Karen had never been more fulfilled than she was in that moment.

As their heart rates slowed and their eyes opened, they connected again in that wordless way. That silence was the sweetest sound of Karen's life. She had been utterly changed.

The chill of late November on the bay finally broke the spell. Goose bumps rose on Bianca's arms and Karen reached to pull the duvet over them. Bianca snuggled close to her, then reached out a hand toward the bedside table. Karen thought she was going to turn off the lamp so they could fall asleep, but instead, she snagged the two paper turkeys.

"We forgot to open them during dinner," Bianca said with a pout.

Trying an imitation of Bianca's sultry tone, Karen said, "I'm ready for another meal."

Bianca rolled her eyes, but did pull her in for a lengthy kiss before handing her a turkey. Karen was about to open it when she realized it wasn't the one she'd written, it was Bianca's.

"You gave me the wrong turkey," Karen said.

Bianca's cheeky smile told her she knew exactly what she'd done. She was already peeling up the tape securing the message Karen wrote all those days ago. She was unaccountably nervous for Bianca to read the words. It didn't make sense, since she'd said them out loud half a dozen times that day, but this was a reminder of the first time.

Bianca's eyes flitted across the words. A sharp intake of breath might have been her preparing to read the words aloud, or it might have been shock at the words themselves. If she had intended to speak, however, she changed her mind. She read the words over and over again, a wide smile on her lips and tears welling in her eyes. Karen pulled her close and kissed her cheek.

Bianca breathed, "You loved me all those weeks ago?"

"I loved you from the moment I saw you across the darkened room at school. I just didn't know how much until that day," Karen said.

Bianca's touch on her cheek was so light, it might have been a breath of wind, but her kiss was firm and sure. After a long moment, she nodded toward the turkey in Karen's hand. Bianca hadn't done anything too extravagant to decorate her turkey, just a couple of Magic Marker necklaces to differentiate it from Karen's. She peeled back the turkey's wing to reveal the message inside, assuming it would say that she was thankful for her sister. Because of her assumption, she had to blink several times to confirm the words she saw were really there.

I'm thankful for Karen, who makes me finally feel like I'm enough. I love you.

Epilogue

"You know there's a reason Alex won't let me do this," Bianca said.

Karen grinned and went back to wiping green paint off the newly painted white trim. Bianca had insisted she could help when Karen announced her plans to paint the kitchen. It was her house, after all, and she wouldn't be the kind of girlfriend who expected Karen to do all the work just because she was the butch one. Karen had argued, but Bianca found very persuasive and sexy ways to make her give in. Maybe Karen should have stood her ground. They'd spent more time cleaning Bianca's mishaps than painting.

"You're a great painter, baby. You just get excited. You can do this," Karen said.

"I don't know if I want to."

Bianca stood with her hip cocked to one side and her paintbrush held limply in one hand. The other hand fanned at her face, trying in vain to ward off the swelteringly-hot July afternoon. Karen's mouth watered at the sight. It was at least ten degrees warmer on the top floor and she for one, appreciated the living room windows that faced due west. Anything to make Bianca shed a piece of clothing or two was good in her book.

"We can't stop now. We aren't even half done with the cutting in. Then we have to roll the walls."

Bianca watched her with a hungry look, knowing full well that neither her eyes nor her mind was on the half-painted walls. She crooked a finger at Karen. "We can at least take a break, right?"

Karen held her brush away from their bodies as she fitted her hips against Bianca's. "Maybe. How long of a break?"

Bianca brushed her lips lightly across Karen's, then slid them around to her ear. "That depends. Are you ready for round two?"

Karen closed her eyes as Bianca dropped kisses down her neck. Her hand slid underneath Karen's T-shirt, her nails scraping against skin. Goose bumps broke out on her skin, and suddenly, completing this project seemed less important. So what if the paintbrushes dried out while they kissed? There were spares in the garage.

They'd only been making out for a few minutes when the front door burst open, banging against the new board and batten coat rack Alex and Karen had installed over spring break. Bianca leapt backward, leaving Karen standing there with her mouth awkwardly open and her heart racing.

"Jesus, Alex. Do you always have to burst into rooms like you're trying to catch me off guard? You know how much I hate that," Bianca said.

"You've had thirty-seven years to get used to it." Alex kicked the front door closed and hung her leather messenger bag on a hook.

"That doesn't make it any less unnerving. You scared Karen."

"She's not the one who yelped like that. Are you?"

Karen shrugged. "A little."

"A two for one. Score," Alex said.

"You're a jerk," Bianca said.

Alex bounded up the stairs and grinned. "At it again? What's that the tenth time I've walked in on your two making out like horny teenagers? It's been months. When are you going to get over the honeymoon phase?"

"We've been working so hard since summer break started we've hardly had a moment to rest, much less act like horny teenagers. We haven't even been out to Kilmarnock yet," Bianca said.

Alex skirted the drop cloths on her way to the fridge for a beer. "What's stopping you? Other than them spending half the summer here with you?"

"We finally got them out from under our feet," Karen said. "As much as I love them, I'm ready for a little time away from my parents."

"Sucks for you then. I'm taking Arthur to a baseball game on Saturday."

Karen grimaced as she grabbed a beer for herself. "It's so weird that my girlfriend's sister is on a first-name basis with my dad."

"No weirder than me walking into my living room just in time to see my sister's tonsils," Alex said.

Bianca stuck out her tongue, but a little zing of joy zipped through Karen. Alex's teasing was her way of showing love, and now that love extended to Karen, too.

"Not to mention getting to hear my sister scream the paint off the walls most nights."

Karen didn't miss the way Alex's teasing smile drifted. The two of them had spent enough time bonding at the backyard fire pit for Karen to know Alex was thrilled to see Bianca happy again. Still, she'd let it slip more than once that it almost made her want to find someone new. Almost. Karen didn't know the full story of Alex's divorce, but Bianca had hinted at lots of infidelity. Alex lost her business up north because of it, so her ex-wife must've done something really gnarly.

"What're you so happy about anyway?" Bianca wrapped an arm around Karen's neck and leaned into her as she studied Alex.

Alex took a long slug of beer and shook her head. It wasn't only Karen Bianca could read like a book. She knew things about Alex's emotions that Alex didn't even know. Apparently, this was how siblings who loved and trusted each other worked. Seeing the dynamic had finally kicked Karen into gear on building something more meaningful with Derek. It would be a long time until they were at this place though.

"I just landed a big job right here in Ashcroft Court," Alex said.

Karen leaned into Bianca. The two of them had talked about moving somewhere together, and this neighborhood was an obvious choice. They would be close to Alex, which would make Bianca happy, and it might be something they could afford. It was an older neighborhood, so prices were lower and the houses had good bones. Not like the matchbox houses builders were putting up these days in a matter of weeks. Those places wouldn't last like the brick ranchers in older neighborhoods like theirs.

"Oh yeah, what's the job?" Karen asked.

"Some old lady just died and left her house to her niece."

Karen winced. "Old Mrs. Cauthorn? That is reason to celebrate."

Bianca slapped her shoulder. "That's rude."

Alex laughed at Karen's cry of pain. She of all people knew how many rings her sister wore. Those slaps on the shoulder could sting. "Every time I mention Mrs. Cauthorn, people say that. She wasn't real popular around here, was she?"

"Definitely not," Karen said.

"That still isn't reason to celebrate her death," Bianca said.

"The only person in town who seems sad she's gone is Carter from the pumpkin patch. She said the old lady was sweet, but her wife didn't seem to agree."

"Carter's almost as new in town as you two. She doesn't know any better," Karen said.

"Well, at the risk of sounding ghoulish, I'm glad she tripped over her cat, too. The house needs a lot of work and the new owner is pouring a ton of money into it," Alex said.

Bianca had clearly tired of the two of them dancing on the old woman's grave, because she picked up her paintbrush and attacked the wall again. As usual, her home renovation work was more energetic than graceful. Karen would have to come behind and clean up those paint strokes. She would never understand how Bianca's artistic flair couldn't translate from canvas to drywall.

Bianca gestured with her dripping paintbrush. "Don't think you can use any of that newfound wealth to buy me out of my half of this house."

Karen swooped in with paper towels to clean up the fat drops of sage green paint that splattered onto the hardwood floor. She didn't necessarily share the sentiment, but she knew it was Bianca's call to make. The more time she spent in this house with the Cassini sisters, the more she became part of their family, and she loved being part of their family. A place of their own could wait.

"You spend half your time at Karen's apartment, why do you want to hang onto this place anyway?" Alex asked.

"We've put our blood, sweat, and tears into this house and I'm not ready to leave it yet."

"You've certainly put your stamp on the kitchen floor. Why didn't you cover all of it with the drop cloth?" Alex asked.

"We couldn't find one big enough." Karen gave Alex a sheepish shrug. Most of her time had been chasing behind Bianca, cleaning up all the messes she made. She would have been quicker on her own, but she'd rather do the extra work to get the extra time together. After all, she was a big fan of chasing Bianca around. She was having the time of her life working on this house together.

"I'm counting on you tripping over your cat someday so we can have this whole place to ourselves anyway," Bianca said.

"Good thing we don't have a cat, I guess."

Karen laughed and pulled Bianca into a hug, ignoring the dripping paintbrush. "She doesn't mean it. She just loves having both of us around to open pickle jars and grab things off tall shelves."

Alex grinned back at Karen. "Femmes, am I right?"

They fist bumped and, as expected, Bianca rolled her eyes. Alex loved annoying her sister and Karen loved being part of the teasing.

"You two are lucky I'm so thankful for both of you. If I didn't love either of you so much, I'd make you both sleep in the garage," Bianca said.

Karen put on her fake pout. "You don't mean it, do you, babe?"

"Yes, I do mean it."

Karen pulled her into a kiss but ended it quickly. She hadn't missed how Alex turned away. She'd told Karen once before, "There's only so much saccharine love crap I can handle." Karen toed the line between her own happiness and Alex's as best she could. Alex took her beer and headed out to her work shed.

Once she was gone, Karen asked, "Now do you mean it?"

"I'm not sure. Kiss me again and we'll see."

About the Author

Tagan Shepard (she/her) is the author of twelve books of sapphic romance, including the 2019 Goldie Winner *Bird on a Wire* and the 2024 Goldie Finalist *Pumpkin Spice*. When not writing about extraordinary women loving other extraordinary women, she can be found playing video games, reading, or sitting in DC Metro traffic. She lives in Virginia with her very patient wife and two ridiculous cats.

Books Available from Bold Strokes Books

Feeling Lucky by Krystina Rivers. What happens when, despite suddenly having enough money to buy almost anything, Lucy and Tanner start to discover that maybe all they need is each other? (978-1-63679-876-9)

Iceberg by Gun Brooke. When Lady Arabella hires Zandra, she never expects to find love, especially not as a disaster looms on the horizon. (978-1-63679-908-7)

It Happened One Semester... by Aurora Rey. After a Pride night hookup, can eager new Assistant Professor Hudson Greene and Dean of Advising Callie Shaw overcome the odds and ace falling in love? (978-1-63679-814-1)

It's Kind of a Bad Idea by Sarah G. Levine. What happens when an emotionally unavailable serial dater meets the one woman she can't help but fall for—who happens to be the one woman who told her not to? (978-1-63679-920-9)

Thankful for You by Tagan Shepard. Everyone deserves to find their person, maybe Karen has finally found hers? (978-1-63679-884-4)

What Happens on Location... by Nan Campbell. How can Helen produce a successful movie when its director is the woman responsible for the demise of her marriage? (978-1-63679-904-9)

When Love Comes Around by Radclyffe and Ronica Black. Can Maya Sanchez and Nolan Wright trust each other enough to build something real, or will the past tear them apart? (978-1-63679-930-8)

Anywhere with You by Margo Glynn. On a road trip through the Great American Southwest, two friends discover nature, hope, and each other. (978-1-63679-907-0)

Burning Bridges by Lesley Davis. Can Clancy and Jude crack the case of eight missing women—and the secrets of their own hearts? (978-1-63679-872-1)

Dreams Entangled by Sophia Kell Hagin. Amid self-doubt, secrets, a pandemic, fear of attack and attempted murder, Pirin and Gracie's attraction turns to love and their lives will never be the same. (978-1-63679-892-9)

Echoes of Love by Catherine Lane. As Hazel's and Jo's paths intertwine, they're swept up in a whirlwind of long-buried secrets, sizzling chemistry, and memories that won't be denied. (978-1-63679-835-6)

Moonlight Obsession by Sheri Lewis Wohl. All it takes to stop a clever killer is moonlight, love, and a silver bullet. (978-1-63679-831-8)

My Boyfriend's Wife by Joy Argento. Amid betrayal and heartbreak, can two women discover a love that could heal their pasts and rewrite their futures? (978-1-63679-866-0)

Tapout by Nicole Disney. A struggling MMA fighter finds her edge in an underground ring, but as she falls for the magnetic and ambitious promoter behind the matches, their dangerous world threatens to destroy everything they've fought to rebuild. (978-1-63679-924-7)

The Fame Game by Ronica Black. Wild child Hollywood actress Luna Kirkman begins dating Hollywood's leading man, only to fall for his straitlaced sister instead. (978-1-63679-858-5)

An Extraordinary Passion by Kit Meredith. An autistic podcaster must decide whether to take a chance on her polyamorous guest and indulge their shared passion, despite her history. (978-1-63679-679-6)

That's Amore! by Georgia Beers. The romantic city of Rome should inspire Lily's passion for writing, if she can look away from Marina Troiani, her witty, smart, and unassumingly beautiful Italian tour guide. (978-1-63679-841-7)

The Unexpected Heiress by Cassidy Crane. When a cynical opportunist meets a shy but spirited heiress, the last thing she plans is for her heart to get involved. (978-1-63679-833-2)

Through Sky and Stars by Tessa Croft. Can Val and Nicole's love cross space and time to change the fate of humanity? (978-1-63679-862-2)

Uncomplicate It by Kel McCord. When an office attraction threatens her career, Hollis Reed's carefully laid plans demand revision. (978-1-63679-864-6)

Vanguard by Gun Brooke. Beth Wild, Subterranean freedom fighter, is in the crosshairs when she fights for her people and risks her heart for loving the exacting Celestial dissident leader, LaSierra Delmonte. (978-1-63679-818-9)

Wild Night Rising by Barbara Ann Wright. Riding Harleys instead of horses, the Wild Hunt of myth is once again unleashed upon the world. Their ousted leader and a fey cop must join forces to rein in the ride of terror. (978-1-63679-749-6)

Heart's Appraisal by Jo Hemmingwood. Andy and Hazel can't deny their attraction, but they'll never agree on the place they call home. (978-1-63679-856-1)

Behold My Heart by Ronica Black. Alora Anders is a highly successful artist who's losing her vision. Devastated, she hires Bodie Banks, a young struggling sculptor as a live-in assistant. Can Alora open her mind and her heart to accept Bodie into her life? (978-1-63679-810-3)

Fearless Hearts by Radclyffe. One wounded woman, one determined to protect her—and a summertime of risk, danger, and desire. (978-1-63679-837-0)

Forever Family by L.M. Rose. Two friends come together after tragedy to raise a baby, finding love along the way. (978-1-63679-868-4)

Stranger in the Sand by Renee Roman. Grace Langley is haunted by guilt. Fagan Shaw wishes she could remember her past. Will finding each other bring the closure they're looking for in order to have a brighter future? (978-1-63679-802-8)

The Nursing Home Hoax by Shelley Thrasher and Ann Faulkner. In this fresh take for grown-ups on the classic Nancy Drew series, crime-solving duo Taylor and Marilee investigate suspicious activity at a small East Texas nursing home. (978-1-63679-806-6)

The Rise and Fall of Conner Cody by Chelsey Lynford. A successful yet lonely Hollywood starlet must decide if she can let go of old wounds and accept a chance at family, friendship, and the love of a lifetime. (978-1-63679-739-7)

www.ingramcontent.com/pod-product-compliance
Lightning Source LLC
Chambersburg PA
CBHW022000010726
47494CB00003B/822